BOOK TWO

Protected
by the
Duke

CHLOE WILLOWFIELD

PROTECTED BY THE DUKE: WEATHERBYS REGENCY ROMANCE
BOOK TWO
First published in Australia in 2025 by Chloe Willowfield

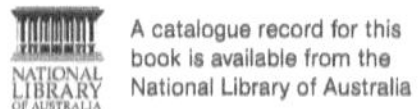
A catalogue record for this book is available from the National Library of Australia

ISBN: 9781763748026
ISBN: 9781763748033 (eBook)

Cover design by Miblart

To MD and the Ding.

CHAPTER ONE

For as long as he could remember, Alexander had been destined to one day fulfil the role of the Duke of Faversham. He had never really questioned this fact, it seemed perfectly logical and sensible, thank-you-very-much.

He hadn't expected to ascend to the title as early as he had done, however. His father's death had been a shock to everyone. Alexander was fresh out of his studies at Oxford when it had happened. He had come back up from university to almost immediately learn the news. He had had to do what he could to protect his mother and three sisters. As the eldest in the family, and the Duke to boot, it was now all his responsibility.

He did all he could that first year to learn the ropes, a little of which he had learnt from his father back when he was still alive.

After a while, he got into the swing of things and became the Duke of Faversham to everyone outside his family and the small circle of friends he kept. To his friends, he was Faversham. And to his family, he was Alexander.

Alexander shrugged his dress coat on. Ordinarily, he wouldn't bother going to a ball like this. What was the point? He wasn't marriage material and it wasn't as though any of the eligible ladies of the ton would want a man like him for a husband anyway. Although he was a Duke, he had cultivated his reputation for being dour and glowering to such an extent that no lady could possibly be interested in him.

He supposed he didn't care. It wasn't as though the Faversham line would die with him. Someone else in the family, a sister or a cousin perhaps, would have a son and continue the family name. After the mess his father had left behind and the precarious position he had left their family in, Alexander had little confidence in his abilities to do much of a better job as a husband or father. Despite what his mother might say.

Tonight, however, he would be making an appearance at the ball. The Landsdownes were old friends and he knew the two eldest sons, Matthew and Joseph, very well from their days at Eton. So even if no lady would wish to dance with him, even if he scared every mama off with his gloom and doom, he could at least look forward to some intelligent conversation with friends.

He strode out the door and into a waiting carriage. Tonight, he wouldn't be on the marriage mart, but this would be the closest he had come to it in many a moon.

"Will you be dancing tonight, Alexander?" Matthew Landsdowne asked. He leaned against the wall of the ballroom and crossed his arms.

Alexander scoffed gamefully. "Not bloody likely."

Joseph Landsdowne leaned across his brother and said, "Aww, I'm sure the young ladies of the ton would leap at the chance to dance with you, a duke."

Alexander shook his head. "Come on. The young ladies of the ton would cower at the prospect of dancing with me. I am the ice-cold duke after all."

Matthew smiled wryly.

Joseph laughed. "They don't call you the most feared man of the ton for nothing, that's for certain."

Alexander nodded with a hint of pride. "And that's exactly the way I like it."

Before either Landsdowne brother had the chance to reply, the string ensemble in the centre of the room struck up and began to play.

The sound of Mozart filled every nook and cranny of the space.

Alexander liked this piece of music. He might even be inclined to dance to it one day. Not that any ladies of the ton would ever find out. He had an image of a cold-hearted, unfeeling duke to uphold, after all.

He turned his attentions to the dancers swirling around the floor. One stood out above all. She was most captivating. No, she was breathtaking. There was no better word to describe her.

He had seen her once before, when she was presented at court at the start of the season. He knew she was the eldest sister of the Earl of Weatherby. One of the ton's most established families. Other than that, he knew very little about her.

Nevertheless, she carried herself with such grace and she had such a light about her that he couldn't help but believe she was the most stunning lady of the season.

That winter's day when she was presented to the Queen, he had been utterly fixated on her from his spot on the balcony above amidst the chattering throngs.

Belinda had focused her energies and her eyes straight ahead of her. Like every debutante, she needed to concentrate on representing her family name and on pleasing the Queen.

But if Belinda had turned her head a little to the right, she would have seen a man in his twenties with dark hair, piercing brown eyes and a hawk-like nose. He had cut a fine figure. Yet no lady of the ton would want to marry him, such was his reputation. He had kept his eyes on Belinda as she was presented to the Queen. Not a single move Belinda made failed to escape his attention.

Funnily enough, Belinda was the only young lady that season who was the subject of his attentions. And if anyone were to ask that man about those attentions, he would have denied them. After all, he was the cold-hearted duke and cold-hearted dukes never found a lady enchanting.

He sighed internally. It was all a moot point. No matter how breathtaking she was, no matter the magnetic pull she had over him, he would never be able to have her as his bride. He would never be able to have any woman as his bride because he was Alexander, Duke of Faversham. No woman deserved the fate of being married to the cold-hearted duke.

Alexander's group began to peel off this way and that.

There was some issue or other with the Landsdowne's second sister and all her brothers hurried off to investigate.

Alexander, for his part, headed towards the gardens for wont of anything better to do. It would be a place, at least, to clear his head.

He shoved his hands in his pockets and headed towards a quiet part of the gardens. Away from the lights of the house and the flames of the torches, the sky would be clear enough to catch a glimpse of the stars above. Even in London, with all her people and buildings and life everywhere, it was still possible to find patches of darkness where one could go to admire the distant lights of the heavens.

Yes, this corner of the garden, near the middle of the maze, was the perfect spot to collect his thoughts before he headed back home to Faversham House.

After bowing to her dance partner at the end of the quadrille, Lady Belinda Weatherby moved to the side of the room and helped herself to a glass of strawberry water. She sipped it gently and focused her mind on what to do next. After three dances, she was beginning to tire out.

The gentlemen with whom she had danced had been nice enough, but it was still only her first season and she did not want to make any rash decisions when it came to choosing a husband. After all, the season was still young and she could spend one or two more unwed before questions would be asked on the ton regarding her suitability as a wife. No need to rush things.

She resolved to spend some time in the gardens and check out the talent out there. As the daughter of an Earl, gentlemen from many of society's most prominent families would vye for her hand in marriage and she wished to appraise herself of her full range of options.

She'd come here tonight in the company of two of her brothers. Edgar, the current Earl, and Xavier, the current heir to the title. She hadn't seen them in a while and presumed they were in some other room inside. Loved them as she did, it would be good to get some respite from their overbearing attentions.

She headed out of the french window doors that separated the ballroom from the patio and past the small crowd hanging around the wrought iron tables. Down the steps, one two three, and then she was on the lawn where ladies and gentlemen walked arm in arm in close tete a tete.

Snatches of conversation made their way to her ears.

"Did you see the coldness in Faversham's eyes?" said a woman's voice. Belinda could not place who had made that particular utterance.

"Oh yes," replied another woman. "He always looks like that. So stern, so mirthless. I could not stand the company of such a man."

Belinda knew that name. Faversham. Duke of one of the most prestigious titles in all of Britain. Though she had never met the man, his reputation preceded him. He was no mere rakehell. He was instead a man known for never laughing, never smiling and having an air of complete disinterest in the general delights of the ton. Likely not the right sort of man for her, Belinda mused. Irrespective of his acclaimed title, she could not imagine herself with a man who did not appreciate the delights of dance and music as she did.

She milled around on the grass for a brief minute before the neatly pruned topiary archway above the entrance to the maze caught her eye. Inviting tea lights lit the way and beckoned her inside. Thinking nothing of it, she made her way down the path.

It was nice and serene in here. So unlike the bustling ballroom of the house. Here was a place where she could explore and be alone with herself, if only for a few minutes. She would make sure to return to the ballroom and its marriage mart whirl after she'd had a rest out here.

She wandered through the maze, following its twists and turns, all the while keen to find its heart. Eventually, she spied it and sped up her pace to reach it.

Such was her excitement that she paid little heed to looking where she was going.

So she did not see a black-clad figure wandering around the very centre of the maze.

He had his back turned to her and was lost in a world of his own.

Belinda kept striding forward, oblivious, until she collided into the figure with a thud. She lost her footing and slipped on a patch of wet mud. And then she was falling down down down.

She hit the ground with an almighty thump. Something snapped near her foot and then a hot, searing pain shot through her left ankle. Blast it! She'd managed to land on it at a most awkward angle. She let forth a groan of pain. She closed her eyes and grimaced.

Rich baritone tones drifted from above her. "My lady, are you alright? Can I assist you?"

Belinda didn't recognise the voice. She opened her eyes and looked upwards.

A man in finely cut jet black pantaloons and matching waistcoat loomed above her. Belinda would have guessed he was in his mid twenties. He had dark hair with a slightly floppy fringe, brown hawk-like eyes and a distinguished aquiline nose.

She didn't recognise him. "My ankle. It hurts."

Alarm filled his features. "I'll help you up," he said.

"Wait." She lifted a halting arm.

"What is it?" he asked, voice curious and concerned.

"Before you assist me, I should like to know your name, sir." If nothing else, she wanted some conversation to help her to take her mind off the pain in her ankle a little.

"Oh yes, of course. The Duke of Faversham."

Belinda's heart froze. She knew that name. He was the most feared man in the entire ton. "Pleased to make your acquaintance," she said with forced politeness.

"And may I have the pleasure of your name, my lady?"

"Lady Belinda Weatherby."

He gave a brief nod. "Well, Lady Weatherby, I am delighted to meet you." He began to bend down to help her. "I had best get you inside. You will likely need a doctor."

He reached out his hand to her.

But before she could take it, a dreaded sound filled her ears.

"What's this? Oh ho ho, Lady Belinda Weatherby, what are you doing?" a voice said.

Curses, thought Belinda. To be caught in a position like this and have the worst possible person discover her. Lady Petunia Reynolds, champion gossip of the ton and all round troublemaker.

"I said, Lady Belinda, what are you doing?" Lady Reynolds' voice grew harsher and louder. Anyone within a ten feet radius of the maze would no doubt be able to hear her now. "Surely you are not taking liberties with gentlemen like a common woman of the street."

The Duke of Faversham looked directly into Belinda's eyes, his hawklike brown eyes boring through to the depths of her soul, and said softly, "I am so sorry, my Lady."

Belinda began to reply and ask the Duke what exactly he was sorry for, but her words went unheard as he turned to face Lady Reynolds and said with a voice as cold as ice, "Lady Reynolds, how dare you speak to my fiancée in such a manner."

A small crowd had formed now behind Lady Reynolds, their attention grabbed by the sound of her voice.

"Well I never," spluttered Lady Reynolds.

One could hear a pin drop. The crowd watched with bated breath, anxious to see how this drama between three of the ton's most prominent families would play out.

Lady Reynolds regained her haughty composure. "Congratulations on your impending nuptials, your Grace, my Lady. I trust you will be most *happy* together." Then she turned on her heel and stomped out of the maze, leaving a tittering audience in her wake.

The Duke closed his eyes for a few seconds, as if seeking strength from some source other than himself, before opening them again and looking down at Belinda. "Pay them no mind, my Lady. How is your ankle? Do you need some assistance?"

Belinda groaned and sat up on the ground. She tried to move the affected foot. Sharp twinges of pain radiated from her ankle, up her leg and down towards her toes.

"Heavens, it hurts. I am not sure I will be able to walk on it," she said.

"I will take that as a yes, then," he replied. He bent down on one knee and offered her both his hands. "Hold onto me steady, my Lady, and then on the count of three I will pull both of us up standing. Here we go, one, two, three."

The pair were then on their feet.

Belinda seethed through her teeth at the agony of placing weight on her injured ankle and held it aloft.

"I do not think you will be able to walk, my Lady," said the Duke.

"I fear you are correct."

He lifted her in his arms and carried her through the crowd and out of the maze. The pair looked a sight, with

Belinda half covered in mud and the Duke having mud on his knees.

Once they were in the main gardens, lit by an array of tealights, the Duke said, "Who are you here with? The Earl?"

"Yes, and Xavier too," she said.

"Then we had better find your brothers and a doctor."

Speak of the devil, at that moment Edgar appeared from the french windows on the patio. At the vision in front of him, his face turned a ghostly pallor and he roared, "Faversham, what in God's name is going on?"

Before the Duke could get the chance to speak, Belinda turned her head towards her brother. "We were in the maze -" She sighed. "Look, it will be easier to have this conversation somewhere inside."

"She needs a doctor," blurted the Duke.

"What?" roared Edgar. He strode towards the Duke, ready to launch into a furious tirade when a familiar voice behind him stopped him in his tracks.

"Edgar, there you are -" Xavier said, with a cheeriness that turned into bemusement when he saw the scene in front of him. "Your Grace, this does not look good."

"She has an injured ankle. She needs a doctor," said the Duke.

"How *dare* you. You will be the one who needs a doctor by the time I am finished with you," hissed Edgar.

The Duke jumped as the woman laying in his arms jerked in a fit of exasperation. "Will none of you buffoons listen? I already said it will be easier to have this conversation inside. Take me inside at once."

The three men immediately fell silent in shock.

"Very well," said Edgar. He walked towards the Duke and took his sister from his arms. "Your Grace, you can tell my brother your side of the story."

With that, Edgar strode inside the house with Belinda in his arms and headed towards a side chamber.

"Call for a doctor," he said to the manservant outside the chamber. Then he walked through the door and placed Belinda gently on a white and beige satin chaise longue. He shut the door, before returning to kneel by her side.

"Whatever *he* did to you, whatever happened, you have nothing to be ashamed of," he said.

"It wasn't like that," she replied. "The Duke did nothing untoward, and neither did I. I was in the maze when I collided with him. I slipped on some wet mud and injured my ankle. He was assisting me off the floor when Petunia Reynolds came along, saw us and started shouting foul insinuations. He then referred to me as his fiancée, which put out Lady Reynolds' fire and she left. My ankle hurts too much to walk on it, so the Duke carried me outside. He was looking for you, Xavier and a doctor."

"Hence why you are half covered in mud and he has mud on his breeches," said Edgar. "You must understand how this looks."

"I do," she replied. "But the truth is nothing improper happened, despite what Lady Petunia Reynolds might think."

Edgar sighed. "This was not how I had planned your first season to go, I am so sorry Belinda. I had intended for you to be able to have the time to choose your own husband, not be strong-armed into an arrangement."

Belinda's usually stoic lip trembled. "It cannot be helped, brother. Tell me, is the Duke a cruel man?"

"No, by all accounts he is not. Which is why the incident outside and how it looked to me took me by surprise. It would have been extremely out of character for him to take advantage of you in any way."

"That is somewhat a relief to hear," she said flatly.

Edgar's eyes brimmed with concern. He rubbed Belinda's shoulder in an attempt at comfort.

This night had gone about as badly as it was possible for a ball of the ton to go. What a disaster!

After the doctor went on his way, Edgar turned to his sister and said, "We must see about getting you home."

Belinda growled internally, half in pain at her ankle and leg and half in exasperation at yet another moment in her life controlled by the decisions of others. Thank you to Lady Reynolds for her snide gossip. Thank you to the Duke for doing the gentlemanly thing and announcing her as his fiancée. And thank you to Edgar for deciding now that it was time to go home. She crossed her arms. "Alright, I suppose."

Edgar stepped outside to call for the Weatherby carriage, leaving Belinda on the settee to wallow in her disappointments.

A short while later and her two brothers returned.

"The carriage is outside," Edgar began. "Here, I will assist you."

He picked her up from the settee and carried her in his arms out of the room, down the hallway and out onto the driveway where the Weatherby carriage lay waiting.

Xavier and Edgar assisted her into the vehicle and she took a seat opposite the pair.

Edgar looked severe but the most significant sign of the evening's dispiriting course of events was on Xavier's visage. His normally cheerful countenance was dour and gloomy.

"What happened to the Duke? Where is he?" she asked.

"Given the late hour and the suddenness of tonight's events, we agreed he would come around to call on you tomorrow afternoon so you can discuss matters with him yourself," said Edgar. He banged on the ceiling of the carriage and, in short order, the coachman gave the horses the office to start.

Belinda chewed her lip and said nothing. What more was there to say in this situation? What could she do to stop this now-inevitable chain of events as it hurtled her towards the altar? If she refused to marry the Duke of Faversham, she would be ruined. Lady Petunia Reynolds and all the loudmouths of the ton would see to that. And then where would she be? Forced to spend the rest of her days as the dependent sister of an earl and decreasing in relevance with each passing year and each heir that was born?

She seethed to herself. There was nothing for it. This marriage had to go ahead. She would become the Duchess of Faversham, like it or not.

The wheels of the carriage turned as it made its way to Weatherby House on Grosvenor Square.

And inside, Belinda's stomach turned and churned in time with the wheels.

CHAPTER TWO

Alexander slunk out the side entrance of Landsdowne House.

He needed to stay away from the hubbub and the carriages that would most assuredly be going on around the front. No doubt people who saw the incident in the maze would be there, gossiping and spreading rumours. Belinda herself might still be there, probably about to be whisked away in the Weatherby carriage by her brothers. For him to make an appearance in the middle of all that would make for a most messy scene indeed.

He'd arrived by hired sedan. No need to waste time and money on bringing out the ducal carriage. He had no need to impress.

So it was easy enough for him to sneak out a side door and leave through a back gate. Disappearing into the night, leaving through forgotten exits, that was part and parcel of his modus operandi.

Now he was on Bury Street, a lesser known thoroughfare in this part of St James's. Still a salubrious part of town, he thankfully was unlikely to come across any footpads here.

The night's watch were ever present in this part of London, after all.

He cut across the moonlit cobblestones quickly and in mere minutes he was out on Jermyn Street.

There was some hustle and bustle but thankfully no familiar faces.

A string of hackney carriages were waiting for hire. He took the first available and jumped in.

"Where to, guv'nor?" The driver asked.

"Faversham House, Park Lane," Alexander said. He leant back into the passenger seat and did his best to relax.

The carriage trundled along through London's streets at a steady pace.

As he moved further and further away from Landsdowne House, the crowds thinned out and by the time he reached the home stretch of Park Lane they were very sparse indeed.

No doubt if he were to go down, at this time of night, to the less salubrious districts he would find all manner of life on the streets. The opera singers and actresses of Covent Garden would be with their protectors or trying to secure one. The molly boys, too, would be looking for clients. And ladies in certain houses in Soho would be preparing for specialised sessions.

Tonight, however, Alexander was making sure to steer well clear of all that.

The events of this evening had changed his life irrevocably and he needed to be away from all human society.

The horses made their final push towards Faversham House. In a few short minutes he would be home and free to ruminate on his thoughts without interruption.

Belinda. Belinda. Belinda. He hardly knew anything about the woman, other than that she was the eldest Weatherby daughter, was the sister of Edgar and Xavier, and had a sweet face.

When they'd bumped into one another in the maze, he had sincerely hoped that that would be the end of it. A chance encounter, an accident that stopped before it ever budded into anything more. Yet Lady Petunia Reynolds, that damned woman, had just so happened to walk in on the scene and start loudly throwing around baseless allegations of the most grievous nature for Belinda's reputation. What choice did he possibly have other than to do the honourable thing and give her the one form of protection that would give her ironclad defences against Lady Reynolds' accusations? What choice did he have but to marry her and take her as his bride?

The hackney carriage entered the gates of Faversham House. It traversed the driveway to pull up outside the main doors.

Edgar paid the driver before getting out and slunking his way inside.

His mother and sisters would be in their wing of the house by now so he needn't take any special care not to disturb them.

A few footmen were still up, hanging around in the entrance hall.

Alexander turned to the most senior on duty and said, "Shut the house up for the night, please. I'll be in my office."

Then Alexander made a beeline for the third story room where he and he alone was in charge as the Duke of Faversham.

He lit a couple of candles and closed the door so he would be truly undisturbed.

He shrugged off his jacket and slung it over a chair.

He poured himself a glass of whiskey and made his way to the window. Outside he could see the rooftops and spires of London spread out before him. The townhouses of the wealthy in Mayfair the homes of the less fortunate in Soho and beyond. In the middle of that Mayfair milieu would be Belinda. She would most likely be home now at Weatherby House. He had never been inside that Grosvenor Square edifice and he only knew Belinda's brothers in passing, but he knew well the Weatherby name. Weatherby and Faversham, two of the most distinguished names in the ton, with lineages going back centuries.

Their two families were soon to be bound in marriage, and shouldn't that be a cause for celebration among high society?

Yet Alexander felt his stomach twist in an uncomfortable knot.

Belinda was only young, her first season out, and she had been trapped in a situation which would mean she would have the misfortune of being married to a man like him.

This wasn't fair on her at all.

He had three sisters and he would hate for any of them to be in Belinda's shoes, staring down the barrel of a marriage to a man like him, all because of an unfortunate run in in a maze that Lady Reynolds happened to witness. The worst part of it all, though, was that Belinda didn't even seem to realise that she *was* staring down the barrel. She could never know, either. Alexander had to ensure she was protected from such knowledge, protected from such innuendo, protected from *him*.

He had seen Belinda before they even ran into one another in the maze. When he had been in the ballroom, standing at the side watching the proceedings, a young woman had caught his eye. He remembered her as well from the court presentation of a couple of months ago. She had been enchanting then, but he had no business with debutantes. He was Alexander, Duke of Faversham and not suitable material for innocent debutantes. He had darker tastes, tastes they needed protection from. The lighthearted boy-next-door or even the studious scholar, those types of men were right for debutantes like Belinda. But a man like Alexander? She needed protection from a man like him, not his hand in marriage.

So when he had seen her on the dancefloor that night, doing a quadrille with Lord Walthamstowe his heart had lept for a minute second at her beauty and how ethereal she was in the candlelight. Only his heart had sunk just as quickly as it had arisen. Because she was the type of woman he could never have. He was too dark, too deviant, too twisted for the likes of her.

But wasn't she enchanting?

He allowed himself to bask in the memory of how enchanting she was on that dancefloor. The graceful way she moved. The shimmer of her luscious locks, so elegantly coiffed in an updo, crowned by a glimmering tiara, to reveal the sweet curve of her neck. She was a vision. But only ever a vision. Though it was now inevitable that they marry, they would never truly be together. If she ever knew his secret, it would harm her irrevocably.

It was highly apparent that she didn't know the truth about him. Otherwise there was no way on earth, sprained ankle or not, she would've allowed him to carry her. To even lay one finger on her.

He turned away from the window and sat on the chair at his desk. Then he took a sip of the whiskey. The harsh liquid burned his throat. He wasn't accustomed to it given he only drank it in very rare, stressful situations like tonight.

He leaned back and ran his hands through his hair in an attempt to unwind.

It wasn't really working.

CHAPTER THREE

The next day, Alexander strode into the green drawing room at the Faversham's London house.

His mother Anastasia, Dowager Duchess, sat on the settee reading a pamphlet while his three sisters had scattered themselves around the room. Judith, who would be having her first season in a couple of years, was at the harpsichord playing a piece of her own composition. Meanwhile, Mary sat at needlework while Diana was on the floor playing with her dolls.

Four pairs of eyes focused on him.

"Mother, may I please speak with you alone?" he asked.

"Yes, yes, of course," the Dowager Duchess said. Then she turned to a maid and said, "Rebecca, please take Diana to the yellow drawing room."

Rebecca took Diana by the hand and led her through the door. Mary and Judith followed, rolling their eyes as they went. Judith shut the door behind her and then it was Alexander and Anastasia all alone.

Anastasia put her pamphlet down and looked at her son expectantly.

"Mother, I am engaged to be married," he began.

She smiled softly. "Congratulations. Who is your bride to be?"

"Lady Belinda Weatherby."

"Ah yes, the eldest Weatherby sister. She is a fine choice, Alexander," beamed the Dowager. "When did this happy development take place?"

"Last night, at the Landsdowne Ball."

The Dowager clapped her hands together. "Oh, this is just the most excellent news!" She raised herself from the settee to stand opposite Alexander. She took his hands in her own. "If your father could see you now, he would be so proud."

Alexander gave a small smile. He could well anticipate what would come next out of his mother's mouth. Such was her level of hero worship of his late father.

Sure enough, the Dowager gushed away. "Your father was such a wonderful husband, the best husband any woman could ever ask for. And such a perfect father too. He never put a foot wrong. I was so happy with him, every day of our lives together. Oh for you to follow in his footsteps would be the greatest thing of all!" She squeezed his hands in delight. "I am so proud of you, Alexander. This engagement is your first step to becoming as great a Duke as your late father was, may the Lord rest his soul."

Alexander nodded and gave a smile. "I can only hope to be half the husband and father he was, mother." But inside, Alexander's stomach churned.

A day later, as the servants cleared luncheon from the table at Weatherby House, Edgar turned to Belinda and said, "The Duke will be here soon, you are to receive him in the drawing room. I will meet with him first in my office. There are some things I need to discuss with him, but you should not have too long a wait."

Belinda nodded.

Edgar continued. "It will all go fine, sister. He has far more to worry about than you do in all of this."

After Edgar left the dining room, Belinda climbed the stairs flanked by her maids and made her way to her bedroom to prepare the final finishing touches before her rendezvous with the Duke.

She decided to remain in her pale rose day dress, her face devoid of makeup and her feet in her favourite pair of pink satin slippers.

"Retie this bun please," she said to one of her maids.

"At once, my lady," replied the maid as she got to work on perfecting Belinda's bun.

After Belinda had given herself an in depth inspection in her mirror and deemed herself to pass muster for a meeting with even His Majesty himself, she went back downstairs to the drawing room and awaited her fate.

She sat on the settee and picked up a light comedy in an attempt to distract herself. Yet it was all in vain, for her mind continuously raced back to the previous night and the sudden dramatic event that had changed the course of her life forever. Certainly, she was now set to be a Duchess but at what cost? She barely even knew the man.

She trudged her way through the chapter, reading some of the sentences several times, until she heard a soft knock at the door.

"Enter," she called as she placed her book on the coffee table in front of her.

A moment later her betrothed stepped through the door.

He made a deep bow towards her. "My lady, how are you faring this afternoon?"

"My ankle is still rather sore, but it will mend. So the doctor says," Belinda replied.

"That's good," Alexander said.

The pair looked at one another for several seconds, before Alexander broke the silence that clung in the air.

"Pray tell, how are you feeling otherwise?" he asked.

Dry husks of apprehension filled Belinda's mouth. What should she even say to the Duke?

Every nook, every cranny of the room was overtaken by a growing tension. Though Belinda and Alexander were two members of some of the ton's most elite families, in this place and on this day it was as if they were on opposite sides of the planet.

Belinda found her voice somewhere through the dryness of her throat. "About as well as can be expected, your grace."

Alexander scrutinised his betrothed through his brown hawk-like eyes. Hell and blast! Evidently she did not trust him at all and, given his reputation on the ton, he could not blame her. It was time for him to take a different tack.

"I fear I have started things on the wrong foot, and for that I apologise," he said.

Belinda furrowed her brows at him. What on earth was going on?

The Duke walked towards her with a solemn expression on his face.

Once he reached where Belinda sat, he knelt on one knee in front of her. "My lady, I swear to you that I will always protect you and treat you with honour."

The arid sensation in her throat began to dissipate just a little. Protection and honour were values she could well understand as a Weatherby. Ever since she was a young girl, she had been brought up to believe that her future husband would both honour and protect her. So it was a balm of comfort to hear those words from her betrothed's lips.

Alexander continued speaking. "This most probably isn't how you wanted your first season to go. But no matter how this started, please know that you will always have my complete loyalty."

Belinda felt the tension around the room subside a little. Loyalty was another value she could well understand as a Weatherby.

She nodded. "Thank you, your Grace."

Silence filled the room.

Belinda turned her mind to the next, most logical point of discussion for any young debutante of the ton. "And what of our wedding plans, your Grace?" she asked. "Lady Reynolds has put us both in a rather difficult spot."

"She has indeed," Alexander nodded.

"The ton are bound to talk."

"That they will."

"Our reputations are at risk if we delay this wedding," Belinda said.

"My lady, I have the utmost concern for protecting your reputation. Which is why I wish for us to wed with the greatest expediency. But protecting your reputation, not mine, is my priority. It's not as though I have a stellar reputation to protect." Alexander's face was stern.

"What of your family's reputation then?" she asked.

"That is important to me, yes." He paused for a beat to think before continuing, "Yet the events of last night won't worsen their reputations. Even Lady Reynolds isn't capable of that. It's your reputation I am concerned about."

Belinda looked down at Alexander and nodded slowly.

He looked deeply into her eyes.

She had not felt the hot gaze of a man's eyes bearing down into hers before. It was scorching. So unlike the glances of the gentlemen she had danced with at the balls during her now-truncated season. Those gentlemen had either been too nervous to look her properly in the eye or else their attentions were only perfunctory.

Alexander's eyes, with their hawklike form and dark brown colouring, made her feel something that she couldn't quite describe. It wasn't unpleasant but it made her feel on slightly uneven footing. Perhaps this was what it was like to be looked at in the way a man looks at a woman whom he wishes to claim as his wife.

She berated herself for following such a line of thought. What foolish fantasies! She barely knew the man and they were only getting married in order to save her reputation.

This was a marriage of convenience, nothing more, and it would behove her well to accept reality.

She shook herself out of her thoughts. They wouldn't do her any good.

"Thank you, your Grace, for your kind concern," she said. "This marriage, it shall preserve my reputation at least."

He nodded slowly. "It shall. It is the best I can offer you and I am truly sorry for that. But rest assured, whatever happens I will always protect you."

"Thank you, your Grace," she said.

They exchanged a few more pleasantries and then Alexander was getting up from the floor and about to head for the door.

"I shall take my leave of you know, my lady," he said. "I shall apply for a special licence without delay. I know you will have much to prepare and so won't need me taking up any more of your time. Farewell, my lady."

He gave a deep bow, turned on his heel and left the room.

Belinda leaned back in her chair. That had been a strange encounter. The Duke seemed to want to do right by her but had little interest in her as a person. She was a marionette being wheeled into place for her big day, in only a matter of two or three weeks.

CHAPTER FOUR

The next fortnight was a giddy whirl of visits to the modiste to outfit her with her wedding clothes in addition to preparing her trousseau.

At the final fitting, her ankle now fully healed, Belinda stood on the box in Jean Cookson's modiste shop with her eyes closed as Jean made the finishing touches to her outfit.

The young woman felt Jean adjust some fabric around her head before the modiste said, "There, my lady, you can open your eyes now."

Belinda duly did so. As she met herself in the mirror, she gasped internally. From the delicate lace of her mantilla veil to the ivory silk folds of her jewelled dress and dainty beading around the neckline and sleeve cuffs, she looked every inch the lady of the ton that she was.

"It is beautiful, thank you," said Belinda. She cocked her head and pondered her situation. She did look beautiful in this outfit, it was a certainty. But what good would it do her in her marriage to a man she barely knew? In her marriage to the cold-hearted duke? She frowned.

Jean, ever the perceptive observer of all the goings-on of the ton, noticed her client's unhappy expression. "My lady, you look unhappy. Is something the matter?" she asked in a gentle tone.

Belinda could have cried at the modiste's question. The past two weeks had been an awful brew of having decisions made for her without her having any real input. Of not having control over her own life. And for Jean to have noticed must have meant that the look was obvious on her face.

"Miss Cookson," Belinda began, "What do you think makes a good marriage?"

Jean took a pause before giving her reply. "Well, though I have never been married myself, I have seen many brides of the ton ahead of their weddings, as well as dressed them after their marriages. And those matches which have been the most successful are those where there is a mutual respect between the couple. There does not necessarily need to be a spark at the start. Remember, sometimes the fastest flames to burn become the quickest to extinguish themselves. The mutual respect can develop during the course of the marriage and from that, trust builds and the couple can have a successful marriage over many years. Sometimes even love develops, although that is not essential for a successful marriage, I hasten to add."

Belinda sucked her cheeks in and gave a nod of acknowledgement. "Thank you, Miss Cookson. You have given me much to mull over."

"You are most welcome, my lady." Jean leaned forward and made a tiny adjustment to the position of Belinda's veil. "There, that is even more beautiful."

Silence reigned in the shop for a few moments.

Then, Jean spoke again. "I do not wish to be impertinent, my lady. I know you never spoke of your husband-to-be directly with me."

Belinda raised a suspicious eyebrow.

Seeing the beginnings of her customer's displeasure, Jean hurried to finish her line of thought. "But from every account I have heard, the Duke of Faversham is not a cruel man. You could do much worse for a husband than him."

Belinda nodded slowly. "My brother said something similar. The night the Duke and I were engaged."

"I can imagine how it's tough to believe. Perhaps you will have to see it with your own eyes."

"Other people's words are other people's words."

"Yes, my lady."

Jean set herself to bustling about the shop, tidying up this and that.

Belinda stared at herself in the mirror. She looked like a beautiful bride in her gown and veil. But on her face, she wore a grimace of fear.

***

The Duke applied for a special licence and two weeks later, Belinda found herself outside the doors of St George's, Hanover Square, with Edgar.

Edgar placed her veil gently over her eyes.

"Sister, you look beautiful," he said with a smile.

Then they headed through the doors and down the aisle to the organ strains of *Trumpet Voluntary*. They reached the altar where the Archbishop of Canterbury stood waiting ready to conduct the service.

The Duke himself stood facing the altar and turned around to face Belinda with a severe expression on his face. Heavens, he had always looked severe whenever Belinda had seen him. She could not recall a time when he had smiled. Edgar had said that the Duke was not a cruel man, but Belinda had her doubts. Surely only a man with malice in his heart would be capable of constantly going through life wearing the same gloomy expression.

Then the Archbishop began the service and before long Belinda was vowing to 'love, honour and obey' a man she hardly knew.

The Archbishop pronounced the couple man and wife and led the congregation in prayers.

Then came the familiar sermon from the *Book of Common Prayer*, where the Archbishop read the duties of man and wife. Belinda noticed that her new husband listened with great intensity to this piece and her heart sank further. What would he expect from her? Certainly, she had heard the sermon before at many weddings but to hear herself referenced, to hear the Archbishop himself say that she ought to submit herself to the Duke as to the Lord, a man she hardly knew, and to see how intently the Duke listened made her feel adrift and rudderless. She had hoped to marry a man of her own choosing, one who she got to know through courtship before she married so when she heard this sermon at her own wedding she would know to whom the Archbishop was referring. But she did not know her husband at all and had no idea of what he expected from her.

Then the service concluded and the Duke took her gently by the arm and led her up the aisle through the crowd of smiling well wishers.

He assisted her into a carriage and they headed down Grosvenor Street.

Other Weatherby and Faversham family members would no doubt be following along soon in their own carriages.

Inside the carriage at the head of the procession, there was an awkward tension brewing.

Belinda wasn't sure precisely what to say. So she remained silent.

Alexander, for his part, didn't say anything either.

Belinda assumed it was because he was such a stern and severe man, so focused on being Faversham and on all his ducal duties. He would want an obedient bride, yes that would be what a man like him would desire. Best for her not to say anything.

They trundled along the south side of Grosvenor Square and Belinda looked out of her window at the familiar scene that would soon be a mere memory. Weatherby House, good old Weatherby House stood as it always did, so sturdy yet ornate. And in the centre of the square were the fashionable gardens where she would take a stroll when the mood took her.

She shook her head at herself. What was she thinking, getting all maudlin like this? Yes, she *was* leaving her family's London home, where she had spent much of her childhood. But she was only moving a few streets away. A quick carriage ride and she would be back in Grosvenor Square anytime she pleased. Well, as long as Alexander allowed it. She hoped he would. Surely he couldn't be that unreasonable?

The carriage reached the end of the street and turned onto Park Lane. Past the green boughs of Hyde Park and then they were out the front of Faversham House. Through the elaborate wrought iron gates and across the gravel driveway to the grand doors of the house.

Liveried servants in the smart green Faversham uniform stood lined up to greet them.

The carriage drew to a halt and a footman opened Alexander's door

The Duke stepped down onto the forecourt before turning around and assisting Belinda.

Her dainty feet in their white satin ballet shoes landed on the gravel with a soft crunch.

Alexander offered her his arm. "This way, my lady, if you please. I must introduce you to your new household."

Belinda gave a small nod and let her new husband lead her over to a portly middle-aged man at the head of the line.

Alexander gestured to the man. "This is Prentice, our butler."

Prentice gave a bow.

Before Belinda had a chance to say or do anything else, Alexander was leading her towards a grey haired woman in a dress that was about twenty years out of date in its cut.

"And this is Mrs Hiddlesthwaite, our head housekeeper here at Faversham House," he said.

Mrs Hiddlesthwaite curtsied with practiced smoothness.

On and on the staff introductions went.

Belinda did her very best to remember them all, each name and position, but even for her excellent memory it was a challenge. Still, as the new lady of the house managing these staff would be her day to day responsibility, so she wanted to do the best job she could.

Finally, they reached the end of the line and Alexander guided her towards the heavy oaken doors.

They crossed the threshold and Belinda found herself on a shiny black and white chequerboard marble floor. She looked up again and saw her own reflection bouncing back at her.

Then she looked back up and turned her gaze towards her enigmatic husband.

"Welcome to your new home, your Grace," he intoned in his deep baritone. "I trust you will be most happy here."

"Thank you, your Grace," she said.

From somewhere to her right, her new lady's maid Miss Dauntsey appeared. Miss Dauntsey gestured to Belinda's bouquet of flowers. "Please, let me take those for you, your Grace."

Belinda nodded her assent. "Oh yes, thank you."

Miss Dauntsey disappeared almost as quickly as she had materialised.

Belinda and Alexander were alone again together.

He tilted his head down towards her and met her eyes with his own dark mahogany ones. "Your Grace," he said. "We have not much time before our guests arrive. I'm sorry there isn't time to give you a proper tour of the place right now, but you'll get one tomorrow. That notwithstanding,

I do wish that you are happy and comfortable here, as befits your position as Duchess."

Belinda was about to open her lips to give a reply to her husband, when the crunch of gravel and a carriage pulling up interrupted her.

Alexander turned his head towards the open door and squinted a little in the light. "Ah, those must be our first guests," he said.

Footsteps on the gravel followed by a few familiar squeals and giggles. Yes, it was none other than her siblings. Edgar led the way, followed by Xavier and Philomena. The three of them were all in good spirits. Edgar was the most severe of the three, hardly a surprise given his status as the head of the family, but he was positively jovial in comparison to Alexander. Bringing up the rear were the source of all the squeals and giggles, her two youngest siblings Lionel and Genevieve.

Belinda looked across at Alexander. Much to her surprise, he seemed unphased by the antics of her two youngest siblings. She had assumed that a dour and sour man like him would recoil at their noise and frivolity.

Edgar strode towards the Faversham couple. "Belinda, Faversham, so good to see you both." He patted Belinda's arm before grasping Alexander's hand in a cordial shake.

Xavier did the same, a warm brotherly greeting to Belinda and then an easy handshake with her husband.

Curiouser and curiouser, Belinda thought. Alexander had a reputation on the ton for being cold and severe and some of his behaviour since she had become entangled in his life certainly reflected that. Yet there were other elements, such as the greetings he shared with Edgar and Xavier that did not align with the image of the dour duke.

Philomena was next with her greetings for the couple.

And then it was the turn of the somewhat rowdy Lionel and Genevieve.

A footman, who had appeared from Belinda did not know where, directed the Weatherbys through a set of pale sage doors off the side of the entrance hall.

Another carriage pulled up and another set of guests materialised. The Dowager Duchess of Faversham and her three daughters.

The Dowager quickly embraced her son and then placed a brief peck on Belinda's cheek. The three daughters stood tittering behind their mother.

Once she had finished with her greetings, the Dowager turned around to her daughters and said, "Come along girls!" She led them through the same pale sage doors that the Weatherbys had entered a few minutes earlier.

Another carriage pulled up and another group of guests arrived.

On and on it went until eventually the stream of the great and the good of the ton dried up.

Alexander turned to Belinda. "That's the last of it, your Grace. Do you need some rest before we head into the banquet?"

"No, I am quite fine, thank you," Belinda said.

"Very well."

Arm-in-arm, they made their way across the entrance hall towards the pale sage doors of the banquet room.

Two liveried footmen opened the doors before them to reveal Prentice.

The portly butler gave a respectful bow towards Alexander and Belinda. Then he turned around to face the assembly of guests. "Ladies and gentlemen, the Duke and Duchess of Faversham!"

Applause broke out in the banquet room.

Prentice stepped to one side.

Alexander and Belinda entered their wedding banquet. Around the room, she could see familiar supportive faces of her dearest family and friends. Conspicuously, Lady Petunia Reynolds was absent. Her heart lightened a little at that realisation.

They took their seats and the meal began.

Throughout, Alexander was respectful enough. And while he didn't exactly smile, he didn't seem quite so severe as he had in the church.

Belinda let out a breath she hadn't realised she had been holding. Maybe this marriage between them could work out after all.

After the fish course, Alexander turned to her. "Your Grace," he said. "How are you feeling?"

"Quite well at the moment," she said.

He gave a brisk nod. "I'm glad to hear it." He paused for a beat before continuing. "I have some news that may please you."

"Oh, what's that?" she asked.

"My mother and sisters will leave for Norfolk tonight."

"Tonight? Why so soon? And what are they doing in Norfolk?"

"There's a Faversham owned estate that way, a sort of dower house if you will. My mother's told me she'd prefer it than hanging around in London now she's no longer Duchess."

Belinda wrinkled her nose slightly. "Well, she needn't feel unwelcome here, if that's why she's in a hurry to leave. I don't want to be the one to push her out by any means."

Alexander nodded. "I expected you'd say something like that. And I believe you. But my mother has her own wiles and I doubt she'd cope well with another mistress of the house. Best for everyone this way."

"Yes, I suppose that makes sense," she said. She waited a beat before continuing. "And you, your Grace, how are you feeling about all of this?"

"I'm trying my best to be calm. Lady Reynolds, well she didn't make this easy. For either of us."

"True, she did not."

"But I am determined to look after you, to protect you." His dark hawk-like eyes bore down at her with a hot ferocity that she didn't quite understand.

Her heart leapt a little.

Then, he continued speaking. "Please be assured that I will do my utmost to protect you, in every regard."

Belinda smiled. It was a relief to hear him speak of protection, as he had the day after the Landsdowne Ball. Clearly, providing protection was something he valued very highly. "Thank you, your Grace," she said.

He nodded but didn't get a chance to reply as Edgar tapped on a glass.

It was time for the formal speeches to begin, starting with Edgar's quasi-father of the bride speech.

After dinner, once they were all alone and the rest of the Favershams had retired to the London dower house, Alexander rose from his chair and knelt on bended knee before his bride.

She looked so charming like this, he thought. With her hair tied in a loose bun and her jewelled gown. She was every inch the duchess. In the firelight, she shone with a radiance he had rarely ever encountered before.

She was a golden orb, even that entereth within the veil, and he was the sceptre.

Belinda looked down at him with a slightly puzzled, expectant expression on her face.

The fire crackled away, a brightly glowing pyre surrounded by a band of darkness in the farthest reaches of the hearth.

Alexander opened his mouth and began to speak. "Your Grace, you are most beautiful. And you will make a most excellent Duchess. I am so very glad that you are going to be my Duchess."

Before Belinda had a chance to formulate a reply, Alexander raised himself from the floor. "Now, if there is anything you wish for, my servants will attend to you," he said.

Belinda scrunched up her nose. "Are you not staying?" This didn't align with anything her kindly maid had told her to expect all those years ago.

Alexander was on his feet. "I must take my leave now, your Grace. I have urgent estate business to attend to."

Belinda nodded slowly. None of this made any sense. But who was she to question her husband?

Alexander bowed to her and swiftly exited the room.

Belinda sat dumbstruck. What on earth had just happened?

After a few minutes, she got up out of the armchair and made her way over to the windows. She cast her gaze out across Hyde Park and Rotten Row. They were enveloped in darkness with the only lights being a line of flaming torches adjoining the road. There were a few figures strolling up and down Park Lane. Who were they? Members of the ton? Some of the figures seemed to be ladies. Belinda hadn't known ladies to be able to walk out at night, so who were they?

She seethed inside. Ever since this damn season began, nothing significant had been her own choice. And ever since she tripped in the maze and Petunia Reynolds found her and Alexander together, the path to the altar was locked and loaded. And to cap it all off, her new husband was behaving very oddly with some strange, unbelievable excuse about urgent estate business.

On the one hand, she wanted to give him the benefit of the doubt. Dukes would have to deal with estate emergencies from time to time. It was the nature of being a duke, after all.

Yet, on the other hand, she could not escape from the thought that it was highly unusual for a groom to effectively abandon his bride on their wedding night. He had been so awkward. Surely a duke, one of the most powerful men in the kingdom, wouldn't be nervous on his wedding night? If anyone would be nervous, shouldn't it be her? The inexperienced young woman bound at the altar to obey him? None of the evening's events made any sense whatsoever.

She clenched her fists in frustration and turned away from the window.

This room, though she hadn't really looked closely at it when Alexander had led her here, was comfortable with a hint of the ornate. Similar to some of the rooms at Weatherby House, so there was that familiarity at least.

Was this all her married life would be? Being shuttled from grand house to grand house, while her husband sequestered himself away somewhere else entirely?

The clock on the mantelpiece chimed nine on the hour.

She sighed. There were still so many hours of the evening to go.

For want of anything better to do, and because she had no idea of where anything important was in this blasted house yet, she walked over to the servants' bell and pulled down the cord.

She stood and awaited whoever would appear before her. She gritted her teeth.

After a few minutes, there was a knock at the door. A woman's voice called through the wood. "Your Grace?"

"Enter," Belinda replied.

A woman in her late twenties, about Belinda's height, stood before her. It was her new lady's maid, Miss Dauntsey.

"Good evening," Belinda said.

"Is there anything I can get for you, your Grace?" Dauntsey asked.

"Say, I've barely seen any of this house yet. Would you give me a tour?"

"Yes, your Grace," Dauntsey replied.

The pair made their way through the door.

At last, Belinda would discover the lay of the land of her new home.

⁂

After a good hour of strolling around, Belinda had seen most wings of the house. The library, every guest bedroom and the three drawing rooms. She had even had a brief wander through the gardens, where the light was terrible and she could hardly see a thing.

Back inside, Belinda noticed a whole corridor she hadn't been down before. "What's this way?" she asked.

"Oh, this is his Grace's wing," Dauntsey said. "I can show you the corridor, though probably not the rooms themselves. That I had better leave to the butler."

Dauntsey led Belinda down a corridor covered in dark green damask wallpaper. As with some of the other corridors in the house, a few oil lamps in sconces lit the way here and there.

Every door was shut. Nary a sound emerged from any of them.

Dauntsey gestured around. "His Grace's chambers and offices."

Belinda nodded before asking, "And where shall I be staying?"

"Ah now, I can show you all of that," Dauntsey said with a smile. She led Belinda down several twists and turns and up a grand, oaken flight of stairs. Another hallway covered in dark green wallpaper lay out before the women. Unlike the duke's chambers, every single door was open.

The lady's maid gestured to each doorway in turn. A study, two sitting rooms, a dressing room, a walk in wardrobe, a bathroom and a finely decorated bedroom. All fit for a duchess.

Belinda walked back down towards one of the sitting rooms. "Say, would you set up some tea in here?"

"At once, your Grace." Dauntsey curtsied and scurried off towards what Belinda presumed were the kitchens.

Belinda made her way into the sitting room and took in her new home.

These were lavish, salubrious surroundings. She could be most comfortable here. But where was her husband? And, more to the point, why on earth had he made such a hasty exit on their wedding night of all nights? None of it made any sense, however much she may want to give him the benefit of the doubt and assume the best of intentions.

CHAPTER FIVE

The next morning, Belinda woke up alone in a strange bed. At first she had no idea where she was. Where was the familiar pink and white embossed wallpaper? Where was her collection of trinkets and treasures? The tin whistle Xavier had brought back for her from Edinburgh, the shells she had collected from the rockpools on that trip to Lyme Regis when she was eight?

Then realisation dawned. She was in the Duchess' chambers at the Faversham's London home. And not as a guest, but as the very Duchess herself.

She rose and padded to the window, drawing her lace dressing gown close around her as she did so. Outside she could see the grand driveway and then beyond the gates that looked out onto Park Lane.

This was her territory as a lady of the ton. She knew Park Lane very well indeed from the regular carriage rides she had taken up and down it over the years. Beyond lay Hyde Park and Rotten Row. Again, places she knew oh so well from the days of her girlhood.

Once upon a time, before her condition began, she had rode up and down Rotten Row with her brothers. She had loved the sensation of being free in the open air. Of travelling at pace. Of working together with her horse to move forwards and achieve a common goal. She had been a keen young horsewoman. But her courses beginning and the associated pains had put paid to all that.

She tried to focus her mind on happier things. Not on what she had lost but rather the things she could still do that she enjoyed.

She loved playing her violin, her books and, when she had the chance, dancing. All those things brought her great joy. She hoped as the Duchess of Faversham she would still be able to pursue them. Surely the cold-hearted duke would not be so cruel as to deny her those pleasures? Both Edgar and Miss Cookson had told her that the Duke was not a cruel man. And the day after their engagement, the man himself had assured her that he would always treat her with honour. Would it not be so harmless to take her husband, her brother and her modiste at their word? And put her faith in her husband?

Belinda walked along the landing and made her way down the stairs. Stationed at various points along the hallways were footmen in sumptuous green velvet liveries. The Faversham family colours.

She entered the dining room and took her seat at the opposite end of the table to where the Duke, as head of the household, would sit. No one else was in the room. It was still rather early so she expected Alexander would be along soon to join her for breakfast.

The butler, Prentice, entered the room carrying a piece of paper and a small knife on a silver platter. He stopped next to Belinda, turned towards her and bowed.

"Your Grace," said Prentice. "His Grace left this letter for you."

Bemusement filled Belinda's features as she reached out and took the wax sealed letter and little knife in her hands.

She thanked Prentice and he bowed with a line that breakfast would be served shortly. Then almost as quickly as he had materialised, he left the room and Belinda was alone again.

She ran her fingers across the Faversham crest on the wax seal with its ducal coronet and two bulls as supporters. She took the knife and sliced open the wax seal. Her eyes widened as she began to read the contents of the letter.

Dear Duchess,

Welcome to the Faversham family. I trust that you find everything to your satisfaction. Though we have spent little time together, from the brief encounters we have had as well as the discussions I have had with your brothers Lord Weatherby and Lord Xavier, I know that you are going to be a most excellent duchess.

Therefore, it is with the greatest regret that I write this letter. By the time it reaches your hands, I will have left London for my Yorkshire estate, Faversham Abbey. It is my intention to reside there for the foreseeable future.

I must tell you not to try to follow me and to instead stay in the south. Of course, you shall have free reign of Faversham

House in London as well as my Bath property. It is a most charming residence, very near the Royal Crescent, so I hope you shall enjoy the delights of that fair city when the mood strikes you. But I must reiterate that I do not desire you to come to Faversham Abbey. I beg you to understand that this desire is not due to any flaw on your part. Rather, I make this decision to protect you and for your own benefit as I do not wish you to be hurt anymore than you already have been.

With sincere regard, your husband Faversham

Belinda sat backwards. She froze in shock. Of all the things she thought might happen on her first full day as the Duchess of Faversham, this hadn't even crossed her mind as a possibility.

Whatever was she to do now?

Surely her husband had a good reason for behaving as he did and vanishing to the north, all while commanding her not to follow him. What that reason was, she had no idea.

Having free reign of two properties was an enticing prospect and one that was so far out of her previous realm experience as a Weatherby daughter. Perhaps it was something she would learn to enjoy.

She might as well make the best of this most confusing situation. She resolved to find what pleasure she could, where she could.

Still, there was a funny churning in her stomach. She didn't think she could face breakfast this morning.

When she finally got up from the table, after what could have been several hours for all she knew, her cutlery and crockery lay completely clean and untouched.

Alexander held his head in his hands.

As the carriage rolled north and every mile pulled him further and further from his new bride, the pang of regret in his stomach stabbed him like a dagger.

How he wished to be in London with her and enjoying the delights of life as newlyweds. Yet his own choices meant it was not in Belinda's best interest to be around him. He had to withdraw himself from the situation for his wife's safety.

If she were ever, heaven forfend, to find out about his choices then it would surely break her heart. He had to protect her at all costs, even if it came at the cost of his own happiness. She was his wife and he had a duty to her to honour and protect her. And Alexander Faversham was a man for whom duty meant everything.

He hated himself for what he had done. For how his own choices had led him to this inevitable decision. He loathed himself for how Belinda would inevitably awaken today to one of the worst shocks of her life. She would surely go down to the breakfast table, expecting to dine with him, only to be greeted by a letter. His letter. Telling her that he was going to Yorkshire and that she was not to follow him.

He had tried to be reasonable. He didn't want her to feel like she had to be cooped up in London or hide herself away. She could do as she pleased in respectable London society, or go to Bath and be part of the ton there. Whatever she liked. But the one thing that he could not allow her to do was follow him up to Yorkshire.

He knew this must make him seem exactly the cold-hearted duke of his rumoured reputation. Any rational observer would surely think so.

But it had to be this way. If he was to protect her, if he was to keep her safe, it had to be like this.

He had no other choice.

This action, once the ton found out, would cause some rumblings. But he knew that ultimately the gentlemen of the ton would see it as a husband's prerogative. And the ladies would think that Belinda was lucky to make such a quick getaway from a man who they believed could only ever be a cruel husband.

Yes, Belinda would be better off without him. It was incontrovertible.

Rain drove down the windows of the carriage. The London summer was becoming merely a distant memory in the rear view window. Ahead, lay only the windswept autumn of the Yorkshire Moors.

The carriage rolled on, ever northwards, carrying Alexander and his regrets with it.

It would only be a matter of a few short days until he was at Faversham Abbey. And Belinda would be truly safe from him.

CHAPTER SIX

Another morning, another breakfast alone. Belinda sat at the table in her usual spot.

The Dowager Duchess and her daughters were well settled into their Norfolk home. That left Belinda alone with the servants. She had briefly entertained the idea of going to stay in Bath but that would change little to nothing of her situation. She would still be alone and her husband would still be hiding from her up in Yorkshire.

It was all so tedious and dull. To be here at Faversham House with no one to talk to but her maid and the rest of the servants. To be without anyone who would stand half a chance of saying anything beyond platitudes and agreeing to orders only as long as they ultimately aligned with the Duke's wishes.

She wasn't going to find much more worthwhile here at Faversham House, that was for certain.

Perhaps she should pay someone a social call?

Frustratingly, her dearest friend Abigail had recently married and left London to start her family in the West Country. So a visit to her today was off the cards.

But she did have some other friends still in town. Theodosia, Maria and Harriet. She would pay them each a call and see what conversation she could find there.

<hr>

A couple of hours later, Belinda was in one of her favourite day dresses inside the ducal carriage and on her way to the mansion where Theodosia lived on St James's Square.

She hoped Theodosia would be a good listening ear.

They'd been friends since girlhood, Theodosia being from the notable Sedgewick family who had known the Weatherbys for generations unto generations.

The carriage drew up outside the Sedgewick residence and, in short order, a footman assisted Belinda out onto the pavement below.

Belinda entered the house and a maid showed her to the drawing room.

Theodosia looked up from the book she was reading and her face broke into a smile to see her friend. She put the book down and lifted herself to her feet. "Belinda! So lovely to see you!" she exclaimed.

"You too," Belinda said. "How are you?"

Theodosia walked towards her friend. "I am well, I am well." She reached Belinda and took her hands in her own. "But tell me, your Grace, how is married life? I want to hear all about it!"

"Oh well, er -" Belinda began.

"How rude of me! Please sit, please sit." Theodosia butted in and gestured to the settee. Then she addressed a maid who stood lingering by the door. "Some tea and sandwiches for us, please."

The maid scurried off to the kitchens.

Belinda sat herself down on the plush settee.

Theodosia joined her. "Oh yes, so sorry. How rude of me to interrupt. You were saying?"

"Well, yes, married life," Belinda said. "It has its positives, but it hasn't proved to be everything I thought."

Theodosia raised her eyebrows and her eyes widened. "How so?"

"The Duke has already gone away."

"Gone away? What do you mean?"

"To his estate. In Yorkshire."

Theodosia brought her hand to her mouth in surprise. "Why? And so soon after your wedding. Was there some emergency that drew him up there?"

"That's the thing," Belinda said. "He's been very secretive about it. He's told me it's for my protection and to not follow him up there."

"That's not good at all. You poor thing." Theodosia shook her head.

At that moment, two footmen entered the room carrying trays of sandwiches and tea. They swiftly placed them on the coffee table in front of Belinda and Theodosia and left the room.

Theodosia gestured to the refreshments. "Don't worry, I'll pour." She set to work and then said, "Surely the Duke must have his reasons though."

"But what could they be?" Belinda leaned forward and helped herself to a cucumber sandwich.

"I suppose there could be many reasons. Perhaps there really is an emergency on the estate, something dangerous could have happened and he wants to keep you well out of it. Perhaps someone up there is ill and he has gone to attend to them and it's contagious. Perhaps there's unrest amongst his tenants and he's gone up there to sort it out," Theodosia pondered, her mind as usual heading to the place of the dramatic.

"Those could be true," Belinda said.

"In any case," Theodosia continued confidently. "He is your husband so surely he must know best and have your best interests at heart."

Belinda nodded, but said nothing. As fun as she could be, Theodosia had led a very sheltered life in a happy family. She was a bit naive to the ways of the world and the ways of some gentlemen. Gentlemen like her unfortunate husband, it seemed.

Theodosia gestured to a cup of tea. "Here, please have this one dearest."

Belinda took the cup and began to drink. Theodosia was well intentioned but this visit hadn't been the balm to her heart that she had optimistically hoped it would be.

⟡⟡⟡⟡⟡⟡ ⟡⟡⟡⟡⟡⟡

Over the next few days, Belinda paid visits to Maria and Harriet. Love them as she did, their reactions to her marital woes had been much the same as Thomasina's.

Belinda sat and stewed in her chambers after coming back from her final visit to the trio. Her friends in town were all still unwed and starry-eyed about her new marriage. Becoming a duchess was about the pinnacle of what they could hope to achieve in life. So it really should have come as no surprise that they weren't able to understand the predicament she faced.

She berated herself for thinking things would be any different.

Poor little rich girl, indeed.

A couple of days later, after another round of shopping on Bond Street, Belinda decided to pay a visit to Weatherby House.

She hadn't anticipated being back so soon, having expected to be living her first weeks of married life with Alexander, but it would nonetheless be good to see her brothers and sisters again.

She wandered into the drawing room where a familiar sight met her eyes.

Her eldest brother, Edgar, sat reading some paperwork.

Around him, her two youngest siblings, Lionel and Genevieve, were on the floor engrossed in some sort of card game.

Edgar looked up from his papers. "Sister, so nice to see you. What brings you here?"

She walked towards him and sat down in an armchair next to him. "I thought I'd come by and see how you're all getting along without me."

"Well we are surviving, but we do miss our beloved sister," Edgar said.

Lionel and Genevieve got up from their spot on the floor and made their way towards their elder siblings.

Genevieve broke into a broad grin. "It's Belinda!"

"Belinda!" Lionel exclaimed in excitement.

The group exchanged pleasantries and Genevieve and Lionel both proudly spoke of how their studies were going.

Then the children's governess arrived to take them to their luncheon, leaving Belinda alone with Edgar.

"What's happening, sister?" Edgar asked. "Shouldn't you be with your new husband?"

Belinda sighed. "That's it. He's gone and left me."

Edgar's eyebrows shot up. "Left you? How? Why? When?"

"The morning after our wedding, I went down to breakfast only to find a note from him advising that he had gone north to his Yorkshire estate. He said it wasn't my fault or anything I've done wrong. He didn't give a clear reason. Instead, he merely said it was for my protection," she said.

"Your protection? So he didn't say what he was protecting you from?"

"No, he didn't," Belinda said firmly. "And he also decreed I shouldn't follow him up there."

"So he wants you to stay in London the whole time?"

"This is perhaps even odder, but no. In his note he wrote about me having the option to live in a house he keeps in Bath as well. And he never said anything about not living anywhere other than his houses either. So I don't think he's trying to keep me prisoner in London."

"No, it doesn't sound like he is," Edgar agreed.

Belinda took a pause before responding. "Though brother, I must ask you something."

"Go on," he said.

"On the night of the Landsdowne Ball, after all the dramatics in the maze, when you and I were alone together. You said to me that the Duke is not a cruel man. Do you still believe that to be true?"

"I think there could be a good explanation for why he's behaved the way he has so far in your marriage. You said he explicitly said it wasn't your fault?"

Belinda nodded. "That's right."

"Well, that's somewhat reassuring that he's not a cruel man. Because if he blamed you for this baffling decision of his, then that would be a sign of cruelty from him," Edgar said.

"It's still a baffling decision though."

"It is, yes. But there must surely be a reason."

"There very likely is. He said he did it to protect you. Perhaps there is an emergency and he needs to resolve it to keep you from harm."

"But what emergency?" Belinda spluttered.

"One can only speculate. Maybe there's been some problem with the tenants on the estate and he needs to go up there to resolve it. Maybe there's been some sort of financial dispute and he has to fix it to ensure your future security."

Belinda tilted her head this way and that. "Might be so, I suppose. What do you think I should do?"

"Until you know more about what he's done and why, I wouldn't rush to take any course of action. I'd bide my time if I were you." Edgar said.

"And then what should I do, if I bide my time and it all turns out that he's been up to something nefarious?" Belinda grew more agitated. "I can't realistically get an annulment, I'd be ruined given what the rumour mill says happened in that blasted maze!"

Edgar reached out and laid a gentle hand on her forearm. "There are still options. You don't have to get an annulment or live with him. He said you could live in London or in Bath, correct?"

"Yes, he did."

"Well, those are still possibilities. You could live in either city, be mistress of your own household and do your best to forget about him. But until you know more about his reasoning, I wouldn't start closing down opportunities for yourself."

"Lady Petunia Reynolds already saw to that weeks ago!" Belinda exclaimed.

Edgar sighed. "Yes, she did. And it's very unfortunate. You have a right to be angry about it. But you can't change the past. All you can do is move forward."

Belinda nodded. Her brother was speaking some sense, as cool-headed as he could be. "You've certainly given me a lot to think about. Thank you, Edgar."

"Anytime we're both in town, I'm here to talk. And when I'm not, you can always send me a letter and I'll write back. I don't want you to feel alone, sister," he said.

"Thank you," she said.

Belinda left Weatherby House with a slightly new optimism. Her conversation with Edgar had been reassuring in some ways. It was a relief to know she still had his support and that he thought there could be a reasonable explanation for the Duke's strange behaviour.

Yet she still had so many unanswered questions.

And Edgar, love him as she did, was never the kind to make her heart light with laughter or sympathy. He was good at dishing out cool-headed advice but that was as far as it went. It was his way of showing he cared, after all. She would have had to speak to Xavier for a pint of sympathy and he was currently traversing the length of Great Britain on one of his many leisure trips.

Such was the life of a young man of the ton, she sighed. Men like Xavier could wait years until they wed and could behave largely as they wished in the meantime. On the other hand, young ladies like her had to be on their best behaviour. Or risk ruination. Or end up in a cold, loveless marriage like hers.

Belinda headed down the Mall in the Faversham carriage. Today she was off to see more family members, this time two of her mother's cousins, Virginia, Countess of Solihull, and Margaret, Viscountess of Bournemouth.

Since her mother's death, Virginia and Margaret had been the two most prominent matriarchs in her life. Perhaps they would have some words of wisdom to set her on the right path. And they had assured her before she wed that she could always count on their full support, after all.

A short while later, and Belinda was standing outside the doors to the drawing room at the Bournemouth London townhouse.

"Her Grace, the Duchess of Faversham, is here to see you, my ladies," the footman said.

Belinda walked into the room and greeted her cousins.

The footman exited the room, leaving the three women to their conversation.

"Belinda, darling," Margaret said, "how lovely to see you. Oh, do have a seat!" She gestured to the sofa where she was sitting.

Belinda made her way over and joined her cousin on the sofa.

A maid entered carrying a fresh pot of tea. The maid poured cups for each family member.

Margaret turned to Belinda. "Now, Belinda, how are you finding married life?" she asked.

Belinda sucked in her lower lip and furrowed her brows, before replying, "It is quieter than I had expected."

"Quieter? How so?" Virginia asked.

"Well, the Dowager and the girls have already moved out," Belinda said.

"To the Dowager House?" Virginia asked.

"No, there's a property in Norfolk they've gone to." Belinda took a sip of her tea.

"Oh, well, I suppose you don't have to worry too much about there being someone else around who used to be the mistress of the house," Margaret said with brisk brightness.

Belinda sucked in her lower lip again. "I suppose so."

Margaret's face fell.

Virginia said, "That doesn't sound like the voice of a happy, newly anointed duchess. Is something wrong, dearest?"

Belinda heaved her shoulders. "Alexander has gone."

"Gone? Where?" Margaret asked.

"To his estate in Yorkshire." Belinda took another sip of her tea. "He left me the full run of the townhouse here, as well as a place he has in Bath, all with good supplies and funds. And yet, I don't understand why he went away in the first place."

"Did he give any reason? Any indication at all?" Virginia asked.

Belinda shook her head. "No, he wouldn't give a clear reason. He said it was to protect me. But, protect me from what?"

Margaret and Virginia exchanged puzzled glances.

Then Margaret said, "Well, you have no reason to doubt that his assertion is true, however cryptic it is." She reached across and took Belinda's hands between her own. "Dearest, from all I know of your husband, he is a most respectable gentleman and he would not want to do anything to harm you. It may be hard to have your husband away, but surely he would have made this decision with your best interests at heart. He has left you the full run of two houses with good supplies, proper funds, yes?"

Belinda nodded. "Yes, that's correct. There's nothing material of which I am in want."

Virginia and Margaret shared another glance.

Margaret spoke again. "It's a challenging situation, no doubt. And I would wager, not what you had expected. But there are ways to make the best of it."

"And," Virginia added, "there are more than a few wives amongst the ton who would be very happy indeed to be left to have the run of not one but two houses, with no husband or other interfering relations to get in the way."

"You do have a point," Belinda said.

Virginis and Margaret's eyes met in a furrowed gaze of concern. Every sentence Belinda uttered was more and more evidence that her marriage was in trouble.

Something would have to give.

CHAPTER SEVEN

A couple of days later, Belinda sat in the carriage opposite Virginia and Margaret.

"So, Belinda, darling, we know you have been cooped up in that house," said Virginia.

Margaret took up her sister's train of speech. "And that is no way for a duchess of the ton to spend her days."

At that, Belinda gave a weak smile.

Margaret continued speaking. "Today is the day you make your debut into the Everaline Club."

Belinda quirked an eyebrow. "The Everaline Club? What's that?"

"Ah, now that is something all married ladies of the ton can join," said Virginia. "And as a duchess, your place is assured, second only to members of the royal family. Your late mother was a member, as was her mother before her."

"So it's a bit like the Lumley Club and the other clubs the gentlemen join?" asked Belinda.

Margaret nodded and smiled. "Yes, it's along those lines. Though I strongly believe that there is no gentleman's club anywhere in the kingdom that can hold a candle to our beloved Everaline Club."

The carriage rattled along the Strand before turning into a courtyard of discrete brick buildings.

This was definitely not the sort of place Belinda would ever have suspected could play host to a prestigious ladies club.

The carriage drew to a halt. A footman opened the door and pulled down the steps.

Belinda and her two relations emerged from the carriage. They were outside a red brick house four stories tall and constructed in the Queen Anne style so popular a century before.

The footman wrapped smartly on a glossy obsidian door and stepped away.

Twenty seconds or so went by and the door swung open to reveal a middle-aged maid.

She gave a curtsey. "My ladies, how lovely to see you."

Margaret nodded. "Thank you, Higgins."

Higgins took the group's cloaks and then led the way down a well-lit pale peach corridor and into a buttercream room. It reminded Belinda a bit of Mrs Buppetts Tea Rooms, only there were no men and a harpist was playing serenely on a small stage in the corner. The tables were bustling with ladies, many of whom Belinda recognised from the ballrooms of the ton.

This was not the sort of place Belinda had imagined would ever be available to ladies of the ton. Why had her mother never mentioned it to her while she was still alive? Perhaps Belinda had been to young, only still a young girl when her parents went down with that ship. Perhaps, Belinda supposed, her mother would have been the one to initiate her into the Everaline Club had her mother lived long enough to see Belinda walk down the aisle.

"Now," Margaret said brightly, "there are some ladies whom I would love to introduce."

Before Belinda knew much else of what was going on, Margaret took her by the elbow and guided her towards a group of women dressed in fine pastel gowns. Belinda guessed they were about ten years her senior.

"Your Grace, may I present to you Lady Elizabeth Greenslade, Viscountess Mere." Margaret gestured to a wiry blonde woman with well-accentuated cheekbones.

"Oh it is a pleasure to meet you, your Grace," said Viscountess Mere. "Please, call me Beth."

And before long, Belinda was on first-name terms with all the group, three viscountesses, a countess and a couple of baronesses.

The party moved towards one of the round oaken tables scattered around the room and took their seats.

Beth said, "What shall we play? How about a game of whist?"

And, with that, the great game began.

Belinda was no stranger to whist, or indeed many of the other card games so popular with the ton, having played many a round with family and friends over the years. But she was no major aficionado. Instead, she used this game as an opportunity to observe and learn more about the ladies around her. Virginia and Margaret she knew very well and she enjoyed seeing them in their element. Viscountess Mere, or Beth as she now called her, was no good at this game. Her face gave everything away to the point that Belinda may as well have been sitting directly behind her. Viscountess Bolsover, on the other hand, had a truly inscrutable face. She was made to play games such as this. The two baronesses seemed more interested in the little cups of sherry the waitresses kept refilling. Whist could go hang for all that pair cared. And the Viscountess Stewart and the Countess of Fishguard were most keen to hear all about how Belinda found the club and was she enjoying it and how much they looked forward to seeing her there on a regular basis.

Though as a duchess she outranked them all, she could not help but feel a little out of place. Not starstruck or unworthy, more someone who had suddenly moved from the world of the marriage mart and an unsecure future to a world where she had a safe position as a duchess. It was all such a whirlwind.

❧❧❧❧❧❧　❧❧❧❧❧

The Bournemouth carriage didn't drop Belinda off at Faversham House until well after the church bells had chimed eleven.

She gave a cheery, quick farewell to Virginia and Margaret and then scurried down the carriage steps and through the main doors of the house.

A few servants were still up and about and the candles in the entrance hall burned bright.

She turned to the most senior footman on duty and said, "Please, shut up the house for the night."

He gave a bow. "Yes, your Grace."

Belinda turned and made her way up the staircase to her chambers.

She stood at the window and looked out towards Grosvenor Square, Mayfair and beyond into Soho. London lay snug before her. Here and there, candlelights were still burning in the windows of the city's most elite households. Mostly though, it was swathes of darkness until Soho. There, as in nearby Covent Garden, there would still be light and life, with the crowds spilling out from the theatres on Drury Lane and heading towards the pubs and gin palaces.

Lost in her thoughts, she startled slightly at a knock at the door.

Miss Dauntsey's now-familiar voice filtered through the opening. "Your Grace?"

"Come in," Belinda called.

Miss Dauntsey swept into the room. "Your Grace, may I get you anything?"

"Some water please and then take down my hair," Belinda said.

"Very good, your Grace." Miss Dauntsey lit a couple of candles and went into the antechamber.

Belinda carried on watching the lights and the darkness of London at night.

In two ticks, Miss Dauntsey reentered the room carrying a pitcher of water.

Belinda turned around and made her way to the dressing table. She seated herself and met her own gaze in the mirror. Through the dim light, she saw her skin bathed in a warm honey glow and her eyes shimmering bright.

Miss Dauntsey placed the pitcher and a full glass on the dressing table. Then she bustled around, looking for the hair kit.

Belinda took a sip of the cool water.

Miss Dauntsey began to remove the complex arrangement of pins from Belinda's hairdo. Each pin made a clink as it hit the bottom of the metal pin case.

Belinda stared at herself in the mirror and felt the water rush down her throat. Not much to do now other than let her maid get on with the task at hand. As the maid worked, Belinda ruminated on what else she could do over the coming week. She hadn't had any new dresses for a while, not since the wedding in fact. A trip to the modiste would be just the thing.

"Miss Dauntsey," said Belinda, "tomorrow afternoon, after luncheon, will you have the coach brought round please. I should like to go to the modiste. A trip to Cookson is in order."

"Of course, your Grace," Miss Dauntsey said with a smile. She removed the last of the pins and picked up the silver hairbrush. She made quick work of the knots and, soon enough, Belinda's tresses were bouncing and smooth.

Belinda made her nightly farewells to the maid then she was alone. Like every night, it seemed, in this godforsaken Faversham House.

The bell jangled at Jean Cookson's modiste shop.

Belinda made her way through the entrance door, leaving Miss Dauntsey outside while she chatted to another maid.

Belinda cast her eyes over the sumptuous array of fabrics that lined the walls. Ivory satin, forest green velvet and navy blue lace shimmered in the brisk morning light.

From somewhere in the back of beyond of the shop, Jean's voice rang clear. "Just a second, madam."

Belinda didn't mind. She had all the time in the world. Too much time on her hands, in fact.

Less than a minute later and Jean appeared through the archway that led to her fitting room. She bobbed a curtsey. "Your Grace, what a pleasure it is to see you! What would you like today?"

"Well, I am in need of some new dresses. Four or five would do," Belinda said.

"Ah yes, your Grace. I have some new fine lace, from Ireland, that I think you really must see." Jean turned and made her way towards a roll of pale pink lace. She pulled it from the shelf and placed it upon a sturdy wooden measuring table.

Belinda walked over to face Jean.

The modiste unfurled a foot of the roll of lace. "Now this, you see, is perfect for trimmings. I could make you some of those empire line pieces, and put this around the hems. And, if this shade's not for you, I've also got the lace in a few other colours. Cream, sage, and periwinkle blue."

"That sounds most excellent, thank you Miss Cookson. Let's try the sage," Belinda said.

Belinda cast her eyes over the pile of fabrics. They were so stylish and luxurious. Any lady of the ton would be delighted to wear a dress made out of them. Hopefully they would serve as a pleasant distraction from her husband's vexing behaviour.

She looked forward to receiving the finished dresses within the fortnight.

The following week, Belinda was in the Faversham carriage for another visit to the Everaline Club

She knew Virginia and Margaret were very likely to be there, veritable regulars that they were. Others of the married crowd would be present too. She had not realised it before she got married, but the true seats of matriarchal power within the ton were not its ballrooms or drawing rooms. Instead, the true matriarchal power lay within ladies clubs like the Everaline Club. They were where the real decisions were made.

Already, she had learnt that the impending marriage between the third son of the Baron Galesville and Miss Thomasina Young was blocked due to a certain member of the club bringing to light revelations of how abominably the Baron had treated his servants. The story had reached Miss Young before the day was out and the engagement was called off with all haste.

It had also transpired that the ladies of the Everaline Club had played a key role in halting the elopement of the fifteen year old daughter of Baron Elliott, Miss Susannah Elliott, and a certain man twice her age. The cad's name was Mr Horatio Ashley and, thanks to the efforts of the Everaline Club and their connections across the Midlands, Ashley's carriage was intercepted on the Great North Road. The pair never did make it to Gretna Green and the notorious bounder Ashley was banished from the ton.

If it were left to the gentlemen of London society, neither Galesville nor Ashley would likely have faced any impediment to their nefarious activities.

Belinda stepped out of the carriage, knocked on the club doors and soon enough she was inside the sitting area.

Several now familiar faces came up to greet her.

"Belinda, darling!" Viscountess Bolsover exclaimed with joy. "Come and join us for a round of Whist."

She joined the table and took up her hand of cards.

The Countess of Fishguard leaned across and said, "How are you, Belinda?"

The pair exchanged pleasantries.

Then Viscountess Mere addressed the table at large. "Have you heard, ladies, about what the Viscount of Daylesbury did last week with several opera singers?"

"No!" the Countess of Fishguard said. "Do tell, dearest."

Viscountess Bolsover added, "Yes do, we are all on tenterhooks to know."

"Well," Viscountess Mere crowed with confidential relish, "I have it on good authority that the Viscount of Daylesbury took three opera singers to his townhouse and none of them left his bedchambers for four days. He has most specialised tastes, I understand. And the opera singers were paid most handsomely for their participation and for their discretion."

Viscountess Bolsover laughed. "They can't have been paid very well to be discreet or else we wouldn't be hearing this story right now."

The Countess of Fishguard smirked. "I believe the story broke thanks to a loose-lipped maidservant who was already leaving the Viscount's employ. It was a bit of a parting shot to her former employer."

"Ah yes, that is always a risk with disgruntled servants," Viscountess Bolsover said.

Viscountess Mere nodded sagely. "Confidences can easily be betrayed. If she didn't need a character for whatever reason, she could have been tempted to spill the beans to all and sundry."

Belinda hummed in agreement.

"That's why," Viscountess Bolsover said, "It's so important to keep one's servants on side."

"And for those that don't," the Countess of Fishguard added, "that's what keeps us here at the Everaline Club in entertainment!"

The group laughed uproariously and resumed their card game.

Belinda decided she liked it here at the club. It was fun, the company was amusing and she was part of a group of the ton's distinguished married ladies. Perhaps she could get used to this.

London was different now for Belinda. All her life she had considered it one of her two homes, the other being her family's main seat of Renfregh down in the West Country, yet now things were greyer and drearier.

She had achieved the apex of all a young lady of the ton could hope for. Marriage to a Duke and the role of Duchess. Anything higher and she would actually be royalty.

Yet obtaining that position hadn't brought with it the glories one might think it would. Yes, she was mistress of a beautiful big townhouse with a retinue of dozens of servants. And yes, wherever she went people bowed and curtsied to her and called her 'Your Grace'. And yes, she was now a member of the prestigious Everaline Club.

But none of it served to remove the grey pall that her husband's sudden, mysterious exile had cast over her life.

She looked out of the window and examined the street below. Park Lane. Carriages clattered up and down it, carrying all manner of people from across the spectrum of London life. Beyond lay Hyde Park and Rotten Row. The place to see and be seen by anyone who was anyone on the ton.

Yes, a ride out on Rotten Row would at least provide a distraction for the afternoon. Another way to while away the hours.

She raised herself from the chaise longue and went to pull the servant bell cord.

In short order, Miss Dauntsey entered the room. "Your Grace," she said in a puffed voice.

"A ride around Rotten Row would do me good. Have a man prepare a coach, please," Belinda said.

"At once, your Grace." Miss Dauntsey gave a curtsey before scurrying out of the room.

Belinda sat in the back of the coach with the roof down. The gentle breeze of summer ruffled past her ears.

She leaned back into the seat and surveyed the world around her.

Autumn was fast on the horizon and the leaves on the trees were clinging on to their verdant colours. In only a short while, however, they would turn shades of amber, gold and russet. And then they would fall off and become dry husks on the soon-to-be snowy ground. But not yet. Not yet.

Hot dust from the street and pavements blew up into the carriage with every beat of the horses hooves.

Summertime in the city and she wanted to take advantage of it.

The coach turned onto Rotten Row. The great and the good and the not-so-good of the ton were out in full force.

Gentlemen on horseback caught her eye and tipped their hats in her direction.

Some of them were handsome and some were eligible bachelors.

Belinda mused how in a different reality, one where she had not had her unfortunate run in in the maze with the Duke of Faversham and Lady Reynolds, she might have been courted by one of those men on horseback. Perhaps she might even be engaged to one. But, she reminded herself, it didn't do to dwell on things that couldn't come true. She was married to the Duke now and that was the reality. She had better make the best of things as they stood.

Belinda sat in the Weatherby family box at the Theatre Royal. Tonight it was *The School for Scandal*.

Xavier and Edgar sat to her left while Philomena and cousin Caroline sat on her right.

It was Caroline's first outing at the theatre, given her tender age of fourteen.

Belinda could not help but smile at Caroline's enthusiasm and how impressed the young girl was by it all. Right from when they had arrived in the lobby, Caroline had gawked and tilted her head upwards to the ceiling in wonderment at the ornate frescos above her. She keenly looked through her opera glasses, not wanting to miss a moment of the performance, and seldom ever took her eyes away from the stage.

So far, Belinda didn't mind the show. Most of the cast were good and there were a few witty lines here and there.

But try as she might to focus on the performance in front of her, thoughts of Alexander kept erupting within her mind. Why had he run away the day after their wedding? What exactly was he protecting her from? And who was he to even make the unilateral decision to not even attempt to make their marriage work?

It was no good. She was seething inside.

She had tried to make the best of this evening, a chance to enjoy a play and spend time with family, but it had turned into a total bust.

What was the point of being a duchess, of having the run of homes in London and Bath and everyone calling her 'your Grace', if she had become virtually the prisoner of the will of Alexander Faversham?

She struggled to find an answer.

She could barely take any more of this. Day after day, she went to the Everaline Club, the modiste, the park, the theatre and other places popular with married ladies of the ton. And nothing ever seemed to change. Nothing served to soothe the feeling she wasn't living her life to its fullest. That something was off. Something was restricted, constrained.

Five days later and Belinda felt a familiar, unpleasant sensation within her abdomen.

The carriage was thankfully only a few steps away, awaiting her out the front of the bookshop.

She quickly paid for her purchases, *Henrietta* for herself and *A Vindication of the Rights of Women* as a gift for Philomena, and darted out of the door.

Her footman bowed towards her. "Where to, your Grace?"

"Faversham House," she replied. She fought not to let a grimace of pain cross her face.

"Very good, your Grace." The footman assisted her into the carriage.

In short order, the horses trotted off and Belinda was on her way back to Park Lane.

All the way, she leant forward and clutched her belly. Every blasted time this happened! She'd been on a merry go round of doctors over the years, tried all sorts of treatments, but the only thing she'd found that worked was blessed sweet laudanum. She didn't really like to have to take it, it was a powerful substance after all and one many unfortunate souls lost their way with, but it was either laudanum or trying and failing to struggle through with nothing. She knew which option she preferred.

After what felt like an age, the carriage drew up outside Faversham House.

A footman opened the door and assisted her out of the vehicle.

Belinda dashed inside the house and made a beeline for her chambers.

Along the way, she called out to a footman, "Tell Dauntsey to come to my chambers at once!"

The footman gave a bow but Belinda wasn't around to see it because she was already darting down the corridor away from him.

After several minutes of her mad, pell mell dash, she reached her chambers.

At last!

She opened the door and made her way inside.

She strode straight towards the chaise longue and en-sconced herself in her chambers.

Laying on the chaise longue, she reached for the little brown bottle and took a few drops of its contents on her tongue. The taste was so bitter. Give it a few minutes and her pains would ease. Yes, sweet laudanum would see her right.

Dauntsey would be along any moment to attend to her.

For now, she would just rest her eyes for a few minutes. Yes, that was a good idea.

CHAPTER EIGHT

Belinda sat on the settee in her chambers. Her courses now over, she felt a wave of energy building within her body. After spending the past week laying in her chambers in an all-too-often laudenum-induced haze, her mind was growing clearer and she could see a way forward.

She was sick to the back teeth of waiting around in London. Fun as the Everaline Club was, it did not cover for the fact that her husband had run away from her with a truly cryptic explanation. As beautiful as her new dresses from Cookson's were, they did not cover for the fact that she was alone in London as a duchess without her duke. And as thrilling as the city's entertainments were, they could not cover for the fact that she was alone in this city not through her own choice but because Alexander had made a unilateral decision without consulting her at all.

Some wives might enjoy being alone, having the free run of a lavish house and no husband around. Perhaps Belinda might have liked that too, had it been her own choice to live that way. But Alexander had taken that choice away from her. Like so many times before, her path in life was set by the decisions of others and not through her own free will.

Well, that was ending now. She was going to make her own decisions and take control.

She wasn't going to hang around in London any longer. Oh, no.

She wasn't going to go to Bath, as Alexander had suggested. She enjoyed that city as much as the next lady of the ton, but going there now would only be because she was tiring of London and at a loss for what else to do. And that wasn't her anymore. Oh, no.

She was going to do the one thing Alexander would never expect. The one thing a lady of the ton should never do.

She was going to disobey her husband. She was going to go to Faversham Abbey and confront him.

And even if it didn't lead to a change in their marriage, at least she would have taken action for herself rather than being an object in the life of her husband.

Come hell or high water, she was going to find out exactly what he was protecting her from. And she was going to decide for herself whether that protection was warranted.

To the north she would ride.

"Your Grace, are you sure this is the best course of action?" said Belinda's lady's maid, Miss Dauntsey. She eyed Belinda cautiously across the drawing room.

"Yes, Miss Dauntsey. However, I am not going to force you to come if you do not wish to. You are welcome to remain down here in London and I shall ensure you retain your position within the household," Belinda said.

The maid nodded. "Very well, then I am coming to Yorkshire with you, your Grace."

CHAPTER NINE

With every mile the carriage drew northwards, Belinda's stomach filled more and more with dread. What had she decided to do? How would Alexander react? Would going to Yorkshire only serve to make matters worse?

The carriage headed northbound, first on the Tottenham road before going past the turning for Yardley Manor, the Weatherby's country bolthole where Belinda had spent many happy days growing up. Then onwards towards Cambridge, stopping to spend the night in Royston, and then she was in completely unfamiliar territory.

After several days on the road, she spent her final overnight stay in York. It was a beautiful city in her eyes, she found the Minster most charming, but she wanted to press on to Faversham Abbey and address the mystery of her husband.

Then they entered the North York Moors and the sights took her breath away. She had never been to moorland before and the rugged purple heather was the sort of scenery she had only ever read about in novels.

Before long, rain began to pelt down and the already slow going due to the winding undulating roads grew ever more arduous. Dusk began to fall and the coachmen had to do their absolute utmost to keep the horses steady. After an hour of hard driving, the horses turned left through a stone and iron archway and down towards a Jacobean mansion with several towers.

Then the horses drew to a halt on a gravel drive and the carriage door opened.

Yet instead of the footman she had been expecting to see, the furious face of her husband greeted her.

The Duke nodded at the coachmen and Miss Dauntsey. "Do not fear, I do not blame any of you for this at all. Your positions are not at risk. Please go inside and have the rest of the night to yourselves."

The three employees quickly scurried off to the servant's quarters without a word.

Then the Duke said to his wife, "Would you care to tell me what on earth is going on, your Grace?"

She scoffed and crossed her arms. "I could ask you much the same thing, your Grace."

He closed his eyes briefly and looked at her with weariness. "You had best come inside."

He offered her his hand and she took it, landing with a soft thud on the wet gravel.

He made his way round the back of the carriage and untied the luggage. He called out to two menservants inside the house, who both walked briskly from the main entrance door to the carriage.

"Please, take this one to the South wing." He gestured to Belinda's trunk. "And the others to the servant's hall."

A stablehand came forward to attend to the horses and the Duke exchanged a few sentences with him.

Leaving the servants to their assigned tasks, the Duke turned to Belinda and said, "Follow me."

He turned on his heel and led her through a grand entrance hall and up a dark walnut staircase. A few more twists and turns down corridors, past vibrant tapestries, suits of armour and imposing portraits, and then he led her up a winding stone staircase to the top of a tower.

He held open a wooden door. "After you."

She walked in and found herself in a room replete with floor to ceiling bookshelves. Two beagles sat dozing in dog beds on the floor. This room was a real blend of snug and library.

In the candlelight she took a closer look at him and realised he was sodden from the rain. Her heart lurched. If the Duke's clothes were in this state after only being out in the rain for five minutes, how much worse off had the coachmen and horses fared? She felt a little rueful of her insistence on making this trip. But it could not be helped, she told herself. After all, the Duke had run off to his Yorkshire home leaving only a cryptic letter behind instructing her to never come to Faversham Abbey for her protection and 'benefit'.

She made a beeline for a sturdy wooden chair, smoothed her skirts and sat down.

Then she looked up at Alexander and waited for him to break the silence.

His dark brown eyes met her steely gaze. "You have had a long journey, your Grace. When did you last eat?" he asked.

"Oh at about one o'clock. We stopped at an inn for luncheon," she said.

"That is too long ago. I will call for some refreshments." He pulled the cord of the servant bell.

The room returned to silence.

Alexander turned away from Belinda to face the small hearth where a roaring fire burned.

Belinda eyed him up and down. He cut a finely severe figure, just as he had back in London. He wore a black waistcoat over a billowing white cotton shirt. Sleek black pantaloons covered his legs and on his feet were a pair of black leather boots. Yet, beyond his appearance, what did she really know about him? He was a duke. His mother, the Dowager, was still alive. He had three sisters. Those were the facts. He was one of the most feared men of the ton, that was what the gossip said. But beyond his convoluted talk of protection and honour, what else did she know about him? Who was Faversham, really? That was an answer she hardly knew. And as for who Alexander was? Well, that was something she didn't know at all.

A knock at the door broke Belinda from her thoughts.

"Enter," called the Duke.

A young manservant walked through the doorway.

"Bring us some supper and refreshments please, some pâté or other meats if cook has it," said the Duke.

The manservant left the room with a bow.

An awkward silence reigned over the room.

Alexander kept his gaze assiduously focused on the fireplace.

Belinda bore her eyes into him. She had come up to Yorkshire to find out his mysterious reason for protecting her and if he wanted to turn his back on her this evening, well there would be other occasions for her to uncover the truth. She could bide her time.

The fire crackled away.

The dogs dozed on.

And neither the Duke nor the Duchess uttered a word.

After about a quarter of an hour, two manservants entered the room carrying trays of food and beverages.

"Thank you, put them on the table and we will serve ourselves. That will be all," said the Duke.

The manservants left and then the Duke and Duchess were alone.

The Duke placed the wedge of pâté and two peeled hard boiled eggs on a plate together with some pickled onions and water crackers. Then he poured two glasses of ginger beer.

He put the plate and a glass in front of Belinda before taking the other glass in his hand and sipping from it.

Belinda looked down at the plate and then back up at him. "Will you not be eating too?"

"No, I had supper about half an hour before you arrived," he said.

"This is rather a lot of pâté, are you sure you do not want some?"

He waved away her suggestion with his hand. "I assure you, your Grace, I am quite alright thank you. It is beneficial for you in light of your condition."

"Who told you about my condition?" Her voice trembled and she did not like it.

His face softened. "Edgar did."

"Well he shouldn't have. He had no right."

"He had every right. He remains your eldest brother and, at the time of his informing me, your head of household also."

"But it wasn't his information to give. He should have left it to me to tell you myself."

The Duke sighed. "And when would you have told me had he done so? He only did it out of genuine concern for your wellbeing."

Her cheeks reddened and she looked away from him, not speaking for several minutes.

The Duke stood and watched her in silence, this enigma of a woman. He had provided for her every lap of luxury, the free run of his London and Bath properties, as well as the plush leisurely lifestyle of a Duchess. All he had required in return was that she refrain from following him north to Yorkshire. So why had she done precisely the opposite? What had possessed her to travel for days across the length of England to find him? They barely knew each other, after all, and only found themselves in this marriage because of their unfortunate run in in the maze a couple of months ago.

Then, the Duke was jolted from his musings by his wife's voice. "Was my condition the reason you wrote that letter and came up here? Do I really repulse you that much?"

Shock overtook the Duke's features and a horrid realisation rose within him. The poor woman. He had made the decision to write that letter and move to Faversham Abbey full time in order to protect her from him, not because of any health condition she might have.

"Never," he said with great ferocity. "Please do not ever ever think that my decision has anything to do with any condition of yours or anything to do with what you may or may not be or have or have not done. It is entirely down to my own matters, nothing that you can control."

She looked at him with curiosity, her cheeks still flaming hot. "Then tell me what those matters are."

"Alas, I cannot. To tell you would mean exposing you to things that would harm you most severely. And as your husband it is my duty and my responsibility to protect you," he said.

"What is it you are protecting me from? Really?" she asked.

"I can't say."

"Don't I have a right to know?"

"Your Grace, I cannot say."

"But don't I have a right to know?" she pressed.

Alexander's voice was sharp as a steel dagger. "You have a right to be *protected*, your Grace. Which is what I am trying my utmost to do. Please, refrain from pursuing this line of enquiry further because it can do neither of us any good."

Belinda sighed internally at Alexander's stonewalling. There was that Faversham coldness so talked about on the ton. She may not find out his secret tonight, but she resolved to do whatever she could to uncover it in time.

She took a cautious sip of ginger beer. The sour liquid hit her tongue and worked to relieve the tightness that had been forming in her throat.

Then she turned to the plate of food and began to pick at the pâté and eggs. In all the apprehension of the journey, she hadn't realised how hungry she was. It was only now, while she was sitting here in this little tower room with a stonewalling husband and his sleeping beagles, that she noticed the pangs of emptiness within her stomach.

Through it all, Alexander stood and cast his gaze in her direction.

For several minutes, the room was silent aside from the quiet sounds of Belinda eating and drinking and the beagles every-so-often letting out soft whines in their sleep.

Until Alexander broke the silence with his deep voice. "Tomorrow I'll give you a tour of the house. It's set to be much too wild weather on the moors for us to go out around the estate, so the house will have to suffice for now I'm afraid."

Belinda looked up from her plate of food. This man was an enigma. Mere minutes ago he had been shutting down her line of enquiry with that trademark Faversham coolness. Yet now he was talking about giving her a tour of the house, as though all this was totally normal and expected procedure between husband and wife.

She said nothing in reply. Best make him sweat a bit.

Alexander rubbed the back of his neck. "That is, of course, if you would like a tour."

Belinda gave a small nod of assent. "Yes, please do." As Duchess, she had better do what she could to get a good understanding of every aspect of the Faversham estates. Her feelings about the Duke aside, she had a responsibility to do what she could for the servants and staff. She was the lady of the house now and she would hate to find they were being neglected. If the Duke's bizarre behaviour towards her was anything to go on, she feared that this may be the case.

⚜

Alexander pressed his arm firmly against the wooden door frame and leant against it in an attempt to steady his nerves.

This evening had been a trying one indeed. The unexpected arrival of his wife had rendered his stomach a pit of apprehension. On the one hand, it was surely a desirable thing for man and wife to be reunited under one roof. Did not the church teach that one of the purposes of holy matrimony was to unite the couple in mutual society, help and comfort? Was not Belinda justified in seeking this?

Yet he had left her in London and headed north because he wanted to protect her. She was only young and had been strong armed into this marriage. Well, both of them had after their run in with Lady Petunia Reynolds in the maze but as he was a man and a member of the peerage he knew he had a responsibility to look after Belinda. Alexander was not wholly naive to the realities of life for young ladies of the aristocracy. Ever since birth, they were primped and prepared to find a worthy spouse on the marriage mart, to please their husband and provide him with heirs. It was the same for his sisters, after all. And so it was for Belinda. Her marriage was always going to be the defining moment of her life. Unlike her brothers, she would never have the opportunity to attend university, to go on the Grand Tour or to take up a profession.

Alexander took a sharp breath. This was not what he had wanted for himself or for Belinda at all.

Chapter Ten

The next day, Belinda awoke to a knocking at her chamber door.

She turned her head towards the noise. "Who is it?" she called.

The familiar voice of her maid rang through the door.

Belinda raised herself up from her pillows slightly. "Yes, please come in, Dauntsey."

The door swung open to reveal Miss Dauntsey. She carried a breakfast tray into the room and placed it next to Belinda's bed.

"Thank you, Dauntsey," Belinda said.

The maid gave a curtsey and left the room.

Belinda reached across to the toothbrush and pot of tooth powder and cleaned her teeth.

Then she turned to the breakfast tray and began to eat the scrambled eggs and kippers. All the while, she thought about the chaotic events of last night. Alexander had been so angry when she had first arrived, but then after he seemed more closed up. More like the man she had met before they were wed. The most surprising thing, however, was when she learnt that he already knew about her condition. Other than her elder brothers, maids and doctors, no one knew about it. And on an intellectual level, she grasped that Edgar had only told Alexander the truth out of concern for her wellbeing. But it still hurt to have the decision to reveal that information taken away from her.

She finished her eggs and sighed.

Like so many other areas of her life, the choice of if, when and how her husband found out about her decision was wrenched away from her. As a young woman in England during the reign of George III, she had few enough choices as it was. And as a young woman with her condition, she had even less choices.

Still, she had a handful of choices within her control. It would not do to lay back entirely and let every area of her life be under the hand of someone else.

She resolved to be the one to make as many decisions as she could when it came to her path in life.

After Miss Dauntsey had put the finishing touches to Belinda's bun, she gave a small smile and made her way out of the duchess' chambers.

Belinda looked at herself in the vanity mirror. She screwed up every ounce of her courage and stood up from the stool.

Then she opened the door and headed down the wood panelled corridor towards the heart of the house: the great hall.

A few minutes walking and she reached the balcony that overlooked the great hall.

Yes, just as she had hoped, a now-familiar dark haired head was seated at one of the tables. He was bent over with a pile of papers in front of him and a quill in his hand.

Two beagles rested in dog baskets near the fireplace behind him. Probably the same dogs as the night before, Belinda mused.

She made her way down the wooden staircase. It was a little rickety and some of the ancient oak steps creaked as she went over them.

But Alexander was oblivious and remained engrossed in his paperwork.

Belinda reached the bare flagstones and crossed over to her husband. She pulled the ends of her shawl together and began to speak. "Good morning, your Grace."

Alexander startled ever so slightly. He lifted his head and looked Belinda directly in the eyes. "Ah your Grace, good morning. Did you sleep well?" He put down his paperwork and stood up.

"Quite well, thank you," Belinda said perfunctorily.

She walked over towards the lead-latticed windows and looked out of them.

They brought the grey light of the moors into the Great Hall. Splatters of rain ran down the glass.

She surveyed the scene before her. "What dismal weather we have today. Wild weather as you said last night."

"Indeed, your Grace." Alexander paused for a few seconds, before continuing. "The barometer forecasts it's going to continue for at least another day."

Belinda turned around to face Alexander. She cast her hand to where the beagles dozed in their baskets. "The dogs, what are their names?" she asked.

"Ridgley, he's the one in the green collar, and Barnet has the blue collar," Alexander said.

Neither dog paid any attention to the sound of their name and instead dozed on.

Belinda, despite herself, gave the tiniest hint of a smile. "Ridgley and Barnet. Are they good hunters?"

"They are the very worst of hunters," he said.

"How so?"

"No fight in them whatsoever. All they wish to do is lie around, eat beef and be pampered everyday."

"That does sound like a life." Belinda's smile reached her eyes.

Alexander gave a nod and a smile. "It most certainly does."

The room fell silent again.

Belinda took a few steps towards the grand table where her husband sat.

She noticed how the harsh, scared look in his eyes when she arrived last night was no more. Instead, there was a slight softness in his eyes and, unless she was very much mistaken, the hint of a smile too.

She gestured to the paperwork on the grand table. "What's this you're working on?"

"Estate papers," he replied. "A letter from a tenant farmer about the matter of some repairs he is seeking. A few notes from the curate about parish matters. Though he doesn't really need my say-so on any of that. He's rather inexperienced and second-guesses himself too much." Alexander picked up a hefty stack, bound in a leather case, "And then there are the minutes from the last area landowners' meeting."

"Landowners' meeting? How often do you have those?"

"Once or twice a year. I like to attend myself in-person, though some others locally will send a steward to attend in their place."

Belinda nodded. "Most dutiful of you."

"I do endeavour," he said.

Another silence filled the room.

Belinda sucked in her cheeks before she spoke again. "Your Grace, why is it that you left me in London and told me not to come here to Yorkshire?"

"I can't tell you why," Alexander said.

"Whyever not?" Belinda asked.

"Because it's for your own protection."

Belinda crossed her arms.

"And I will always say it," Alexander added. "Because I am your husband."

Belinda took a deep breath before replying. Don't I have a right to know what you're protecting me from?"

Silence filled the air.

Neither said anything. Neither wanted to break the silence and make the first move.

They stood like that for several minutes.

Until, finally, Alexander couldn't bear it any longer. His voice cracked. "Please, your Grace. Please don't ask me any more about what I am protecting you from. I only wish to keep you safe."

Belinda took several deep, anguished breaths. Clearly, her husband was pained at the prospect of telling her just what he was keeping her safe from. But that didn't mean he would be able to hide the truth from her forever. How she wished he would tell her now and not stonewall her attempts. She stewed internally. No matter. She may have lost the battle today, but she would win the ultimate war.

Her voice was flat and cold. "Very well, your Grace. I won't ask you any more about your secrets today." Then, her tone brightened a little. "Now, last night I believe you said you would give me a tour of the house today?"

"That is correct, yes," he said.

"Is now a good time to start?"

"It is. Please, follow me."

And so the pair spent a rainy and stormy morning exploring almost every nook and cranny of Faversham Abbey.

At every turn, Belinda marvelled at the ancient building's gothic charms. It was all so different to the refinement of her childhood home.

And as for Alexander? Well, he spent the morning doing his level best to ensure Belinda didn't notice him marvelling at her. He could only hope he was successful.

CHAPTER ELEVEN

After she had been at Faversham Abbey for a few days and there was a gap in the many hours of rain, Belinda decided it was time to explore the grounds.

She headed down the gravel pathway, her feet crunching on the tiny stones as she went.

She dove her dainty hands into the pockets of her luxuriant amber velvet cloak. The wind was brisk today, but she could cope with the chill. She was a hardy soul and she had been through much worse.

The gardens lay spread out before her.

Despite the wind, the rays of summer sun shone over the verdant trees and hedges. The neat rows of roses were a patchwork of red, pink, white and yellow.

Belinda was glad to be out in the fresh air.

She kept walking until she came upon a man pruning some bushes. This wasn't someone she could remember seeing around the place before.

She didn't want to disturb him too much from his task, but also would it not be stone cold to simply blank him entirely? "Good day, sir," she called.

He stopped his pruning and doffed his cap. "Good day, your Grace."

"May I ask what your name is?"

"Gibson, your Grace."

"I am very pleased to make your acquaintance, Mr Gibson," she said.

He nodded. "Likewise, your Grace, likewise."

"Have you been with the Favershams for long?"

"Aye," he replied. "For over forty years now. I remember the days before his Grace was born."

"Has it changed much over the years?" she asked.

"In some ways. Some things have modernised, there's indoor plumbing now and oil lamps. But they still like to keep the old traditions alive," he said.

"I'm glad to hear it." She dug her hands deeper into the pockets. "Well, I shouldn't keep you any longer. Thank you, Mr Gibson. It was very nice to meet you."

"Likewise, your Grace, likewise," he said.

Belinda continued down the path. With every step, she surveyed the gardens around her. She liked them. They were charming and, so far as she could tell, well-kept. That gardner was certainly fastidious in his duties, for one.

Eventually, the path came to a halt and she reached a low wooden fence. Beyond the fence lay the rugged moors covered in shimmering heather. She wasn't sure where the Faversham estate began and ended, but at least some of those moors would likely belong to the dukedom.

While the path ahead of her had ended, to her right lay a narrow, winding trail. She followed it, through a gap in the row of fir trees, and found herself in a yard. Fir trees bordered it on every side, with another path diagonally opposite the one she had walked down.

In the centre of the yard sat a white stone fountain. No water ran through it, yet around the base was a small pool of water.

Belinda made her way to examine it.

Out of the corner of her eye, she spied a figure in black.

"Your Grace," the figure called.

It was Alexander.

She stopped by the fountain.

"Good day, your Grace," she cried over to him. She gestured at the fountain. "What can you tell me of this?"

He quirked an eyebrow and made his way over towards her. "Tell you of that? The fountain?"

"Yes, the fountain."

"Well, what would you like to know about it?"

"Why isn't it running? How long has it been here for? Do you come here much? Does anyone come out here to see it?" she fired off.

He replied in a volley of answers just as rapid as her questions. "It's not running because it's too costly to keep it so. It's been here since the middle of the last century. I come by here most days but other than the staff, no one else would."

She nodded but said nothing.

He cocked his head a little. "Say, why are you so interested in the fountain? Not that that's a bad thing, but it does strike me as rather obscure. It's a relatively hidden piece of ornamentation in a relatively forgotten garden on a remote estate."

She gave a small smile. "Well, now I am duchess, I see it as my duty and responsibility to familiarise myself with all matters relating to the houses and the gardens and the servants. I am mistress of several houses, after all."

"Touché," he said.

If Belinda didn't know any better, she would've thought she had seen a slight glimmer of amusement in her husband's eyes. However, she knew better. A man like the Duke of Faversham could never find amusement in simple, innocent matters.

They stood in silence for a minute or two.

Belinda turned to observe the spiderwebs that clung to the fountain's sturdy stonework. They were shimmering in the air and no flies were trapped in them. Yet still they were strong, lying in wait to catch some food for their weaver.

She turned back to Alexander. "What else is there in the garden?"

"I can show you if you wish."

"I should like that."

He offered her his arm and she took it.

Then he pointed at the way he had entered the yard and asked, "Have you seen this part yet?"

"Not yet."

"Excellent. We'll start there then."

He led her down the path and through the fir trees.

A walled herb garden came into view.

"Now this," Alexander began, "This is where most of the herbs and spices for the house are grown."

Rows of basil, coriander and mint nestled next to the brick walls of the herb garden. There were also a few chilli plants clustered in the mix.

Belinda reached down to one of the basil plants, plucked a leaf and popped it in her mouth. "Very nice," she said. "How many gardeners look after the estate? I met one of them earlier."

"Four. Was that Gibson?"

"Yes, Gibson was his name. He was doing some pruning."

Alexander nodded in recognition "He's been here forever, longer than I've been alive. Very hardworking and loyal."

Goldfinches chirped around them and a light breeze rustled through the foliage.

Alexander said, "Come, I'll show you where the vegetables are grown."

Together, they walked down a set of small steps, past some more herbs and through an open, French blue door.

Along the way, Belinda noted to herself how her husband's arm felt intertwined with her own. It felt good, strong and protective and she could feel his warmth against her body.

Past the blue door and a view of a productive vegetable garden presented itself before them.

"And this is where some of the vegetables for the Abbey are grown," Alexander said. "The rest we buy from the tenants or from the village over the other side of the moor."

Belinda nodded. This sort of arrangement was familiar to her from her days at Renfregh. "Are you one for gardening yourself?"

"Me? No. I'm not the most practical with my hands. I prefer to leave that to the expert gardeners we have here," he said.

They walked a few more steps together.

Then, Alexander asked, "And you, your Grace, do you enjoy gardening?"

"Not really," she said. "Like you, I'm not the best with my hands. But I do enjoy walking through them and seeing the fruits of the gardeners' labours."

They walked further through the vegetable garden, past rows of peas and beans growing on wooden trellises.

Belinda continued speaking. "I take it you like walking in these gardens too, your Grace? You said you are here most days."

"I do, yes."

"Then we should meet up for these walks on a regular basis," she said with a smile.

"We should do that. Consider it arranged."

"I shall." Satisfaction bloomed in her chest. Finally, an in. A chance to understand more about what made her husband tick. And also, a small opening in his deep suit of armour that shielded her from the truth about why he had left her behind in London.

They reached another open, French blue door.

When they walked through it, the strains of a woman singing wafted over the lawn towards them.

"He'll be there from Monday to Saturday,

Johnny's so long at the fair," the merry voice intoned, slightly out of tune.

Belinda turned her head upwards to Alexander's. "Who's that?" she asked.

"Hmm, it sounds like Mrs May, the assistant cook," he said.

The voice continued its questionable rendition. "Oh, dear, what can the matter be?

Johnny's so long at the fair!"

Alexander said, "I know she's not the best singer, but then again neither am I. I suppose it helps the day go by quicker for her."

They kept walking up the lawn and then Alexander guided her to a winding pathway on the right.

"Say, are you one for singing?" he asked.

"A bit. I had lessons from a singing master for years. I'm not a natural, though I can carry a tune. I like playing violin, that's my favourite instrument."

"Ah, so you had lessons?"

"Yes, for many years on the violin. And also piano, though I prefer playing violin. Those two instruments and singing, they're my musical accomplishments. As all young ladies of the ton should have."

"Indeed," Alexander said. "We don't have any violins here at the Abbey. And I don't think you brought one up from London?"

"No, I was in too much of a rush."

Alexander nodded. "Understandable. Would you like to have one here? I could have one sent in, from York perhaps."

"Oh, I should like that, very much," she said with a grin.

"And I should like to hear you play."

"But of course, your Grace!" she exclaimed with a joyful note in her voice.

"Tell me, your Grace, have you other accomplishments?" he asked.

"Yes, drawing and watercolours. Needlework of course. And French and Italian. I have had lessons in those since I was a young girl."

"A very accomplished lady of the ton," he said approvingly. "Would you like to do those other accomplishments here too? I don't really have much that's relevant, apart from some books in French and Italian, but whatever you need I can organise."

"Yes, I should like that please."

"Very well, I shall make the necessary arrangements."

"Thank you."

They walked a few more steps before she let forth a small sigh. "It's rather a shame though that I never really got to show any of them during my season. Our unintentional maze meeting taking place before much of the season had gotten underway."

"It is a shame, I agree. You would have been splendid showing off your accomplishments on the marriage mart. And you were splendid on the marriage mart, anyway -"

"Your Grace," Belinda interjected. "Please do not speak in jest. I wasn't splendid by any means."

"Ah but you were, and I do not speak in jest. For what little, fleeting time you were on the marriage mart, you were splendid. I have eyes and ears and I know things."

"But your Grace-" Belinda began.

"Trust the word of a duke on these matters. You were truly splendid. I saw you that night, you know, before we encountered each other in the maze."

"You *what*?" Belinda was baffled. This was the first she was hearing of Alexander having seen her at the Landsdowne Ball before their unfortunate run-in in the maze.

"Yes, it was in the ballroom about half an hour beforehand. You were dancing with Lord Walthamstowe and you were shining like an orb. You lit up the room," he said.

"If that's true," Belinda said with a definite note of scepticism in her voice. "Why didn't you ask me to dance?"

"Well I don't dance as a matter of course. It would be rather out of keeping with my reputation. And I wasn't seriously looking for a bride at that point in time."

They kept on walking until they reached the point where the path intersected with the one Belinda had walked down solo earlier. Again, Alexander guided them to turn right and again, Belinda was strolling down that same path.

Gibson, the gardener who had been pruning the bushes, had finished his task and headed off somewhere else. It was just Belinda, Alexander and the landscape surrounding them.

They reached the fence and came to a halt.

"Of these moors, which are part of the Faversham estate?" Belinda asked.

"Most of what you can see here," Alexander said. "Everything to the north and west that you can see with the naked eye, and the majority of what you see to the east as well. Then beyond that, in every direction, is crown land."

"How do you manage it all?" Belinda asked.

"With the assistance of some most excellent land stewards. Though when I am up here, I do try to be hands on with it. Riding to see what's happening in the surrounding villages and with the farms and livestock. I do love riding there. I find it relaxes my mind."

"I used to love horse riding as a girl, before..." Belinda said.

Alexander's eyes filled with concern. "Before your condition began?"

"Yes," she nodded. "Now with the pain, I find it hard to consistently support myself sitting upright for that amount of time. But I would love to see the estate though."

He bit his lip and nodded, cogs turning in his mind. "I have an idea. What about a phaeton ride? With all the rain we've been having, the ground is too muddy at present. But once the weather clears up, I could take you out."

"I would adore that!" Belinda exclaimed.

"Then please consider it arranged, your Grace," Alexander said.

Alexander sat at the desk in his office. Tension brewed in his guts.

How had he and Belinda ended up in this wretched situation?

If he had not gone to the ball that night, none of this would have happened. If he had not decided to enter the maze, Belinda would have been left alone in peace. If Lady Petunia Reynolds had not blurted out her nonsense, Belinda could have married for love and would not have been saddled with him.

He had tried to protect Belinda, of course he had, but she had rightfully wanted more than he was willing to offer. She had wanted more than the pampered life of a maiden-like wife that he had placed on a platter in front of her. So she had taken matters into her own hands.

For that night, oh that notorious night, would live in his memory forevermore. Her arrival had been the last thing he had been expecting. And it had changed everything.

No longer was he alone in the Abbey with only the servants and his own maudlin thoughts to keep him company. No longer was he prowling the corridors and ruminating in his own thoughts of how, try as he might, he wasn't able to stop himself from repeating his father's grievous error. The error of putting his family at risk. Of jeopardising his wife's happiness and wellbeing.

Regret stabbed at his heart. For so many years, he had sworn not to make a mistake like his father had done. Yet he had done a similar thing.

As a result of decisions he had made long before he ever met Belinda, long before he had ever even heard of her existence, he had put her at risk. He had jeopardised her. He would have jeopardised any bride because of his choices. He was wholly unsuitable as a husband for anyone.

Now he had a young, naive woman living at the Abbey. Who thought she had to please him and adhere to his wishes. That was how she surely would have been raised, was it not? But he didn't want her to waste her time trying to please him. He wanted her to be happy and safe, somewhere far away from him living as free a life as it was possible for a lady of the ton to lead.

Now he had a Duchess with him at the Abbey who had been very brave and very bold. She had travelled all the way to Yorkshire to confront him about his leaving her behind in London with only the vaguest of explanations.

He had to admire her courage and tenacity. He wasn't really surprised that she had them in spades. Edgar, when he had met with Alexander the day after the Landsdowne Ball, had told her Belinda possessed those qualities. He had told Alexander how she had suffered for many years with her condition, of the bravery and fortitude she had shown throughout. He had told Alexander how Belinda had been wrecked by her parents' deaths back when she was a girl, but that she had always been a strong and consistent northstar for the Weatherby family.

Alexander could see what strength she possessed, what determination she had etched on her every layer, right down to the very core of her soul. He admired her so feverishly because of it. It would make her a most excellent duchess.

His insides still churned with regret and apprehension. He had a young woman at his side who had the makings of an outstanding matriarch of the ton but he was terrified out of his wits at the prospect of hurting her. He was like a beast who could not help but hurt the ones he was supposed to protect.

Chapter Twelve

Dearest Belinda,

News of your leaving London for Yorkshire has inevitably reached me.

I cannot pretend to understand the reasons why you took such a decision. They are, of course, your own. But I pray more than anything else that you are safe and doing what you wish of your own accord.

Please do let me know if there is any way in which I can assist you. Though the full force of English law regarding matrimony makes things harder than when you were Lady Weatherby, I promise you that I will do everything within my power to make sure you do not come to harm.

I remain your most affectionate brother,

Edgar

Belinda returned to her chambers after a walk in the gardens that was cut short by yet another rain shower.

What she had witnessed over the past few weeks had taken her by surprise.

Alexander had a reputation on the ton for being so stern and severe and cold. It only stood to reason, therefore, that he was a harsh and unyielding employer as well. His reputation couldn't be a false reflection of reality, could it?

Yet his treatment of his employees hadn't been harsh in the slightest. From everything she had seen here at Faversham Abbey, he treated all in his employ with respect and care. Moreover, if she thought back further to her time living at Faversham House on Park Lane, she could not think of any evidence for his being a cold and overbearing employer.

Similar to her brother Edgar, he was a fair and respectful employer.

However, unlike Edgar, the ton didn't regard Alexander as one of its better employers.

Belinda wondered why this was. Why the discrepancy in the two lords' respective reputations?

She had to laugh at herself as well. She had arrived with real concerns for the staff. There were so many gothic tales of cruel, unyielding masters in remote country houses and haunted abbeys that it had been all too easy to paint Alexander as one such cruel man.

And yet, and yet, and yet, her mind couldn't help but turn to Alexander's cold act of abandoning her within less than twenty four hours of marrying her. Oh, he said it was for her protection. But protection from what precisely?

She made her way to the bench in the window alcove. Along the way, she pulled the cord to ring for a servant. A pot of tea was in order. Yes, she would sit and try to calmly think through the situation and all its many contradictions.

Chapter Thirteen

Dearest Belinda,

Well! Your news was quite the shock! This year has been one of incredible change for you, my dear. One moment you were being presented at the Palace and the next you were engaged to Faversham. I must say, I always thought you had it in you to become a Duchess. You have always been one of the brightest lights. Though Faversham may have been a surprise to us all, and I barely know the man, my Archie assures me that he is a most respectable man and will make a loyal husband for you.

But dearest Belinda, I pray you know that whatever happens between you and your husband, whoever he really turns out to be, you will always have my full support. And if your husband does not turn out to be the man my Archie believes he is, please do be assured that I can help you leave if such an eventuality should ever occur.

I do so hope you are happy.

To go all the way to Yorkshire, to leave London and its society behind. But you are your own woman and I know you as one of the sharpest minds of the ton. You would only take such a decision if you believed it to be the correct and most appropriate course of action. So I must surely concur that it was and remains the correct and most appropriate course of action.

You asked me how the babies are going. Little Maisie and John are both coming along so fantastically. You must meet them when we are next all in London together. We're planning to stay down here in the West Country until next autumn, to give the babies the best chance with all the fresh air of the countryside in this, their first year of life. I'll confirm the dates once we're sure of what we're doing, but I would love to see you in London in the autumn.

How is it in Yorkshire? I have never been, not even on my honeymoon. We ended up going to Wales instead! Is it as wild and romantic as people say? Oh I would love to come and visit you at the Abbey, once you are all settled in and Maisie and John are a little older.

Oh, it is so exciting now that we are both married women. Mistresses of our own households at last!

Please, do write back soon and let me know all of your news.

Your friend,

Abigail

Belinda sat in the Great Hall, replying to a letter from her dearest and oldest friend Abigail.

Around her, a few servants bustled to clean the room's elaborate Jacobean wood carvings.

Precise footsteps clacked along the flagstones behind her. Then they came to a halt.

"Your Grace," her husband's deep voice intoned.

Belinda turned around to face him.

He was holding a sturdy wooden box about two feet long and a foot wide. "This arrived for you just now," he said.

Belinda's eyes widened with interest. "Ooh, what is it?"

"Well, I have an inkling what it might be," Alexander said with a slight smile in his eyes. "But I think you had best see for yourself." He placed the wooden box on the table, to Belinda's left side, avoiding her letters.

She shuffled down the bench so she was facing the mysterious box. She plucked at the clasps and they unfastened with a click. Then she lifted the lid of the box to reveal a pile of bunched up green velvet. In the centre of the luxurious pile sat a sight that brought pure pleasure to her heart.

A black violin case!

"Oh, how fantastic! It's arrived!" she exclaimed.

Then she undid the clasps of the violin case to reveal a beautiful violin and matching bow, plus neck rest.

She turned around and beamed at Alexander. "Thank you, this is excellent. I'll have to tune it before I can properly play it, though that shouldn't take very long."

"I'm glad you like it," Alexander said.

Belinda turned back to the violin and picked it up between her dainty hands. The violins she had growing up were nice, and she still had a decent one at the Weatherby's Bath townhouse, but this was better than any of those. The quality of this new violin was absolutely exquisite. Lovelier than anything she had imagined.

Later on, in her chambers, Belinda took the violin out of the box and admired it. This was such a wonderful gift from Alexander!

The wood of the instrument was smooth and sleek in her dainty hands.

She plucked the A string. It was a little sharp so she adjusted the tuning. Then she repeated the process with the other three strings. Then she picked up the bow, tightened it and rubbed rosin along the horsehairs. She was ready to play.

It had been about eight or nine months since she had last played so she was a little out of practice. But it wouldn't take her too long to get back into the swing of things.

She started playing Vivaldi's *Spring*, one of her favourite pieces.

Her fingers moved up and down the fingerboard and she swayed the bow with vigorous rhythm. It was good to be making music again.

After she had been playing for about twenty minutes, there was a knocking at her chamber door.

Belinda put the bow down. "Who is it?" she called.

Alexander poked his head around the door. "Your Grace, that is excellent playing. May I join you?"

Belinda smiled and nodded. She wouldn't have described her playing as 'excellent', rather accomplished, but each to their own. "Please do," she said.

Alexander strode into the room. "Was that Vivaldi's *Spring*?"

"Good ear, it was. Would you like to hear some more?"

"Yes, please."

Alexander leant against the arm of an upholstered chair, his head tilted expectantly.

Belinda picked up her bow. "See if you can guess this one, your Grace," she said to Alexander.

She began to play. Another Vivaldi piece, *Autumn*.

⁂

The music swirled around the room.

Alexander was a man transfixed. Belinda was highly accomplished at this instrument. He'd meant what he'd said when he called her playing 'excellent'.

She knew what she was doing and clearly her playing was the result of years of diligent training and practice. That diligence and its fruits were most admirable to him.

When he had been walking along the corridor near her chambers, the strains of Vivaldi had stopped him in his tracks.

He'd knocked on the door not because he wanted to disturb Belinda but instead because he wanted to see her play and enjoy the work of someone who put a great deal of effort into their art.

Belinda's acceptance of him into the room had pleased him. He knew he really had no right to impose his presence on her, especially after the cryptic way he had abandoned her the day after their wedding. But he hoped some sort of friendship could develop between them. They were bound together for life now, come what may. But he couldn't dare to hope for anything more than friendship. No, he could never ever hope for more than that.

He sat back on the chair arm and let the sweet melodies of Belinda's talents soothe his soul.

And yes, he knew what piece she was playing. It was *Autumn* by Vivaldi, of course.

$$\text{\textbf{·}}\!\!\rightsquigarrow\!\!\text{—}\bullet\text{—}\!\blacklozenge\!\text{—}\bullet\text{—}\bullet\text{—}\!\rightsquigarrow$$

CHAPTER FOURTEEN

The west wind howled through the moors. Summer was over and autumn had well and truly arrived.

In her bedroom in the South Wing, Belinda tossed and turned on the bed. Nights at Renfregh could certainly be windy but they had nothing on the worst she had experienced at Faversham Abbey. And tonight was about the worst night so far.

She lay, tossing and turning this way and that, trying to get to sleep for at least an hour. Finally, she gave up and decided to head to the library to choose a book. Maybe that would distract her from the noisy storm and help her get some relaxation.

She climbed out of the bed and stepped into her pink velvet slippers. Then she walked over to where her blush lacy dressing gown hung and tied it over her white lace and cotton nightdress.

She grabbed a candle and lit it. She looked at her pocket watch and sighed. It was three o'clock in the morning and she had not slept a wink thanks to the storm.

Then she made her way out of the door and through her chambers to the corridor connecting the South Wing to the

North Wing where the library was located. Not another soul was around. Lucky for them to be able to get some rest on a wretched night like this, grumbled Belinda to herself.

About halfway down the corridor, she came by the Duke's office. Belinda almost walked straight ahead, such was her single-minded intention to get to the library. But out of the corner of her eye she noticed something most unusual. Light was seeping through the slightly ajar door of the office.

She stopped in her tracks.

Listening closely, she heard the soft sound of a quill scraping on parchment followed by the rustling of papers.

Who was making that noise? Was it her husband himself? Or perhaps one of the servants?

Her curiosity piqued, she snuck a look through the door and saw her husband sitting at the desk buried in paperwork with intense concentration.

She knocked at the door and called out, "Husband, may I speak with you?"

The Duke startled at the intrusion before regaining his composure. He got up and walked to the door.

Dark eyes met Belinda's through the crack in the opening.

"You may, your Grace," he said and opened the door. "What are you doing up and about at this hour? Are you feeling unwell?"

"The storm is giving me difficulty sleeping, but otherwise I feel well. I thought I would try to find some reading material in the library to take my mind off it," she said. "What about you? Same trouble with the storm?"

"Yes. These blasted storms are probably the worst part about living up here on the moors." He rubbed the back of his neck. "Say, would you like to come in?"

"Please," she nodded.

He held the door open and she crossed the threshold before he closed it again most of the way.

"Have a seat," he said.

She took a place opposite his desk and settled herself on the maroon leather upholstery. She peered across at the pile of papers and books on his desk and noticed an accounts ledger open directly in front of where her husband had been sitting.

"So what were you doing before I so rudely interrupted you?"

"Ah it was not rude at all. I was doing the accounts. Thought I ought to do something useful since sleep was eluding me."

"Accounts, Edgar seems to spend half his time doing those," she said. "I take it you do as well?"

He nodded. "Indeed, such is the reality for gentlemen of the aristocracy in this country. Well, gentlemen who take their responsibilities seriously anyway. Say, am I correct in understanding from Edgar that your governess taught you accounts?"

"She did, yes."

"Your brother said you had a head for figures, that's one reason I knew you would be an excellent duchess," the Duke muttered to himself.

Belinda sat still and waited for her husband to make the next move. Whether it was tiredness at the late hour or some other cause she did not know, but he seemed preoccupied with some other thought beyond her stumbling upon his late night bookkeeping efforts.

He rubbed the back of his neck and closed his eyes briefly. Then he opened them and looked directly into Belinda's eyes. "I have never told another living soul this information and before I share it with you, you must swear to keep it as a secret between the two of us. Can you swear to it, your Grace?"

"I swear," she said.

"Very well."

The Duke walked to a heavy oaken bookshelf and pulled out a ginormous tome from the bottom row. Then he carried it to where Belinda sat and placed it on the desk in front of her.

"After my father died and I inherited the title, I was at a loss for what to do. For the first couple of days I could not even tell you what I did, I was that numb to everything. But then on the third day a notion came to me that I ought to start acting like the Duke of Faversham. I had little idea of what to do, so I guessed the accounts would be as good a place to start as any. At least then I would *feel* like I was doing something worthwhile, even if I was merely pushing pieces of paper from one side of a desk to the other. So I sent for the account ledgers from my father's time. The first one is in front of you."

Belinda reached for the ledger before looking up at him with a question in her eyes.

"Yes, go ahead and read it," he said.

She duly did so. As she turned the pages, her eyes grew ever wider. The figures in front of her did not make any logical sense for the accounts of a *Dukedom* of all things. With every page, vague outgoings whittled down the value of the estate with expenditures consistently outpacing incomes.

"This is preposterous, how could a title of such high standing as Faversham have such perilously paltry finances?" she asked.

"Those were my thoughts exactly. It took me a while to work out what had happened. But do you see those, the mysterious ones with the strange initials?"

"I do indeed," she said.

"Well after much digging around and investigation that took me the better part of a month, I came to learn that they were all gambling debts."

"*Gambling debts*? Whoever would accrue that amount in gambling debts?" she asked.

"My father."

"Your father did that? Put your family in such a precarious position? But he was a gentleman," she said.

"Regrettably he did. Thanks to him, my sisters had no dowries, we were on the verge of not being able to pay the staff, to name only a couple of problems. And the worst part is that had he not died when he did, had this carried on for even another couple of years more, the estate would have been ruined completely."

He walked round to the ledger he had been working on and placed it on top of the one Belinda had been viewing. "Take a look."

Again, she did as he instructed and read the ledger with close attention.

"This one looks much more normal, a healthy balance. I take it that is thanks to your efforts?" she asked

"That is correct. It was a long hard road."

"How did you do it?"

"Mostly by cutting spending where I could justify it. I kept all the employees on, but there were some underperforming investments I let go. My mother did not like it and that has compounded the distance between us. I try as much as I can to keep my mother and sisters in the state they have always been accustomed to, but I do not like waste so keep what I can understated. You may have heard there has not been a Faversham hosted ball since before my father died. As of last year, I finally got the estate back in the black so we may be able to host the occasional ball."

She looked down at the ledger and then back up at the Duke. "It appears these sheep are proving profitable."

"They are, yes. That and the printing press and paper mill I bought stakes in, those investments are proving the winners. I am on the look out for other investments too though, but they have to be of a moral nature."

She nodded. "I have heard rumblings of some morally dubious ones going on around the ton."

"Yes, great rates of return on a lot of those, at least for a while, but the moral cost does not sit well with me at all."

"This makes so much more sense now, why you are the way you are."

"A cold-hearted miser with no sense of fun?" he smirked.

"Well, your Grace, that is what I heard the season just passed in London. But I think there is more to you than meets the eye."

"Perhaps there is. You are not going to be able to change me though."

"I would not even want to try, your Grace. There is little point in attempting to change a grown man, not unless he himself desires to change," she said.

"That is very wise," he said.

She nodded.

The room fell silent for a minute or so.

Then, Belinda broke the silence. "Are you angry at your father?" she asked.

"I was at first, but now my feelings are mostly pity. To do what he did, it was a compulsion and an illness. It was really wrong what he did, but he was a deeply unwell man," he said. "He must have been struggling so much but none of us ever knew. I doubt anyone even suspected."

Belinda nodded. "The amount of gentlemen of the ton who frequent all those gaming hells and go to the races, it's a wonder we don't hear more of gentlemen getting into debts."

"It's kept fairly well under wraps from the younger members of the ton. But it certainly does go on," Alexander said. "Though those cases are not usually anywhere near as severe as the situation my father ended up in. And I've tried my best to keep all of this under wraps. I don't want the Faversham name associated with a debacle like this."

"Understood. But would you ever tell anyone else? Other than me?" She tilted her head.

"I can envisage telling whoever my heir might be one day. But no one else," he said.

"What about your mother?"

"Good Lord, no. She hero worships my father to this very day. In her eyes he can never have done any wrong."

Belinda gave a small sigh. "It's tough when people worship the ghosts of the past. It can be a very tempting proposition."

Alexander quirked his lip a little. "You speak from experience then?"

"Yes. My parents, when they were lost at sea, I worshipped their memory for many years. Edgar still does to this very day. It shapes every decision he makes for the Weatherbys. On his mind is always the question of what our father would have thought, and what would our mother's opinion have been of such and such a decision. But in time, as I got older, I came to realise that they weren't the perfect idols I'd made them out to be in my head. They had their flaws just as we all do," she said.

"What made you realise they weren't perfect? If you don't mind my asking."

"When I would have been about twelve or thirteen, I started to recall how my father could be very rigid with my two eldest brothers in particular. Unfairly so. He had so many rules for both of them, rules that he didn't have for me. And our mother, she cared, but she could be overly harsh with the servants. In a way I never hope I am. All I can suppose for why I realised those things at that age is because I would have begun to think about my place in the world, about who I wanted to be when I came of age," she said.

He nodded. "Don't we all start realising things when we get to adolescence?"

"I think many of us do indeed," she said.

Alexander cast his hawklike gaze over Belinda before a firm resolution developed in his eyes. "Say, you can call me 'Alexander' if you wish. I feel like you know too much to persist with only calling me 'your Grace' any longer," he said.

"As you wish, Alexander," she smiled. "And if you so desire, you can call me 'Belinda'."

He gave a gentle smile. "I would like that, Belinda."

CHAPTER FIFTEEN

Dearest Belinda,

Receiving your letter brought me great comfort. I am most relieved to hear that you decided to go to Yorkshire out of your own violation. I pray your time at Faversham Abbey is good for you.

In your last, you asked me how your siblings are getting along. Philomena remains focused on her dreams of saving the world. Every week she seems to get five new pamphlets arriving at the house. Genevieve and Lionel are as lively as ever and are proving a handful for their tutors. And as for Xavier, well he is Xavier. He still hasn't settled on a curacy and, I believe, is spending much of his time traversing the country.

We do so miss you in London and hope to see you again soon. Be it in London or Yorkshire or Bath or somewhere else entirely. Whatever you do, I am sure you are doing it well. For my eldest sister would never do anything else, I know it.

Before I sign off, I should like you to know that if you should ever need my help, I will do my utmost to fulfil whatever you need.

I remain, as always, your most affectionate brother,

Edgar

A week later, the weather finally cleared up and Belinda at last found herself sitting in Alexander's phaeton propped up on several plush velvet cushions. Alexander tucked a blanket around her and then took his seat beside her. He took the reins in his hands and then they were off.

The horses trotted along as Alexander pointed out various sections of the estate. The deer park, the arboretum and the fields for sheep grazing. On one level, Faversham Abbey reminded her of Renfregh but it was so much more rugged. Whereas Renfregh was smooth and refined, Faversham Abbey was danger and dark velvet. Autumn mists swirled in the distance and the purple heather highlighted the intimate scene.

Where had she thought of that word? Intimate. It was unlike her. Yet being in the company of her husband brought the concept to mind. Other than her brothers and her father, she had never been alone in the company of a man before she encountered Alexander that fateful night in the maze.

Alexander continued to point out sights along the way, but Belinda found herself distracted by his presence. He was serious, which she was surprised to find she was growing to like, and she enjoyed his athletic body and pleasing face with its deep brown eyes and handsome nose. If only he weren't so secretive about what he was protecting her from, maybe he would make her a good husband. But alas, she could not bring herself to trust a man who kept such a secret from her.

They rode past the arboretum. Vibrant shades of scarlet, orange and gold abounded on the trees. Autumn was well and truly here and making its presence felt.

"What do you do with the arboretum?" she asked.

"That, we use for scientific study and also as a sort of park if you like," he said.

"Scientific study? What are you looking at there?" she asked.

"A lot of botany, how the different trees are faring in this environment and so forth. And also studying the animals and insects themselves, their life cycles and habits," he said. "So far we've not made any major discoveries, you won't read about this arboretum in the papers of the Royal Society anytime soon, but perhaps we will one day."

Belinda nodded. "And who works to make the discoveries?"

"Myself, some of the land stewards and groundskeepers. All amateurs to science."

"I didn't know you were a gentleman scientist!" she exclaimed.

"Yes, well, you could say that. It's really just a hobby for me when I have time. A way to escape from other things going on in the world. My grandfather and great-grandfather both maintained an interest in it too, my father less so. In fact, it was my great-grandfather who planted the arboretum in the first place about eighty years ago, give or take."

"Well I never! I don't think many on the ton would know about all this," Belinda mused.

Alexander's lips quirked into a slight smile. "No, they probably wouldn't. We Favershams can be full of surprises. Any memory of my great-grandfather's establishing the arboretum would be long since gone."

By now, they were almost at the arboretum itself.

Alexander turned to Belinda slightly. "Say, would you like to take a quick detour through the arboretum?"

"Yes, let's," she said with a grin.

"Very well." Alexander turned the phaeton onto the track that ran towards the arboretum's entrance.

Soon enough, they were heading through the arboretum.

Left and right, striking autumn foliage surrounded them.

Belinda asked, "What sort of animals have you found here?"

"Stoats, hedgehogs and sometimes red squirrels," he said.

A robin flew across their path.

Alexander gestured to the reins in his hand. "Would you like a try?" he asked.

Belinda nodded. "Yes, please."

Alexander handed her the reins and explained a little of how to use them. "Now, try showing the horses that you want them to slow down."

Belinda pulled on the reins gently and the horses drew down to a trot.

Alexander gave a nod of approval. "Very good. Now try getting them to speed up again."

Belinda released some of the pressure on the reins.

The horses responded and picked up the pace.

Belinda smiled to herself.

"Excellent," Alexander said. "And now if you want to turn to the left, pull gently to the left. For the right, be sure to do the same but on the right."

"Alright," Belinda nodded slowly.

The horses trotted along until Belinda directed them to the left.

Then the carriage turned onto the track that led down to the bluebell grove.

Belinda turned her head to Alexander's slightly. "So are you one of those lords who takes a big interest in politics and parliamentary business?" she asked.

"I'm not massively into all that, I must admit," Alexander said. "I know that's not the best thing for someone in my position to say. I should take more of an interest, being in the Lords, but there's just been too much to handle with the estates and getting the finances back on track."

"I doubt you're the only lord of the ton in that position," she said.

"That's true. But I still feel I should do better. I do try to attend the key votes. Wilberforce keeps trying to get his abolitionist bill through. Has been for years. I never miss those votes, he needs all the support he can get."

Belinda nodded. "I've read about that in the pamphlets."

"I didn't know you followed them," Alexander said with a smile.

"Yes, I do keep up with them, the main stories at least. I'm not the most avid reader of that sort of thing. My next eldest sister, Philomena, is. It's more her bag than mine. But the world is changing so I can't afford to bury my head in the sand and let things simply pass me by."

"Very well put," Alexander nodded. He tilted his head and pondered before continuing. "I do wonder, sometimes, if it's not the most beneficial to have men like me with an oversized voice in the House of Lords."

"How so? Isn't it your duty, by virtue of being a Duke?"

"It is, yes," he equivocated. "But I question if others, who don't get much of a say now at all, shouldn't have more of a voice in the political goings on in this country."

"That's almost republican of you!"

He laughed. "Maybe a tiny bit. Though I wouldn't go very far with it. Hypocritical as it might be, I would like to remain a Duke. However, I do question whether those from outside the peerage and gentry, as well as women, should have more of a say than they do now."

Belinda's eyebrows raised when he mentioned 'women', but she said nothing and instead let him continue with his monologuing train of thought.

Alexander said, "I do worry that if nothing changes, this country could end up like France."

Belinda's eyes widened. "Really?"

He nodded. "Yes. I fear that if nothing much changes, resentment will build and build until it eventually, inevitably, overflows into something far uglier and more dangerous."

"Such as happened in France?"

"Perhaps, as a worst case scenario," he replied. "Though we must all pray that it never comes to that."

"We must indeed," she said.

"And those in the Lords, like myself, have more responsibility than anyone else to ensure that what took place in France doesn't happen here. And I don't mean by stamping it out. We need to stop acting in such a way that builds resentment in the first place," Alexander said.

Belinda screwed her eyebrows together in thought. What Alexander was saying made sense, but revolution wasn't a subject she'd really concerned herself with thinking about before. She was a daughter of the ton, after all. Primed and prepped to be a society bride. While some young ladies like Philomena did try to involve themselves in revolutionary matters, Belinda had always wanted to stick to the straight and narrow, comply with the wishes of her brothers and do right by her family.

The horses trotted on down towards the bluebell grove as the couple kept up their discussion of the great matters of state.

The carriage covered several miles of the Faversham estate that day.

When it had reached the highest point on the moors and the mists thinned slightly, Alexander looked across at Belinda and thought how wonderful she was.

Her face shone with delight at the experience of whizzing around the estate.

Though she was a beginner, her dainty hands held the reins with aplomb.

She let out a giggle and steered the phaeton round a bend in the path.

Alexander said, "Seems you're enjoying this. Would you like a phaeton of your own? To ride around the estate?"

"Oh yes, I would love that please," she said eagerly.

"Then it's settled. I'll have the stablehands prepare one for you. It'll be your personal phaeton from now on."

Belinda's eyes shone achingly bright.

When Alexander looked across at her, he was struck by how radiant she was. More radiant than ever before.

After the phaeton ride had finished and Belinda had gone to her chambers to change, Alexander was by himself in the gardens for a stroll in an attempt to clear his head.

He cast his eyes over the land before him. Most of what he could see was Faversham land. He'd run away up here all those months ago in an attempt to free Belinda from being chained to a man like him. His being up here, on his estate, was meant to keep Belinda safe. He could lock himself away up here and keep her safe from him, that's what he'd planned.

What he hadn't banked on was Belinda. She'd done precisely the opposite of what he'd wanted, of what he'd told her to do.

And now, and now, and now he couldn't keep her safe from him. But he couldn't send her away and abandon her all over again. For one, it would be cruel. There would also be no guarantee that she wouldn't try to find him again. And, worst of all, he was too selfish. Over the past few weeks, he had come to a painful realisation. One he wished with all his soul were not true.

He loved Belinda.

He'd learnt so much about her since the night he had bumped into that beautiful woman in the maze at Lands-downe House. With every new discovery, he more and more gained a fuller picture of her as a person. Her likes, her dislikes, her successes, her flaws, her history, her life. The way she played her violin with such skill and dedication. The way she got on so well with the beagles. The way she had stood up to him and found him and refused to give up on him.

Yes, he loved her. And she could never know. Not if he was to protect her and keep her safe. From him.

Protecting her was everything.

CHAPTER SIXTEEN

Belinda entered the small tower library-like snug where Alexander had taken her when she first arrived all those weeks ago. The night with the pâté and the eggs and where she had learnt that he already knew about her condition. Oh, how humiliated she felt at the time, that he of all people should know something so private and so intimate about her. Yet now she could not imagine her husband not knowing. True, Edgar and Xavier had known for years and had always been most supportive. But brothers are not the same as husbands, after all. Moreover, with Alexander there was never any underlying current of trying to keep up appearances at public events for the sake of finding a husband. Because *he* was her husband.

Yet there was always something below the surface with Alexander that she could not figure out. Initially, before they were married, she had thought it was a disappointment at being strong-armed into the marriage by circumstance. Once they were married and he disappeared into the north, she had thought that she had done something to offend him, despite his reassurances in that letter. When, after she had been at Faversham Abbey for a month, he had shared with her the difficulties and the debts his late father's gambling addiction had caused, she had thought that that was the cause of his distance. A friendship had now developed between them and she firmly believed in Alexander's commitment to protect her. But still it did not feel as though they were truly husband and wife. Still it felt like he was hiding something of tremendous significance.

This was his private space, she knew that, but what harm was there in exploring it more? She had been in all the rooms of Faversham Abbey on her side of the green baize door and, barring this small tower room and Alexander's bedroom, she knew each nook and cranny of every room. Besides, he had never explicitly told her not to enter his chambers or study or snug.

She scanned the bookshelves. An eclectic collection! Here in the middle were several editions of the *Complete Works of Shakespeare* and beneath were *The Blazing World* by Cavendish and the collected poems of Milton and Pope respectively. On the other side of the room were books by Swift and Defoe as well as manuals on hunting and estate management.

Her eyes drew downwards to the bottommost shelf. There sat a small, ornately-carved wooden chest. How strange.

She walked over to the shelf and bent down in front of the trunk. It had no lock so she simply lifted the lid. More books and papers greeted her. A book called *Memoirs of a Woman of Pleasure*. Books with titles containing unusual words such as 'Flagellant' and 'Domina'. And several pamphlets that on closer inspection were directories of 'Houses of Discipline' in London.

Utterly bemused, she picked up each publication one by one and began to read. Only snippets of each here and there at first, she did not really understand what she was reading to begin with. She had heard whispers on the ton of books that discussed 'sophisticated subjects' that young ladies of fine breeding such as herself were never meant to read. Not wanting to risk the merest hint of a scandal and sully her reputation, she had always made sure to steer well clear of such content lest anyone find her associated with it. But now she was a married woman the state of play was different and she had no scandal to fear so long as she was faithful to Alexander.

Some of what she read did not surprise her all that much. At Edgar's planning, one of her maids had sat her down when she was younger and informed her about the changes her body would soon experience and the matter of how a woman came to be with child. In hindsight she supposed she should have expected some of the information given the behaviour she had witnessed of some of the four-legged inhabitants of Renfregh. Her kindly maid had explained the pleasures of Christian marriage which, Belinda ruefully reflected, she had yet to experience despite being married in a service conducted by the very Archbishop of Canterbury himself.

About two years after the talk from her maid, Belinda had begun her courses and thereafter had gone through a merry go round of doctors and midwives, such were their general heaviness and agonising cramps which only sweet laudanum would relieve. They all agreed something was out of sorts with her body, but none could say what apart from the doctor who droned on about hysteria before Edgar told him to get out and not return.

"I will not have anyone talk about such nonsense, Belinda." Edgar had said. "I am sorry about that doctor, you will not see a quack like that ever again. His treating you as though it is some fictitious disease when any rational person would see full well that it is real."

She read and read and read. There were all sorts of words of which she had only previously heard whispers. Words for acts she had only heard alluded to in satirical pamphlets and cartoons.

It was all rather eye opening.

Alexander certainly had a lot of this content.

She didn't feel repulsed by what she was reading.

Instead, it was all rather curious. She had heard some of the concepts before. After all, she understood what congress was, her kindly maid had explained that to her many years ago. But the combination of activities that were being combined with congress in these pamphlets was mind boggling. There was flagellation, a lot of pamphlets about that. And men being tied up in all sorts of positions both indoors and outdoors, in barns and on vessels at sea and every other place imaginable. Women giving men orders, telling them to bring them items and perform tasks for them. Some of the tasks were menial and others involved what the women called 'worship'. Though it was unlike any worship Belinda had ever heard of before. And, in some cases, there was no congress whatsoever. Only the activities.

Belinda continued reading the contents of the trunk and came to the realisation that aside from *Memoirs of a Woman of Pleasure*, every piece focused on the idea of a man acting as a kind of servant where he was subordinate to a woman.

Belinda supposed that this must be a special area of interest for Alexander. Or else why would he have so many pamphlets and directories about it? Was this something he enjoyed reading about? Was it something he wished to participate in? *Had* he participated in it already?

The very concept of a man being subordinate to a woman as she was reading in these pamphlets was something that she hadn't really considered before. It wasn't the way of things in England during the reign of George III. Not at least as far as she knew.

She and Alexander had been married in the Church of England, after all. She had vowed to obey him. And while she knew that didn't mean subordination, not of the kind these men were experiencing in the pamphlets, it still implied some sort of structure, didn't it? Some sort of structure where it would be against the rules for Alexander to ever be subordinate to her.

But what rules? And whose rules? Her maid hadn't discussed any such rules with her. And nor, come to think of it, had any vicar or minister. Nor had her father nor her brothers. Nor her governesses nor her tutors nor anyone who had ever been important in her life.

So where had she got that idea from? Some sort of conduct manual, she thought. But it was only a conduct manual and what did they know? She had never met the author, didn't even know who wrote those sorts of things. So why pay any heed to them? She didn't have any answers.

On and on and on she read.

So engrossed was she in the books and pamphlets that she heard neither the door creaking open nor the footsteps on the floorboards. In fact, the first moment she realised she was no longer alone was when a distinctive male voice thundered.

"Belinda, what in God's name are you doing?"

Her husband stood before her, his face a deathly pale pallor and eyes bulging from their sockets.

Belinda's first instinct was to tremble and apologise, but then her mind turned to how Alexander had hardly been upfront with her about what he wanted and who he really was. Was this interest of his the real reason for his initial distance and continued guardedness?

She rose to her feet and took a few steps towards him.

"I am trying to find out the truth about why you are so closed off with me all the time, about why you are unwilling to be candid with me about the personal matters of yours that you feel the need to protect me from," she said.

"So you thought you could simply wander around in my private rooms?" he said icily.

She placed her hands on her hips. "What choice did you leave me? At every turn you have put up barrier after barrier, always in the name of protecting me and for my so-called benefit. Why do you have those books and pamphlets in the box?"

"Belinda, those are private, they were never meant for your eyes."

"Oh I understand they were never meant for me. The horse has well and truly bolted and I have seen them now."

Alexander rubbed the back of his neck in a gesture of self-comfort. He looked at the floor before returning his gaze to Belinda. "Yes, I suppose you have," he said as if in a daze.

"So why do you have those items in the box? Are they things you wish to do? Things you have done before?" she asked.

"Yes and yes to some of those activities." He bit his lip and wetness formed in his eyes.

Belinda looked at him with a steely gaze. "If it is something you wish to partake in, why did you not ask me if I would like to be involved?"

"Because it is neither right nor proper for you to even be exposed to these things," he replied.

"I will choose for myself what is right and what is proper," she spat. "Am I not your wife? Are we not to share with each other all the secrets of our hearts?"

Alexander was a broken man. "I only ever wanted to protect you."

Her face softened. "I respect that, really I do. And most of the time I *want* you to protect me. I relish it in fact. But I do not need protection *from* you."

"But you do." Alexander's voice quivered.

"If I really needed protection from you, then how could I trust you to even decide whether or not I needed that protection? If you were so dangerous then you wouldn't be capable of making any decisions about protecting me."

"But I'm your husband. I have a duty. I'm supposed to protect you."

She nodded. "All of those things are true. But you don't have a duty to protect me from you. Not in this way."

Alexander rubbed at the back of his neck in a gesture of self comfort. "Well, I did a fine job of it in any case. It's not like I succeeded."

All the steel had gone from Belinda's eyes by now. What remained was a softness. Mostly sympathy. And a tiny bit of familiarity. "No. But I can understand your intentions. Even though they hurt me."

"I'm sorry I hurt you. Truly, I am. I never wanted to cause you the slightest bit of pain."

"I know now that you didn't. But you did hurt me." She clenched her fists at her sides.

"I wish I could do anything to change it. To change hurting you. I am so sorry I hurt you."

"Then please don't continue hurting me by trying to protect me from you. I do not need protection from you."

He nodded sharply. "You're right."

"Yes, I am." She unclenched her fists.

He looked at her through glassy eyes. "I just don't want to hurt you. And I have. Which is terrible. But I don't want to keep hurting you."

"Then please be honest with me. Because I am going to ask you some questions."

"As you wish."

"Would you ever have told any wife about this?"

He was a little taken aback by her question. Of everything she could have asked him, this one wasn't anywhere on his list of possibilities. "What? No! It wouldn't have been appropriate for any lady."

"What if she were willing to participate?"

Another question that Alexander had never anticipated. Tonight was getting more and more bizarre by the minute. He felt as if he had stepped into a house of mirrors.

Belinda kept her gaze on him and said nothing.

The ball was firmly in his court.

He gulped and then forced himself to say, "Well, that would be a moot point. No lady would be willing to participate in such things."

"That's quite some statement. Are not the women you have done this with before ladies?"

"Not many would call them ladies. They are professionals."

"But do they not deserve the term? Whoever they are? Those governesses? Just because they're not members of the ton doesn't mean they aren't worthy of the term 'lady'."

He tilted his head in equivocation. "You do have a point, yes. I suppose it is possible to call them ladies. But they're not bred to be ladies of the ton. They can be exposed to things you can't."

She let out a sharp laugh. "Why is it acceptable for them to be exposed to something and not me? That's insulting to both myself and those governesses! If I shouldn't be exposed to those activities, then neither should they. And if they can choose to participate in those acts, then why can't I? What is the real difference between them and me? Upbringing? We are all women, we are all flesh and blood."

Alexander rubbed the back of his neck again. "You are right. I must admit I've not thought of it that way before. But you are right."

"I'm glad you see it my way," she gave a small smile. "Which brings me to another point," she said. Inside, her voice shook but she forced herself to maintain a steady voice. "If I, the daughter of an earl, am not a lady then I am not sure who qualifies as one in this country. Tell me, am I a lady in your eyes?"

"You are, of course you are," he implored.

"Then it is possible for a lady to be interested in participating in your secret activities."

Alexander's eyebrows shot up. "Are you serious?"

"I do not speak in jest."

"But you don't know what it means. What it entails."

"I can learn. If I so desire."

"You could. But I'm not going to corrupt you."

She crossed her arms. "No, you'd rather put me on a pedestal. Keep me as a glass statue who can never move, never run the risk of falling and smashing."

"That's not what I'm trying to do."

"Then what is it you're trying to do?"

"Protect you. Keep you safe," he growled in frustration.

"And you can still do that. But I am my own woman, my own rational mind. And I should be able to choose for myself what is right for a lady."

Belinda kept her arms crossed and her gaze firmly on her husband.

Neither Faversham said anything for a good minute.

Alexander did his best not to be the first to break. But eventually, he lost the battle. "Very well, make your own choice," he sighed.

"Oh, I shall," Belinda said. She uncrossed her arms. Then she turned and walked towards the heavy mahogany desk. She sat down on the floor with her legs stretched out in front of her and her back against the desk.

Alexander raised his eyebrows in surprise. "Your Grace - Belinda - what are you doing?"

"I do not wish my legs to tire. And I foresee it being a long night ahead of us."

"But why not a chair?" he said in bafflement.

She cast a dismissive hand at his question. "Now that would be too formal, too rigid. I would feel as though I were conducting some interview in a salon. I cannot cope with formalities tonight."

"Alright," Alexander said slowly, still confused at his wife's apparent ease.

"Now, bring me a bottle of sherry and come and join me." She patted the carpet next to her.

He made his way over to the drinks cabinet and took out an almost-full bottle of Pedro Ximénez. He carried it over to her and plonked himself down on the floor.

※※※※※ ※※※※※

Alexander and Belinda leant against the desk together.

The bottle of sherry was over half empty by now.

He passed the bottle back to her.

She took a final swig.

His sleeves were rolled up in an attempt to keep cool in the heat of tonight's confrontation.

Belinda, for her part, was still mostly put together. But she was yawning every minute or so, and she was fighting a challenging battle to keep her eyes open.

She looked across at Alexander. "I don't know about you, but I for one am absolutely shattered. I don't think I can stay awake much longer. I would like to reconvene tomorrow. Not to argue, you understand. But to discuss."

"I do understand. At least I hope I do," Alexander said.

Belinda nodded. "So shall we say one o'clock tomorrow afternoon? In my sitting room?"

"Yes, let's meet then and there."

And with that, they retired to their separate chambers to get what rest they could ahead of whatever tomorrow would bring.

❧ — ◆ — ❧

CHAPTER SEVENTEEN

L exander roused himself out of bed. He looked out of the window and surveyed the lands which the Dukes of Faversham had held from generations unto generations.

The vision that met his gaze was one he had seen hundreds of times previously. Mists swirled around the heather coated moors and trees jutted out here and there at seemingly random points.

Yet on this morning he was a different man.

Belinda knew his deepest, most secretly hidden truth and from her he could no longer hide.

Yet though there had been tears, he had not received those things he feared most of all from her. Complete rejection and disgust.

His heart was tight in his chest as he made his way over to his armoire and began to dress himself. If this were an ordinary day, he would have called on his loyal valet to perform this task. But this was no ordinary day.

In her sitting room, Belinda sipped her tea.

Deep in thought, she at first did not hear the rap at the door.

After a few moments, there was another knock and a maid's voice called, "Your Grace, may I come in please?"

"Enter," Belinda called.

The door swung open to reveal one of the housemaids holding a small silver platter. Atop the platter were a couple of boiled eggs, some pâté and crackers.

The housemaid placed the platter on the table in front of Belinda. "Luncheon, your Grace."

"Thank you, that will be all," said Belinda.

The housemaid curtsied and left the room, shutting the door behind herself on her way out.

Belinda served herself the food. It reminded her of that first meal she had eaten all those weeks ago, back when she had arrived at Faversham Abbey on a bleak evening and was met by a furious Alexander. Yet she knew much more now than she did back then.

At first when she read through his most secret papers, she hadn't properly understood what she was looking at. But as she read and read and read, she had realised she was reading of the sorts of sophisticated subjects young ladies of the ton were never meant to know about. Well, she knew something about them now.

She didn't want to cry or run away or dash off in a carriage back to London. No, she was made of sterner stuff than that!

Instead, what she wanted was to understand why Alexander was interested in what was in those pamphlets and directories.

When she thought about this whole new world, however, a strange sensation brewed within her. She kept coming back to the thought of what it meant to be dominant. If someone wanted to be dominant, did it make them inherently cruel? Did it mean they lacked any morals whatsoever? Did it make them a monster? Surely, wanting to have control over someone else was unnatural and wrong.

The thought sat uncomfortably within her. And she couldn't quite put her finger as to why.

She finished her meal and raised herself from the settee. It was time to meet with her husband.

She made her way to the dressing table and rearranged her shawl around her shoulders. She met herself in the eye in the mirror. Yes, this was how she wanted to look. Confident, prepared, a Duchess of the ton.

There was a knock at the door. An unmistakable rhythm. It could only be one person.

Belinda walked towards the door and opened it.

In front of her, looking bashful and sheepish but very much present, was her husband.

"Please, come in," she said. She turned away and made for the settee.

"Thank you." He entered the room and then shut the door behind him.

Belinda sat herself down and watched him with expectant eyes.

He rubbed the back of his neck. "I am truly sorry. For last night and for everything. For abandoning you in London. For not telling you the truth."

She nodded slowly. "Thank you for your apology."

The room fell silent.

Belinda took a sip of tea from the cup in front of her. She wanted to make him wait. She wanted to make him sweat for all he had done to her, however good his intentions might have been.

Alexander shuffled a little on the spot.

After a few minutes, Belinda spoke again. "I am not going to apologise to you, you must understand. Neither for last night nor for coming up here to the Abbey in the first place. You started this, not me. And you are a duke and a man and you have far more power in this world than I ever will. So you left me with little choice. That's why I did what I did. It was either that or wait around forever for an answer and an explanation."

"I do understand," he said.

"Very well," she said. "Then, please, come and sit. Would you like some tea?"

"Yes, please." Alexander took a seat in the armchair opposite her.

She poured him a cup of tea.

"Tell me, why a man as powerful as you, a duke even, would ever want to give up his power? Don't all men seek power?" she asked briskly.

"This might sound odd and I don't wish to be facetious, but sometimes the power and having to make choices are too much for me to handle," Alexander said. He cast his eyes down at the floor for a brief moment, before forcing himself to return to meet Belinda's gaze.

Belinda nodded slowly. "So you don't want to be able to make choices?"

"At least for a little while, yes," he said.

"But not for your whole life? You still want to be the Duke?" she asked.

"Well, yes," he said. "At least some of the time. I do have responsibilities and duties after all. To you, to my mother and sisters, to the tenants, to the estate and to the king. I can't run away from them completely. But to escape, to get some sort of respite, that's what I like."

Belinda leaned back on the settee and pondered her husband's words.

On the one hand, she struggled to understand how someone who had long held such power, who was leader of his family and responsible for hundreds of people's livelihoods and homes as the Duke of Faversham, would want to give away any modicum of power. She herself held so little power, had so little say over her own life, that the idea of someone wanting to give up any of their power struck her as most bizarre indeed.

And yet, and yet, and yet. Maybe what Alexander wanted wasn't so strange. If she was living in a world where she had little power and wanted more, wasn't that a sign of dissatisfaction in her life? So it stood to reason that Alexander's desire to give up some of his power represented his own dissatisfaction with his life.

But she still could not help but come back to the idea that anyone who was interested in dominating someone else had something twisted and wrong deep inside of them. Wasn't there something wrong about a person who wanted to control someone else? Who wanted to strike someone else?

Who wanted to deny someone else something? It could only be the idea of a true deviant, couldn't it?

She resolved to ask Alexander. He was the one, after all, who had brought these concepts into her life so immediately, however unintentionally. Certainly, she could have found out about them some other way, at some other time. But his interests and subsequent secrecy had led her down a trail of breadcrumbs that brought her to the door of his snug. So he could give her some explanations. It was the least he owed her after his months of obfuscation and unilateral decision-making.

She leaned forward again. Her eyes were cautious and her facial muscles tight. "Something that's been bothering me about this. You say you want to give up control. And that is all well and good. But what about the person taking that control from you? Are they not a monster for wanting to control you?"

"You are right to be concerned," he said. "I think it would be a sign of a highly worrying person if they didn't find this concept at least a bit concerning. But I would say to you that I make the choice to give up control for a set period of time out of my own free will. Noone is forcing me to participate. I would also say that there are many people, usually men, in positions of power and control in society. Bishops. The Prime Minister. Dukes such as myself. And most of those are not monsters. By no means saints, but rarely are they monsters either. And, in the case of most of those men, other people have little to no say in who they are. Whereas I have complete and final say in whoever I submit to."

Belinda bit her lip. Alexander's words did make sense to her. The thought of being a monster had terrified her. But why? Why had she even been concerned? Something she had felt deep down last night, but hadn't been able to articulate in words burst to the forefront of her mind. Perhaps the reason she was so scared of being thought a monster was because the thought of being one of the dominant women, like in Alexander's forbidden pamphlets, intrigued her. Perhaps it was something she might like to try. If she had read those pamphlets and directories and been wholly uninterested in the content, then surely she would not have been afraid of what someone in the dominant role might be. Because it being dominant wouldn't ever be a possibility for her.

She didn't want to give the game away to him that his words made some sort of sense to her. Not yet, anyway. Instead, she widened her eyes with intent and kept her gaze focused steadily on him.

She took a sip of her tea. The tannic taste swilled around her mouth. No milk, no sugar.

When she had had her fill, she put the cup down. "So, wanting to be dominant does not inherently mean one is a monster. That is all well and good," she said. "But what am I supposed to do now that I know about your interest in submission?"

"You could forget you ever knew," he offered.

"Oh that is not by any means a possibility, your Grace. One cannot find out such information about one's husband and simply erase it from one's mind. So what am I supposed to do now?"

"I don't know what you should do. The choice is yours to make. But to answer your question, your finding out about my interest in submission doesn't mean anything has to ever happen between us," Alexander said.

"Well, no nothing ever does have to happen between us," Belinda said. "But I am human, as are you and I can't deny myself from aspects of life just because I'm not obliged to participate in them. I'm a human being with my own free will and therefore I should have the right to choose what I do and do not participate in."

"Yes, you do have that right." Alexander bit his lip in fretful concern.

"Then what's the problem?"

"I'm worried I'm forcing your hand. That to choose to participate in this with me would be forcing you to do something you didn't want to do. And that you may never have even known about if it weren't for me."

Belinda took a sip of her tea before replying. "It's true, I may never have known about this if it weren't for you. However, who is to say that at some point I wouldn't have discovered it for myself anyway? I can read, after all. Maybe I would've found those books myself at some point. You found them and got them yourself. And on the point of forcing my hand, I could call a carriage right now and have him take me to Bath and spend the rest of my days there if I really wanted to."

"But as your husband, it would be my right to stop you," Alexander said.

"Therein lies the rub. I don't believe you would. There's nothing you've done at any point to lead me to believe you would force me to stay. You *ran away* from me, for heaven's sake!" Belinda said.

Alexander looked sheepish. "For that I can only apologise."

"I accept that. Now I want us to be able to move forward."

"I don't know what that looks like. But I really want to try. More than anything," he said huskily.

"I want to try to," she said. "And I don't know what that looks like either. But that's why I'm here. To talk. To see what you and I can do."

Alexander pinched the tip of his nose between thumb and forefinger. "I just don't want you to feel like you have to do anything, least of all anything to do with what you discovered last night. I don't want to be the sort of husband who makes his wife do anything she isn't comfortable with."

"But what if I want to try those things?" Belinda asked.

Alexander's eyes widened. "Well, uh, that would be a different matter. Though I fear you'd only be doing that out of obligation."

She raised an eyebrow. "Oh, I assure you, I am well past the point of doing anything out of obligation. I was obliged to stay away from Faversham Abbey but I came here anyway."

He nodded slowly. "I understand."

The room fell into silence for a few minutes.

Eventually, Belinda's firm voice broke it. "Those books you have, in that box, are there others?" she asked.

"Not at the Abbey. I do have some at Faversham House though," Alexander said.

Belinda nodded. "And are there others available? From wherever you get them?"

"Yes, there would be. Do you want other titles?"

"I'm curious to see them, yes. How do you acquire them? Mail order?"

"One can. Or there are a few discrete shops, or sometimes back rooms at conventional bookshops, where that sort of thing is available. In London, Bath, Edinburgh, I think Manchester and Birmingham too. And York."

Belinda's eyebrows raised briefly. "In York?"

"It's only one of the back rooms though. Well, in that case it's in the attic of a conventional bookshop."

"Can ladies attend?" There was a little note of excitement in her voice.

"Yes, but you'd have to be discreet."

"Noted." She nodded. She took a sip of her tea. It was starting to get cold. Then she said, "Could we pay a visit to York soon?"

Alexander's eyebrows shot up briefly. He coughed in surprise. Then he regained self control and his expression became one of interest. "That can be arranged."

"I look forward to it." She put her cup and saucer down on the table. "You have given me a lot to think about today."

Alexander's eyes filled with concern. "Oh, Belinda, I hope I haven't made anything worse."

"No, you haven't. In fact, you have given me a lot to think about in a good way. But I need to do some thinking on my own before I discuss any more of this with you."

He nodded. "I understand."

She cast her gaze to the window briefly. "The sky is look-ing clear. What say you to a phaeton ride this afternoon?"

"I should like that, Belinda. I should like that very much indeed," he said with a small smile.

❧ ·•· ❧

CHAPTER EIGHTEEN

Belinda and Alexander sat in her chambers.

Outside, the autumn leaves swirled in the gardens, their russet and gold leaves forming a blanket on that ground that lifted and moved with each gust of wind.

Inside, the howling of the wind made its way through the window panes with an eerie tone.

Alexander and Belinda paid it no mind. They were well-used to life on the moors by now.

Instead, Alexander poured tea for the pair. He ventured, "Did anyone ever explain to you the matter of how marital congress works? Before you arrived here, I mean."

Belinda could not help but make a tiny, brief smirk. "Well, if they hadn't before, I would've found out from some of that reading material you have in the snug! But seriously, I did already know. My brother is not the kind of man to want to leave his sisters wilfully blind to all realities of life. He had my maid explain it to me many years ago." She took a sip of tea. "So he made sure to spare you that task."

"Oh thank heavens." Alexander pinched the top of his nose between thumb and forefinger.

Belinda smiled a little. "So I am very sorry my brother was prudent and deprived you of that privilege."

"I am glad he did."

She took another sip of her tea.

Alexander said, "I don't want you to feel pressured into doing anything too quickly, before you feel ready."

Belinda nodded. "I know you wouldn't try."

"Thank you for your trust. Really, it means a lot. I certainly wouldn't try, but even if you think I'm pressuring you unintentionally, you must let me know. Because I would hate for you to ever be pressured into anything," he said.

"I will let you know. You can count on that. I am not someone who is unafraid to stand up for myself, as you have seen in recent months."

Alexander gave her a small smile. "I most certainly have."

Belinda took another sip of her tea. She was a little nervous, but she wanted to make her own decisions. Ever since she decided to take her life into her own hands and disobey Alexander, things in her life had slowly improved. She had more control. She was more able to be her own woman. "If we were to do anything, I don't feel ready for intercourse yet. I wish for you to know that."

Alexander nodded. "Understood. And I respect that."

"Though, there may be other things I wish to try."

He bit his lip. "And what might those be?"

"Hands to start with. And potentially cunny-lapping." She waited a beat. "I have read through that entire box from the snug over the past week. It was most enlightening."

"I would say, 'oh heavens, what have I done' to expose you to such things, but like you've said before, you could have found out about those matters yourself through other means." he said.

"So what will you say instead?"

"That I respect you greatly for having the confidence to tell me what you just did. And that I hold you in the highest esteem, always."

Belinda leaned back in her chair. She appreciated his words. Despite everything that had happened since that night in the maze, not least his unilateral decision to run away on the night of their wedding, she swore she could still detect a note of sincerity in his voice. Even so, she was having this conversation because she wanted to take ownership over her own body and have more of a semblance of control over her own life. Not because she wanted to please him. If she had solely wanted to please him, she would never have come up to Yorkshire. Rather, she wanted to be Belinda, Duchess of Faversham, and not some young chit who whiled her life away living to please the desires of men.

"Thank you, Alexander," she said. "You know, high esteem is one of those things that society always talks about. The high esteem of the ton. One's reputation amongst the great and the good. But it can mean so many things and some of them I am not sure I even want. Can you imagine having the high esteem of Lady Reynolds?"

"Oh heavens, that would be terrible." He shook his head at the awful thought.

"I do, however, like having the high esteem of my husband."

"And you shall always have it," he said.

She took a sip of her tea. "Say, am I given to understand that these activities, with dominants and submissives, happen in sessions? That some people call scenes?"

"That's a term some people use, yes," he said.

"Right, scenes it is," she said. "Well, we should think about how these scenes might happen. Would you like to kneel at my feet during such scenes?"

Alexander spluttered a little in shock, before he regained self control. "I would like that very much indeed, Belinda."

Belinda smiled to herself. Her first suggestion and Alexander had liked it. Not that she wanted to act with the focus of pleasing him. She had to consider what she wanted too. She would only do something where her and Alexander's interests aligned. Society and the church said a wife had to obey her husband. But these scenes were one area of life where she wouldn't adapt to please Alexander. At least not yet. She was so inexperienced and she had so much to learn. She didn't want to start adapting herself to suit someone else before she even knew who she really was. Maybe when she became more experienced, she would be willing to compromise. But that day was a while off yet.

And right now, a blend of being the respected duchess in public and a dominant woman in private was most enticing to her.

She leaned closer to Alexander. "Just think about it, me by your side as your attentive wife in public and you kneeling at my feet in private," she said. "It's a beautiful vision indeed!"

Alexander looked at Belinda in wonderment. "How are you real?"

"Oh I am as real as you are. We were both made by our creator to enjoy this life and everything it has to offer," she said.

"You are more incredible than I think you even realise," he said.

"It might be so." She gave a little laugh.

Belinda liked Alexander's praise. But she also wanted to make their talk a reality. She was a woman with feelings and hopes and ambitions and she didn't just want to sit around and talk the rest of her life away. She wanted to do and to be as well.

Belinda took a sip of her tea. She pondered the man before her. "Tell me, Alexander, what do you envision calling me as part of these scenes?"

"Whatever you wish," he replied immediately.

She tilted her head in thought and said nothing.

Silence enveloped the room. But it wasn't an uncomfortable kind of silence. Rather, it was the sort of silence you might find between old friends or a couple who had been together for many years.

Belinda took another sip of her tea.

The companionable silence continued.

After several minutes, Belinda began to speak. "Well, I've been called 'My Lady' enough times in my life already. And 'Mistress', it puts me too much in mind of opera singers and actresses and courtesans. I like the Latin term 'Domina'. It has a similar meaning to 'My Lady' and 'Mistress', but not the same connotations for me."

Alexander broke out into a genuine smile. "Domina it is then."

"And you, what should I call you during these scenes?" she asked.

"Just 'Alexander' is fine." He paused for a beat. "Though also, I would like to be called 'Pet'."

Belinda nodded. "'Alexander' and 'Pet' it shall be." She took another sip of her tea. "And as for our first scene together, is there anything you wish to try?"

"I just want you to be comfortable. To feel safe. And to feel good," he said earnestly. "So long as I can make those things happen, I don't mind much what we do. There isn't much you could suggest that would surprise me, believe me."

"Is that a challenge?"

"Not so much a challenge. More reflecting the realities that I've seen in certain houses in Soho," he said.

"Very well," she said. "Here's what I propose."

And so they spent a pleasant hour discussing the intricacies of Belinda's wants and desires for their first scene together. The pair of them could hardly wait to enact their plans.

Chapter Nineteen

Miss Dauntsey tied Belinda's stays around her bust and then pulled the quilted silver and ivory gown over her head. A pink velvet robe and pink satin shoes completed the ensemble.

"You look beautiful, your Grace," said the lady's maid.

"Thank you, Miss Dauntsey. That will be all, please go and have the rest of the night to yourself."

Miss Dauntsey gave a knowing smile and curtsied before leaving the room.

Now Belinda was alone in her chambers. As she and Alexander had discussed, tonight was going to be their first ever scene together. And the first ever scene of Belinda's life.

She looked at herself in the full length mirror.

The combination of swirling gold plating and flickering candlelight cast a sparkling radiance over Belinda so that she was an ethereal queen.

The vision that met her gaze made her feel confident and powerful. Exactly how she wanted to feel tonight and all nights.

She glanced over at the carriage clock on the mantelpiece. It was five minutes to eight.

Alexander would be along at eight on the dot, if he knew what was good for him.

She turned her eyes again to her reflection in the mirror. She was absolutely stunning, if she did say so herself.

She let herself feel the excitement that had been building inside her ever since she had first met with Alexander to plan out tonight's activities. The warm, enticing sensation in her belly was beginning to bloom.

Lost in her thoughts, she was pleasantly surprised when there was soon a knocking at her chamber door.

Two quick knocks followed by three fast ones. It was the code she had arranged with Alexander.

A broad smile formed on her lips.

She turned her head slightly towards the door. "Enter!" she called.

A few seconds passed and the door swung open to reveal Alexander.

She turned fully to face him and drank in the sight of him. He cut a more dashing figure than he ever had before, and that was saying something because every day she saw him she thought him more and more handsome. He wore a black waistcoat and matching black pantaloons as well as a billowing white cotton shirt. On his feet he wore black leather riding boots shined to perfection. His hair was exactly how she liked it, coiffed to perfection to show off its wonderful raven colour.

"Come here pet, and shut the door behind you," she commanded. She tried to school her features into those of a commanding governess rather than a very excited young wife.

He did as she bade and crossed the room to face her.

Then, just as they had discussed, he fell to his knees and placed his hands on his thighs. He raised his eyes to meet hers.

"Good evening pet," she said. "Are you ready to serve me?"

"Yes, Domina," he said. His eyes glowed with reverential admiration for the woman who stood before him.

"Very well." She offered him her hand. "Kiss it."

He did so with eagerness and placed a gentle kiss atop her dainty hand.

She gave a tiny nod of acknowledgement. "Then we shall begin."

She walked over to the blanked-covered, plush pink tufted settee and settled herself atop it.

Alexander remained kneeling on the floor and tilted his head towards her so he could maintain his reverential gaze.

She issued her next command. "Remove your shirt and waistcoat. You may stand to do so."

Alexander rose to his feet. First he took off his black silken waistcoat.

Belinda felt her pulse begin to race a little. So far in their marriage she had not seen Alexander remove a shred of clothing beyond his coat and hat. So to see him begin to remove a more intimate article, and at her very command to boot, was most enthralling.

His waistcoat gone, Alexander turned his attentions to his billowing white cotton shirt. He undid each button with due care to reveal dark black hairs atop his chest.

Belinda drew a sharp intake of breath at the sight. This was quite something!

One by one, the buttons of his shirt fell away and, soon enough, he was shrugging himself out of the shirt.

He looked at Belinda in expectation of her next command.

"Tidy those up and put them away," she said.

Alexander quickly moved to carry out her order. He folded his waistcoat and shirt and placed them in one of Belinda's chests of drawers. Then he returned to his original spot and lowered himself to his knees.

"That's very good, pet," Belinda praised.

The room fell into silence and the only sound that could be heard was the crackling of the candle flames.

Belinda sat back and got comfortable on the blanket-covered settee. She relished the sight of Alexander as he knelt topless before her. His athletic muscles were quivering with tension, with the delight and the desire of being part of this scene with her.

Her idea to keep him in his pantaloons and boots was an inspired one. She congratulated herself. This way, she got to enjoy the beauty and prowess of his arms and chest but she also got to look at a distinguished gentleman of the ton brought to his knees out of his desire to serve her.

Belinda spoke again. "Now, pet, come to me. Stay on your knees."

Alexander crawled towards her, his well formed limbs padding on the ornate Persian rug that enveloped most of the floor of the room.

Belinda wouldn't have stood to have him crawl on bare floorboards or stone, however much Alexander may have wanted to. Because she knew best and she cared about his safety. She loved to see him like this, his prowess being directed solely to serve her pleasure. She had seen so many gentlemen of the ton over the years, dressed in their dark pantaloons and waistcoats and leather boots and all the rest of it. While many of them exerted and demonstrated a special kind of prowess, not once had that prowess been directed for her enjoyment. So tonight was most wonderful indeed. The delicious sensation that had bloomed within her began to spread to the rest of her body. She was alive with electricity and the excitement she felt at being with Alexander tonight as part of this scene.

He came to a halt at her feet and returned to his kneeling position.

"That's very good pet, well done," she said. "Now, remove my shoes and provide some relief to my aching feet."

"At once, Domina," Alexander said. If he had a tail, he would have been wagging it right now, such was his happiness and delight at the situation.

One by one, he removed Belinda's shoes with practiced deftness and gentleness. Then he turned his attentions to her weary feet and placed firm circles on the soles with his strong, masculine hands.

Belinda let forth a moan of pleasure at his attentions.

Alexander's lip quirked upwards when he heard how much she was enjoying his efforts. He wanted nothing else tonight other than to please her and make her feel safe and cared for.

Then he rubbed his knuckles along the ball of each foot. "Oh pet, that feels so good," she moaned.

He kept up his attentions for countless minutes. It would not do to disappoint his Domina!

Eventually, when she had had her fill of his wonderful hands on her dainty feet, Belinda opened her lips. "You may stop, pet. You did such a good job. I am most pleased."

She felt herself grow wet with need. She had not felt this way about Alexander before, for a long time she had been so vexed with the cold-hearted duke that he wouldn't have been able to elicit such a feeling from her. But now she had him exactly where she wanted him and he was the most desirable man on earth in her eyes.

She reached through the skirts and petticoats to find her sopping slit. Her thatched mound was slick with the juices of her desire. She rubbed her fingers along her labia and enjoyed how plump they felt. Then, and only when she was good and ready, she moved her fingers deeper to find her pulsating clitoris.

She was practiced at this, with years of experience, so she knew her own body well and she knew what she wanted.

She ran her finger in delicate circles round and round her clitoris. Her finger moved easily through her smooth juices.

Alexander kept his eyes focused on her at all times.

She looked down at him. He had gone beetroot red and his pupils were as wide as saucers.

She felt powerful and strong and in charge of her own body. All woman, woman, woman!

She felt herself climbing that delicious precipice and teetering on the edge. It was as though she was at the top of a cliff face and beneath her were the rolling azure waves and it was all she would need to do but to let herself fall down down down into the tempting waves below.

But she didn't want release just yet. This was a night where she wanted to savour her pleasure.

She removed her hand from her skirts and brought it to her lips. The sweet taste of her juices was exquisite.

Beneath her, Alexander drew an audibly sharp intake of breath.

Belinda looked down at him through hooded lids. "Oh you liked to see that, did you pet?"

"Yes, Domina. You look absolutely radiant." He said. Then, his lip quirked up a little cheekily. "May I please have a taste?"

She tutted. "Not tonight pet, you will have to earn that privilege over time."

"Yes Domina, thank you Domina," he said. His voice was desperate with need.

She returned her hand to her skirts and resumed her delicate attentions on her clitoris. This time, she stroked up and down. Her hips bucked a little at the new sensation.

"Oh, pet," she stammered. She was fast approaching the edge of the precipice again.

"Domina," Alexander groaned.

She switched things up and stroked round and round her clitoris in teasing circles. This was a most delicious sensation.

But perhaps even more delicious was when she let herself experience the fullness of her ecstasy. It was time again.

She pulsated her hips forward and back, forward and back, forward and back. In that moment, all that existed were her and the man who knelt before her. She kept her eyes on him through hooded lids as the wondrous sensation washed through her.

When she had had her fill, she opened her eyes fully. Now it was time to try something else.

"Bring me that brush you spoke of," she said.

"Yes, Domina," smiled Alexander. He made his way to the dressing table.

"And do not dawdle!" said Belinda.

Contentment washed over Alexander. All of life he had been primed to fulfil the role of Duke of Faversham, to lead and to protect. But now he had a new cause in life too. During sessions like this he was also bound to serve and obey his darling wife Belinda and he revelled in the thought.

Alexander reached into the dressing table and pulled out a fresh medium sized silk brush. Then he returned to where Belinda reclined on the settee and knelt in front of her offering the brush. An act of true reverence.

Belinda took it in her hands. It was about six inches long, with a sturdy wooden handle and a set of bristles at the tip.

She brought the bristles to the point where her legs met.

Alexander had said to her during their planning discussion that some ladies enjoyed the sensation of soft bristles and that using a brush would make it easier to control. Belinda had only ever used her fingers before, but had been enticed by the new possibilities Alexander had mentioned.

The bristles tickled her labia. It wasn't unpleasant. Rather, it was a sensation of which she had never experienced the like before.

She looked down at Alexander. He still knelt on the floor, with his eyes gazing reverently up at her. Exactly as she had specified. He was fast proving to be a most obedient submissive and that fact pleased her greatly.

She pushed the brush further inside her, her legs spread wide, and relished the new sensation.

Her slickness soon made the brush shiny and wet. It teased against her labia and it was all she could do but to buck her hips forward to get more of that oh so delicious sensation. How she adored the way it felt!

She moved the brush over her clit. She shivered at the sensation. This was far more delicate, yet pinpointed, than her finger. Up and down, up and down, she moved the brush.

She let forth a small, breathy moan of pleasure.

She continued the tantalising motion of the brush over her pleasure pearl. Her hips rocked back and forth all the while. The delicious sensations kept building and building within her. And soon enough, she was on that precipice of pleasure again. And it was all that she could do but to let herself experience the exquisite bliss of release.

She let the wave of climax wash over her.

When she had finished, she gazed again down at Alexander. This time her lids were hooded with need and desire.

He was oh so handsome kneeling on the floor before her. The shimmering candlelight cast a warm honey glow over his bare back and torso. This man, this duke, this leader of the ton, submitting to her and surrendering himself to her made her feel powerful and strong. The very thought made her long for another climax.

She brought the brush back to her clit and rubbed it around in circles.

She let forth a gasp of shock and delight.

A salacious idea struck her. What if she tried new directions, not just circles and straight up and down, but other shapes and even letters?

She moved the brush into the shape of a triangle, then a star and then another circle. Every new move felt wonderful!

She grew wetter and wetter with every stroke of the brush.

Then she moved the brush to spell out an F, then an A, followed by a V and then more letters until she spelled out the word 'FAVERSHAM'.

Claiming the name that united them for her own pleasure was a most delectable idea.

She looked down at Alexander again. Another idea sprang to her mind.

She would claim his name for her pleasure.

She began the proprietary act. First, she moved the brush to trace the letter A over her pulsating clit.

She couldn't help but let forth a small whimper of delight.

Then she continued stroking the brush betwixt her legs, to spell out eight more letters so she finished spelling out the word 'ALEXANDER'.

When she had spelt out that final letter R, she became overcome by the thrilling knowledge that before her knelt her husband, ready and willing to do her bidding, and that she had claimed even his very name for her own pleasure.

Fizzing jolts of pleasure began to radiate from her core, spreading throughout her limbs and down to her fingers and toes. She let herself relax fully into the wondrous sensation. Another orgasm rippled through her.

She was absolutely soaking already, but involuntary spasms betwixt her legs made sure she released yet more slickness. The blanket beneath her was totally sopping wet.

When she had ridden out her orgasm fully and to her desired completion, she put the brush down next to her and drew her legs slowly together. She pulled her robe around her for warmth.

She addressed the man who knelt before her. "Pet, you did fantastically. Please, come and join me." She patted the seat next to her on the settee.

Alexander lifted himself up from the floor in a graceful, fluid movement. He walked the few steps over to her and sat down. "How are you?" he asked fervently. "Can I get you anything?"

"Spent. But in a good way," she laughed. "I would like some water please, and be sure to get some for yourself as well."

Alexander nodded and went up to perform his task.

But before he could fully rise to his feet, Belinda said, "Oh but please do sit here with me a while first."

Alexander sat back down.

Belinda said, "And, how are you feeling? Is there anything you need?"

"Like the luckiest man alive," he said with a genuine smile. "You were incredible, Belinda. Absolutely incredible. I just hope it was good for you?"

"Oh it was wonderful, truly wonderful," she replied contentedly. She leaned back a little on the settee, moving to find the best position of comfort. "Are you sure there is nothing else you need tonight?"

"No, all I need is here."

"Very well. Please fetch us some water."

He went off to perform his task and quickly returned with two glasses of water.

He handed one to Belinda and sipped on the other.

"That was fantastic, though, you know," Belinda said between gulps. "And you were fantastic too."

"As were you," he said.

"We should do that again soon." She looked at him expectantly, hope sparkling in her eyes.

He gave a broad smile. "That can most certainly be arranged."

They finished their glasses.

Then they each went over to a dresser to perform their nighttime ablutions.

When they had finished, Belinda walked over to where Alexander stood.

"I wish for you to stay with me tonight, Alexander," she said sleepily.

"Of course, sweetheart," he replied.

She kicked off her shoes. Then she removed her pink robe.

Alexander reached out to take it. "Here, let me take care of that for you."

She gave a small nod. "Thank you."

He went to hang up her robe in the wardrobe.

Several candles still flickered around the room. He busied himself with snuffing them out.

All the while, Belinda lay back on the bed and pulled one of the quilted blankets over her.

Alexander finished putting out the candles. He turned around to face Belinda.

She patted the spot on the bed next to her. "Come and join me."

He walked towards her and climbed onto the bed.

Belinda turned around to face him. "What are you doing tomorrow?"

"I've got to meet with the land steward in the morning, around eleven o'clock. There are some papers I need to sign. But that meeting should be over and done quickly. It's more of a perfunctory thing than anything else," he said.

"And in the afternoon?"

"No plans as of yet." He fought to stifle a yawn. Belinda's tiredness was contagious. "Say, what about a phaeton ride in the afternoon? The barometer predicts it will be a clear day tomorrow."

"Yes, I do like the sound of a phaeton ride. Let's do that after lunch."

"I look forward to it."

Belinda went to reply, but before she got the chance she dozed off. Such was her tiredness after the night's most exhilarating activities.

And what of Alexander? Well, he joined Belinda in the land of dreams in mere moments.

CHAPTER TWENTY

Dearest Belinda,

How is Yorkshire treating you? Oh I must say I was so surprised to learn that you had left London and headed up to Faversham Abbey. But I suppose one cannot keep a wife away from her husband!

Oh, to think we debuted together only the season just gone and you are already a duchess! A duchess! One can hardly hope to achieve anything better in life. I do so hope to achieve the same one day soon.

I did not know this during our season together. But I have recently learnt a most interesting tidbit which I believe you will be gratified to know. Your husband could hardly take his eyes off you when you were presented at court to Her Majesty! Yes, it is true. I have it on the good authority of one of my aunts that Faversham watched the presentations from the balcony and he barely cast his gaze over any of the debutantes. Save for you. When you were presented, he kept his eyes on you the entire time. He was a man enraptured! So I suppose it comes as little surprise that he is now your husband. Despite what some may think, I believe Lady Reynolds had little hand in your marriage. Rather, it was fate.

Do write back soon with all your news! I can't wait to hear more about your life as a duchess!

Your friend,

Euphemia

Belinda delighted in her new phaeton. It was so sleek and freeing, giving her a whole new way of seeing the world. She adored going riding in it, all around the estate and sometimes the windswept moors.

Not since she was a girl, before her courses and condition had started, had she known such joy of riding around the countryside and exploring the world that lay before her.

And that led to a problem which had never before occurred to her. She had no riding clothes.

She had been wearing some of her ordinary dresses out in the phaeton. But satin and lace weren't the most suitable for riding.

No, what she needed were some proper riding outfits. Tweed and tailored and oh so stylish.

She had no idea who would be able to make such garments or where she could find a modiste. If she were in London, then Cookson's would be the obvious choice. But this was Yorkshire and they did things differently here.

She was sitting at her dressing table as Dauntsey pinned her hair into an elaborate updo. She had some shiny amber hair beads that really brought out the truth of her beauty.

"Dauntsey," Belinda said. "If one wanted to get riding outfits made in these parts, where would one go?" Belinda asked.

"I honestly don't know, your Grace. I can make some enquiries if you like," the maid replied.

Belinda gave a brief nod. "Yes, please do that."

Later that day, Belinda leant back into her armchair and sipped her tea in her sitting room. The taste of a good cup of bohea was so refreshing.

A knock at the door. It sounded like Dauntsey.

"Come in!" Belinda called.

Dauntsey entered the room and gave a curtsey. "Your Grace, I have been asking around and have it on good authority that York is where you shall find the best modistes locally For riding gear and any other garments you may desire."

"That is very useful to know, thank you," Belinda said.

She finished the last of her tea and Dauntsey cleared the tray. So York it would be then. It was a whole new world up here in the north.

She had only had a brief opportunity to see York on her way up from London, such was her rush to find Alexander and confront him. So she was intrigued about what the city was really like and who its denizens were. Would it be similar to other parts of England she'd spent time in, perhaps Bath? Would the people of York have similar interests and concerns to their compatriots down south? What was the fashion like there? The entertainment scene? Her mind was brimming with questions

Chapter Twenty One

"You can take a carriage to York if you want," said Alexander. He was seated opposite Belinda on the settee in his chambers.

A pot of tea and cups rested on the low table between them.

Belinda raised a quizzical eyebrow. "Aren't you going to come too?"

Alexander bit his lip. "I would not wish to disrupt you."

"Disrupt me? Whatever do you mean?"

"Well, I know I'm not always the best company -"

She butted in sharply. "Alexander, please don't say that!"

He continued with his explanation. "I don't wish to hinder your enjoyment of York. You're a young lady about town. Having some old duke at your side all the time might be a drag."

She raised a quizzical eyebrow. "Two points to what you've just said. One, you're not that much older than I am. Twenty-seven years of age is hardly old at all! And two, do you actually want to come to York? Because it's sounding to me like you're looking for an excuse not to go. If you don't want to come, then for heaven's sake please just say so."

"It's not that I don't wish to come to York. I like visiting there. It's my favourite city in all of England," he said.

"Well, then I implore you to come with me," she said with a small smile.

Alexander's eyes crinkled with delight. "I would like that very much, Belinda."

"That settles it," she said firmly. She took a sip of her tea. "Tell me, what shall we do in York?"

"There's an assembly rooms," Alexander said. "Perhaps you would like to attend?"

"Oh yes, it would be good to see what society is like up here. Do you often go?" Belinda said.

"From time to time, when I'm staying at the Abbey. It's not somewhere I make a regular point of going, but there are people there I like to see and catch up with. The Morworths, the Devitts and a couple of other families," he said.

Belinda nodded. "Then we should most definitely go."

Alexander laughed a little. "Consider it added to the itinerary, your Grace.

The carriage trundled its way through the city gates of York at Monk Bat.

Alexander turned to Belinda. "So, what are you looking forward to seeing while we're here?"

"Well when I was here last, I got to see the Minster and liked that. But I was in such a hurry to come up to you that I didn't take the time to see anything else," she said. "The city walls, and the Shambles, we'll have to stroll those. Oh and St Mary's Abbey, I should like to see that too. And I would like to see what York's modistes and milliners have to offer."

Alexander smiled. "That is quite a list. We shall do it all, mark my words."

"Have you been to those places before? Perhaps not the modistes though?" Belinda asked.

"All of them at one time or another." Alexander rubbed her hand gently. "Though not all on the same trip. And yes, I have been to the modiste a time or two. With my sisters every now and again. We have all the time in the world for each of those things on this trip. All the time in the world and more."

Belinda and Alexander strolled arm-in-arm through the streets of York.

At this time of day, the streets were alive with people.

Belinda looked around her with curiosity. She had briefly spent time in York on her way up to Faversham Abbey all those weeks ago, but back then she hadn't had much opportunity to see what was going on. So focused had her mind been on finding Alexander.

The people milling about looked a similar sort to those in Bath. A prospering provincial city with its inhabitants of all ranks.

They turned into the Shambles.

This area wasn't anything like Bath. It was a narrow cobbled street with higgledy-piggledy Tudor buildings on either side. More like parts of London such as Holborn and Tower Hill.

A little way into the street, a small band was busking.

There were two on the fiddle and one on the tin whistle.

Belinda didn't recognise the piece. "Do you know it?" she asked Alexander.

"No, not one I've heard before. It could be a local folk piece, or perhaps one they've made up themselves."

Belinda decided that she liked the piece, in any case. She tossed them a few coins.

Alexander's voice reverberated in her ear. "Come, there's a shop here I think you'll like."

"Lead the way, please," she said with a smile.

In short order, they were outside a bookshop. The windows gleamed brightly, polished to perfection, to reveal an illuminated display of ornate tomes.

Belinda cast her eyes over the selection. There were several Ann Radcliffe titles as well as Goethe in translation. Most thrilling of all, though, was a stunning edition of *Songs of Innocence and Experience* by William Blake. She had never read that work, but had heard good things back in London. It would be a nice memento of her time in York, she resolved.

They headed inside, down a small corridor and to the right.

The room itself had several other clientele. From their dress, they looked a mix of the landed gentry and the middling classes.

Belinda looked around her in excitement. She always loved a good bookshop and this place was brimming with potential.

She turned to Alexander. "Come, let's look at the poetry section."

"Yes, let's."

She guided him towards a section filled with shining leather tomes. "There was one in the window that caught my eye, an illuminated one by Blake. I want to see if I can find it over here."

He looked at the shelves in front of him. "B, B, where are the Bs?" His eyes scanned the topmost shelf and he found what he was looking for. "Ah! Here they are - oh here's one by Blake." He reached for the book and took it in his hands.

The cover read *Songs of Innocence and Experience* in swirling embossed letters.

Alexander ran his fingers across the words. "Is this the one you're interested in?"

Belinda peered down at the book. "Why yes it is!"

"Here, have a look." Alexander gave her the book.

She palmed through the pages in excitement. Here, on one page was a stunning illustration of a tiger. Then, on another, she saw beautiful angels, almost otherworldly. The artist of this work was highly talented. And Blake's words struck a chord with her.

"Listen to this," she said.

'O Earth, O Earth, return!
Arise from out the dewy grass!
Night is worn,

And the morn
Rises from the slumbrous mass.
    'Turn away no more;
Why wilt thou turn away?
    The starry floor,
    The watery shore,
Is given thee till the break of day.

"I do like that," he said. "It's mysterious and evocative. Takes one away to another plane of existence."

She weighed the book in her hands. "That's a good way of putting it. Oh, I'm definitely getting this one," Belinda said. She looked up at Alexander. "Are you getting anything?"

"I'll have a look at the agricultural books. There might be something new that'll help with the estate management."

He made his way over to the agricultural section.

Belinda followed behind.

Alexander turned back to face her. "You don't have to come to this section, if it's not of interest to you. I really don't mind."

She gave a little smile. "It's not an area I know much about. But perhaps you can show me the types of titles you read. It would be useful for me to know about this too, being a duchess and all."

Alexander nodded. "That's fair enough."

He walked over to the agricultural shelves and placed his hands on his hips. He scanned through the hefty tomes. "Yes, they've got it. The latest edition of Wickett's."

"What's that?" Belinda asked.

"It's a guide to the best crop rotation practices, soil testing, most profitable crops and so on. Especially for Great

Britain." He reached up and plucked the book from the shelf. "This is definitely one I'm getting. Very useful for a lot of us running the estate."

She nodded. "I look forward to reading it."

"It's a bit dry, but useful nonetheless," he said. "As for your question about other titles I read on agriculture, the rest of the really handy stuff I already have at the Abbey." He gestured to several titles on the shelves and called out their names in turn. "There's *Stewart's Guide to Harvesting*, *The English Companion for the Arborialist* and the *Encyclopedia of British Flora*. All really worthy titles, though none of them make for the lightest of reading."

Belinda laughed. "I suppose the subject matter doesn't really support light reading."

"No," he said with a smile. "Such is the life of running an estate. We who, if we wish to do a decent job, are obliged to train ourselves using some of the driest husks of books known to humanity."

"What poor people we are," she said wryly.

"Indeed," he said. "Is there anything else you'd like to look at while we're here?"

"Oh yes, now that you mention it, I'd be keen to see some of the novels."

"Sounds like a plan."

And with that, they spent a happy half an hour perusing the shop's wide selection of novels and reading favourite passages aloud to one another.

A day later, clouds hung low in the sky. The city walls today weren't bustling. Nonetheless, a few brave people were out and about exploring them. Belinda and Alexander were amongst their number.

The wind whipped around Belinda, ruffling her hair and making her velvet cloak billow and ripple. But she didn't care. It was good to be back in York. When she'd been here a few months ago, she had been in such a rush to get to Faversham Abbey and find Alexander that she'd barely done anything beyond take a quick look at the exterior of the Minster.

She turned to Alexander. "Walking along here, it makes me feel as though I'm in the Medieval times."

"Oh yes, I can envision how that would be so," Alexander said.

Belinda's skirts rustled against his legs in the gusty wind.

It would be blowing a gale soon.

"It's getting rather cold out here. Would you like to head inside?" Alexander asked.

Belinda struggled to hear him over the howls of the wind. "Sorry, what was that?" she shouted.

Alexander raised his voice to match hers. "I said, it's getting rather cold. Do you want to go somewhere indoors?"

"Yes, let's. Now that you raise the point, it is getting rather cold out here." She cast her eyes about the heavens. "And that sky is looking ominous."

"I'll take you to a tearoom. There's a good one round the corner."

Belinda smiled. "I'd like that."

Alexander led her down the steps and onto the cobblestones of the street.

They walked for a minute or two and then came to a halt in front of a sturdy brick building, two-stories high. A sign creaking in the wind read 'Prewett's Tea Shoppe'.

In short order, they were inside and sitting at a table near the hearth.

There were a few other customers here and there, but the place wasn't exactly bustling. Wild, windy days like this kept the population of York in their homes it seemed.

Belinda perusing the menu. "What do you recommend?" she asked.

"It's all pretty good. The honey pastries are a real standout in my view," he said.

"Honey pastries it is then." She glanced down at the menu. "Oh and what about some of the jam tarts? I do so love a jam tart."

A waitress came and took their order and soon enough they were enjoying the delicacies of Prewett's Tea Shoppe.

Belinda bit into a honey pastry. Alexander was right. They really were delicious. Though the jam tarts certainly passed muster with her too.

They chatted throughout the meal. Alexander spoke of his previous trips to York with his family and Belinda shared her own experiences with family trips.

"Lyme Regis, what's it like down there? I've never been," Alexander said when Belinda mentioned she'd gone there with the entire Weatherby clan regularly over the years.

"Oh, I love it down there! There are rock pools teeming with crabs, little fishes and so forth. And the landscape is really charming. It changes with the weather too. When there's sun, the sea glistens and the cliffs are shining white. But if you're there on a stormy day, it's like something out of the tempest." She took a sip of her tea before continuing. "When it's stormy or overcast, Lyme Regis is eerily similar to the moors around the estate."

Alexander quirked his lip. "And what of the smugglers? I hear they're to be found in Lyme Regis."

Belinda let forth a rippling laugh. "By all accounts I've heard, Lyme Regis is a haunt for smugglers. So are several other places along that part of the coast. Their close proximity to France being a benefit to bringing over brandy. But I must say, I've not seen much evidence of smuggling myself. I don't think the Weatherbys move in the right circles for that."

"I am glad to hear it," he said. Then he took a sip of his tea.

They finished the last bites of their food.

Before either of them had a chance to think about what they'd be doing next, there was a loud screech at the door.

A cat burst through a flap that Belinda hadn't noticed before.

"Get that thing out of here!" shouted someone from the kitchens.

A teenage girl who was working on the front counter turned her head to reply. "Oh but it's Mr Crimblepaws, do let him stay. That's what the cat flap is for anyway," she whined.

Mr Crimblepaws ignored all the commotion and instead made a beeline for the hearth. He was a sizable tabby with a nimble gait.

He came to a halt at Belinda's feet and curled up around her.

Alexander laughed. "He likes you."

"Is he here regularly?" Belinda asked.

"Yes. And every time I've been here, there's been the same fracas between the cook and the waitresses. The cook hates that cat but the rest of the staff adore him," Alexander said.

Belinda reached down and gave Mr Crimblepaws a pat.

"He's a real character here," Alexander said.

"How do you think a cat might go at the Abbey? Would the beagles tolerate one?" Belinda asked.

"I think they likely would. They're very docile dogs, useless as hunting hounds with hardly any fight in them." He took a sip of his tea. "Would you like a cat? I can arrange one if you like."

"Oh yes please," she said with a grin. "I've never had a cat before. Our family only ever had dogs."

"Then it's settled. I'll make some enquiries and we'll get a cat soon."

York Assembly Rooms were most elegant.

Belinda, in her lack of familiarity with anything further north than East Anglia, had had no idea of what was on offer here.

As in Bath and London, couples swirled around the dancefloor. The ladies in pastel nouveau-empire gowns and the gentlemen in fine-cut frock coats, waistcoats and pantaloons. Not a wig in sight! Belinda scrunched up her nose at herself. Not a wig in sight indeed! Why on earth would that be so surprising? What a silly assumption on her part. Why would society in another part of England be twenty years behind the mode just because they were far away from London? Her assumptions said more about her than they did about society here in the north. Wigs, indeed!

She turned her head to Alexander's. "Shall we dance?"

"It would be my pleasure," he replied. He offered her his hand with a slight smile.

She took it and together they glided to the ballroom floor.

The string ensemble struck up another tune and the strains of Bach swelled through the air.

Belinda looked at the man before her, her husband.

Earlier in the year, she had shared some dances with eligible bachelors of the ton. It had all been very proper and above-board and the young men with whom she had danced were generally genial and always polite. At all of those balls, with all those dance partners, she had never seen a man look at her the way Alexander was looking at her right now.

His eyes bore into her. But not with a cold icy gaze. Oh, no, not with any gaze that suggested coldness or dispassion. Instead, in his lay the depths of red hot stars. This

Alexander, the one who danced before her, was unlike the cold, dead-behind-the-eyes Duke of Faversham that the grapevine whispered about, that if she hadn't known any better, she would have had trouble reconciling Alexander and the Duke of Faversham as in fact being the same person.

She had never before seen him dance at a ball. His reputation, from all she had heard, was not that of a man who enjoyed dancing, not a man with any flair or passion or sense of sensibility. Well, the man before her put paid to all of that!

She danced in time with him, letting him lead her deftly around the ballroom floor.

This wasn't at all what she had expected from this night. And she was absolutely loving it.

After they had taken a few dances, Belinda turned to Alexander. "I think that's it for me for the moment," she said.

"Are you feeling unwell? Or would you just like to sit down?" he asked.

"The latter," she replied with a smile.

"I'm relieved to hear it. Come and sit down, there are some people I would like for you to meet."

"Well, lead the way," Belinda said.

He linked his arm with hers and led her towards a group sitting near the fireplace.

One of the men in the group, a gigantic redhead, turned towards the couple. "Faversham!" he exclaimed and broke out into a hearty grin. "And this must be the very Duchess herself!"

Other heads within the group turned towards the Favershams. They too, all greeted the couple with smiles and excited eyes.

A woman, who was perhaps a couple of years Belinda's senior, called, "Come! Come! Oh I must meet you, the lady who was crazy enough to marry Faversham!"

"Violet!" another woman exclaimed half in reprimand, half in amusement.

Alexander paid the exclamations of the two women no heed. Instead, he addressed the group at large. "Ladies, gentlemen. May I present to you the new Duchess of Faversham, and my most enchanting bride, Belinda."

A chorus of hearty hellos and how-do-you-dos struck up from the group before Belinda.

Alexander gestured to each member of the group in turn and introduced them to Belinda.

The red haired giant of a man was in fact the Viscount of Morworth. And the woman who had half-outragedly exclaimed 'Violet' was the Viscountess of Morworth.

Violet was really Lady Violet Devitt. And seated next to her was her husband, Baronet Michael Devitt.

Belinda had heard of the Morworths and the Devitts when she was down in London. Yet she had never laid eyes on them before, so far as she could recall. She turned to Violet, "I don't think I've seen you before. Not at any of the season's events."

"No, you wouldn't have," Violet said with a friendly smile. "Michael and I, we've never been ones for all that hustle and bustle down in London."

"Me neither," the Viscountess of Morworth added. "And nor is Percival. He's my husband." She gestured to the red-headed man. "I'm Eunice, by the way."

Violet said, "I don't think you're crazy, I hasten to add."

"Oh no, Belinda giggled and sat down next to Eunice. "I didn't think you did. Just a figure of speech."

"Though I'm most pleasantly surprised to see Alexander wed," Violet added.

Eunice nodded. "So am I. In fact, I think I speak for all of Alexander's circle of friends up here in the north when I say that you're a very pleasant surprise."

"You do indeed," Violet said.

At that moment, a footman came round offering a platter of goblets of red wine.

The women helped themselves to the drinks.

Belinda took a sip. It was rich and plummy and filled her whole mouth with its tannins.

Violet leaned towards her. "How are you finding life at Faversham Abbey?" she asked.

"Pleasant. The moorlands are so different to where I grew up. In Wiltshire, I mean." Belinda said. "Have you been to the Abbey?"

"No, nobody in our group ever has," Violet replied.

Belinda's eyebrows raised a little. "Really?"

Eunice nodded. "It's true, not in all the years I've known him. We usually host Alexander at one of our homes instead."

An idea formed in Belinda's mind. "Well, that will have to change. Now I am here, I shall have to play hostess. You can expect an invitation from me."

"We would like that a lot, thank you," Eunice said.

Violet clapped her hands together in glee. "Oh, this is a turnout for the books! We shall finally all get to see just where Alexander and his new bride live!"

Belinda took another sip of her wine. "And where are you living?" she asked.

Eunice said, "Morworth Hall is about twenty miles to the west of here. We're here most of the year."

"And we're towards the coast at Devitt Towers. It's a couple of hours from here in the carriage, on a good day," Violet added. "And we should love to host you, when next we have a house party."

Eunice nodded. "As shall we."

The three women spent a happy couple of hours chatting and sharing stories of their seasons in London.

Belinda enjoyed meeting Eunice and Violet. It was good to be moving into society here in the north and learning its ways.

◦◦───◦◆◦───◦◦

CHAPTER TWENTY TWO

The next day, the carriage pulled up outside the entrance to the Shambles.

Alexander leapt down onto the wet cobblestones and turned around to assist Belinda.

She took his hand and landed on the street with a dancer's flourish.

It reminded Alexander of how she had danced that night at Landsdowne House.

Though she wasn't dressed for a ball tonight, she looked just as ethereal as she had the night they had encountered one another in the maze. Now she wore an amber velvet cloak over a silver satin dress. Atop her head she wore a matching silver satin hat with a lace and gauze veil falling down her back and face.

She turned to him with a soft smile. "Well, lead the way, your Grace."

He took his arm in hers. "As you so command."

Together, they walked down the Shambles. Nearly every shopfront was in darkness, though candles were burning in some of the upper windows where the owners lived above.

The street saw very few souls other than the Favershams at this time of night.

She murmured in Alexander's ear. "Do you come here often, your Grace?"

"A couple of times a year," he replied with a little, slightly embarrassed smile. "I know the owner, and you can be assured of absolute discretion."

Belinda was intrigued. "Who is the owner? Anyone I know?"

"As it so happens, you may well do. The Marquess of Scarborough. Though he is never there himself, he leaves the day to day running of the shop to his most trusted staff. But he is quite the connoisseur."

"Well I never!" Belinda exclaimed. "Does the Marchioness know?"

"Yes, I believe she's involved in choosing and commissioning the books."

"Well, the ton really is full of surprises!" Belinda didn't know Lord and Lady Scarborough much on a personal level, but being established members of the ton, she knew their names and a little of their basic information. They were a couple in their fifties, based in Buckinghamshire, who had never had children and who came down to London for the season with clockwork regularity. In fact, Belinda had danced with the heir, the Marquess' nephew Mr Francis Burns, a couple of times at balls and had found him nice enough. But he didn't cut half the enticing figure that Alexander was now beginning to.

"This is it," Alexander's deep voice murmured in her ear.

They were in front of a small bookshop, one they had looked at the other day. Back then, it had been a bustling little nook with rows and rows of the most popular literary tomes. The illuminated window display had featured several beautiful titles too. Belinda had purchased a lovely, richly illustrated edition of William Blake's 'Songs of Innocence and Experience'. She was very much looking forward to reading it back at the Abbey.

Now, all seemed dark on the ground floor.

Belinda wondered how they were going to get in. Could this really be the right place?

Alexander gave three quick knocks on the door, then two slow knocks, followed by another three quick ones.

About fifteen seconds went by and the door swung open to reveal an unassuming reedy man of about thirty years of age. He gave a nod of recognition to Alexander. "Good evening, right this way please," the man said.

"Thank you," Alexander replied.

The door shut itself behind the Favershams.

The reedy man disappeared almost as quickly as he had arrived, leaving Belinda and Alexander alone in the narrow hallway that led to the main bookshop on the right.

There was a tall tapestry hanging on the wall directly opposite the Favershams.

Alexander walked towards it and moved it aside to reveal a door.

He opened the door and said, "Right this way."

Then he led Belinda up two flights of wooden stairs and into a softly lit room replete with rows of bookshelves.

Purple and blue velvet curtains adorned the walls and also hung as dividers along the rows of books.

No one else was in the room.

Belinda turned to Alexander. "There's no one up here it seems. What if I want to buy anything?"

"Ah, it operates on an honesty system. Once you're in and known, you can simply leave the money at the desk."

Alexander gestured to a wooden desk with a padlocked moneybox atop it.

Belinda nodded. "I see." Her eyes scanned around the room through the lace and gauze of her veil. "Hmmm...where should I start?" She took a step towards the nearest row of books.

"I'll be over here." Alexander gestured to an armchair near the curtained windows. "Take your time."

"I shall endeavour," she laughed.

She examined the shelves in front of her, peering through the small gap between her veil and her chest. Most of the books had titles like *Titania's Night in the Woods* and *Tales of the Enchantress*. She skimmed through a few of the tomes but they didn't really grab her interest. She was a woman of gothic tastes, not magical nymphs.

She moved down to the next row. There she found *Deflowering Miss Jacqueline*, *My Night with Sweet Cassandra* and *The Progress of Fair Sarah Clancey*. Again, she skimmed through the pages and again, nothing really held her interest. They were reminiscent of the book called *Fanny Hill* at the Abbey. She'd read that from cover to cover already and so she was looking for something different.

She moved down to the next row. This one had titles all with men's names. She had a look at some of the books and could find little to no mention of women within them. Instead, these books focused on men together. She took what seemed to be the most well-written, *Wulfric*, and held it in her hand. This was an intriguing piece and one she wanted to purchase.

Carrying *Wulfric* in her hand, she made her way to the following row.

Now this was a section of great intrigue! All sorts of titles graced the shelves.

She palmed through them. *Lessons for Amelia* and *The Life and Times of Miss Harriet Quimby* were well-written but were both about women submitting to men. Some of the scenes of a carnal nature were appealing such as when Amelia's beau worshipped her cunny with his tongue, but the rest of the content wasn't to her taste. It might appeal to some women, and that was all well and good, but it wasn't doing much for her. She had spent her whole entire life being subject to the decisions of others, particularly the decisions of men, and well-intentioned as some of the decision-makers had been, the lack of free will chaffed her enormously. For once, she wanted to be the one in charge.

She came to a book inscribed *The Scandalous Journey of Lord Sebastian Edwards*. This might be more up her street. She opened the tome and began to read.

Lord Sebastian Edwards was a distinguished member of the ton who was visiting a professional Domina. His escapades involved being tied up in various positions and in various places. The park. The Domina's bed. And in one scene that had her heart pulsating at fifty horsepower, in the private chapel on his estate! And throughout, the book contained a lot of scenes of something the characters called 'discipline', though it didn't really seem like Lord Sebastian was learning much since the discipline was administered with astonishing regularity. Sometimes the discipline took the form of a birching, other times it was a spanking with an open hand or with a leather paddle. Whatever the method, Belinda found an exciting heat building within her and a growing wetness between her legs.

Seemingly, this was the sort of content attuned to her tastes. It met a deep, and until very recently, unfulfilled need within her. She found she liked it.

She added *The Scandalous Journey of Lord Sebastian Edwards* to her to-buy pile.

She picked up another book nearby. This one was called *Mistress Grace Cottlesworth and her Legion.* It featured a woman, the said Mistress Cottlesworth, who ruled over a whole household of men who served her. This book, too, made her feel intrigued and desiring of someone's touch. Hers. Alexander's. She didn't know, but there was a pleasantly tense ache building within her.

Back in the carriage, Belinda turned to Alexander and said, "Touch me."

Alexander bit his lip. "As you so command. Where would you like for me to touch you?"

"Betwixt my legs," she said.

Alexander knelt on the floor beneath her and drew his hand up through her petticoats and skirts to find her most secret place. He worked his fingers through the thatched mound delighting in the softness and symbol of her mature womanhood. Already, her mound was slick with the wetness of her own juices. He considered it a privilege that she was willing to share this part of herself with him. He was pleased to see she was so confident, so at ease with herself. No matter the circumstances behind why they wed, the fact was that she was his wife now and as such he wanted her to be happy and confident in herself. For her own sake. She was a most wondrous creation, after all. And like all of God's wondrous creations, she deserved to be happy.

He moved his hand through her thatched mound to find her clit. He reached that dainty organ's nub, so perfectly designed to give her pleasure, and ran his index finger in teasing circles.

Heavens, she was absolutely sopping wet!

He moved his finger around her clit with gentle deftness. She was so close to the precipice of pleasure already that it wouldn't take much to send her over the edge.

Belinda shifted one leg ever so slightly. "Alexander...more...Alexander," she moaned through sweetly parted lips.

Alexander dipped his finger once more against her. Then he brought his finger to his mouth and savoured her sweetness.

Belinda opened her eyes a little and looked down at him through hooded eyelids.

"You liked that, did you?" she giggled.

"Yes, oh yes," he moaned.

She offered him her hand and helped him up onto the seat alongside her.

Alexander poked his head out of the curtains that shielded the Favershams from the world outside. Not long now, they were almost at the inn.

Chapter Twenty Three

Back at the Abbey, Belinda settled down into her chambers to read her purchases.

She had a stack of books on the table, a pot of tea at the ready and the fire ablaze on the hearth. She was ready to go.

She picked up *The Scandalous Journey of Lord Sebastian Edwards*. The first title at the bookshop that had truly piqued her interest that night.

It was perhaps not the best written piece of literature she had ever read in her life, but nonetheless it tugged at something deep inside of her. It was most thrilling, if a little scandalous, to be reading about the exploits of such a gentleman of the ton who time and time again got himself into all manner of disgraces.

She leaned forward and took a sip of her bohea tea. The rich and malty flavour washed down her throat.

She returned her attention to the book. Lord Sebastian was facing the discipline of a riding crop in the stables on his estate. For reasons the book failed to elucidate, he had displeased his Domina and she had ordered him to present himself at the stables on a brisk spring afternoon. When he arrived at the stables, the only things greeting him were his Domina, a wooden spanking bench and a vast selection of riding crops. Lord Sebastian was soon enough bent over the bench with his pantaloons around his ankles and his Domina applying swift, firm strokes of the riding crop to his poor backside.

With every line she read, Belinda felt herself grow more and more tense between her legs. This book was awakening desires within her that she didn't even know she had. She liked the sound of being the Domina and applying firm discipline to a misbehaving lord.

Lord Sebastian's antics got more and more outrageous as the book went on. Every chapter brought a parade of sinful images to her very eyes. And she loved it all!

She felt herself get wetter and wetter between her legs. She was pulsing, aching with desire.

She reached down and pushed her hand through her voluminous skirts and petticoats. The velvet brushed against her hand as she did so, sending an exciting frisson of static through her already needy body.

She pushed her hand up, up, up to the thatched mound where her legs met. She ran her fingers briefly through it. It was soft and growing slick with her juices.

She giggled a little to herself at the sensation.

Then she moved her hand through her sleek slit and past her plump labia. She wanted to get to her pleasure immediately and didn't want the build up of a tease today. After all, she could save that for when she was next with Alexander. What mattered now was reaching that most delicious sensation of climax as quickly as she possibly could.

With practiced deftness, her index finger found her budding clitoris. She moved her finger round and round. A wonderful warm feeling built within her belly. With every stroke, the lovely warmth spread to the furthest reaches of her body. Until, after less than a minute's worth of clitoral attention, she felt her full climax building within her. Her hips convulsed in an effort to extract every ounce of pleasure she could from her swollen bud.

She closed her eyes.

She moaned softly. Her breathing intensified and accelerated. Doing this felt so good. She felt so free and alive. Her body was truly her own and she was in control.

Eventually, after she had danced on the edge of pleasure for exactly how long she didn't quite know, she let herself come down. Her breathing began to return to her normal pace.

She opened her eyes and the honey-light of the room returned to her.

Despite everything that had happened with her body over the years, the loss of control she felt at her condition and status of being a young lady of the ton, moments like this made her feel powerful and as though there were new possibilities and other paths available to her. If only she had the courage to seize them.

She knew that her status as a bride meant that the rigid rules of society still applied to her, at least some of the time. But when she was alone, in private, it was a completely different story. She was her own woman and she was learning what she liked.

She leaned forward and looked sceptically at her tea. She felt the porcelain of the cup and, just as she had suspected, it had gone cold while she was enjoying herself.

But she didn't want to be done yet with the afternoon's fun.

She righted her clothing, got up and walked over to the servants bell cord. She gave it a swift tug.

In short order, a maid appeared.

"Another pot of tea, please," Belinda ordered.

"At once, your Grace." The maid gave a curtsey before she cleared the old tea tray and left the room.

Belinda put down *The Scandalous Journey of Lord Sebastian Edwards* and picked up *Mistress Grace Cottlesworth and her Legion*. She wondered with eagerness at the revelations that might await her inside.

Later that day, Belinda made her way downstairs to meet with the housekeeper, Mrs Bartholomew.

In her first months at the Abbey, she was already getting into the swing of managing the household.

It was true that Alexander had technically left her in charge of the London property, but his sudden absence had meant that it wasn't the same. In London, she had been hampered by the questions of what had happened with Alexander and why he had left and so she hadn't been able to put her mind to any of the duties of a duchess.

However, at the Abbey she had a sense of purpose in the role. Though the Abbey and its estate were remote, it was the centre of activity for all the villages from miles around. So making sure that the heart of everything ran smoothly was of paramount importance.

She knew well the saying that the devil makes work for idle hands.

Here at the Abbey she could not afford to be idle for long. Not if she wanted to perform the duties of a duchess properly.

She needed to meet with Mrs Bartholomew to discuss catering plans for the coming weeks, now that the harvest was over.

Then tomorrow she would be hosting the vicar's wife for plans for advent.

It was a busy life for a duchess and one she was enjoying immensely. All her health troubles notwithstanding, she had no intention of being the kind of aristocratic lady who lounged about all day and achieved nothing much of any note at all.

She wanted to leave her mark. But most important of all, she wanted to perform her duties as best as she could. She was a Weatherby to her core and Weatherbys were raised from the cradle to value duty above almost all over things.

She strode into Mrs Bartholomew's office and sat down. The day's duties were upon her.

CHAPTER TWENTY FOUR

Dearest Belinda,

I was thrilled to receive your last and see the news that you have taken up phaeton riding. How liberating and wonderful it is to be able to ride wherever and whenever one wishes!

And York as well. Oh I remember my days there, when I was a younger woman. It is such a charming city with so many delightfully unexpected corners.

You asked how everyone at the club is doing. We are getting along as we always do. Which is to say, there is a marriage or two that won't be going ahead thanks to our intervention. None of us could bear to leave those poor chits to such disastrous fates as 'men' like that!

What are your plans for Christmastide? Will you be coming down south or staying in Yorkshire? Margaret and I will be in London if you are coming south.

Love from,

Virginia

"What do you do for Christmas?" Belinda asked from her spot on the settee in the library.

"I'm always up here. It's tradition for the Duke to host a celebration for the whole Faversham estate here at the Abbey. My mother and sisters attend too," Alexander explained. "And you, Belinda, how do you normally keep the season?"

"With the Weatherbys in London," she said.

"We could alternate years, have one year down in London at Weatherby House and one year up here at the Abbey. We could have your family up here at the Abbey for it too."

"I should like that," Belinda said with a smile. "Though are you sure you can cope with my youngest siblings? Lionel and Genevieve can get rowdy at times."

Alexander nodded and laughed. "I can handle them. I've got experience thanks to my three sisters. They can be a handful when they want to be."

Belinda's eyes widened. "Oh dear. The thought has just occurred to me. The five of them together, in this one house."

"We can cope, I am sure. Well, not exactly sure. But hopeful," Alexander said.

"That settles it then. We'll have Christmas here at the Abbey with your side. Then in future years we can alternate, or invite my side up here too."

"An excellent plan." Alexander gave a firm nod.

⁂

Belinda felt the briskness of the late autumn air as she drove her phaeton over the moorland.

Frost covered the ground all around her. Winter would soon be upon the Favershams. But she didn't mind for she was already thinking of something else. Another, much more enticing line of thought.

She bit her lip and smiled to herself. An idea began to form in her mind. The perfect idea.

All her life, she had been confined by her position as a Weatherby daughter. Certainly, being a member of one of Britain's most illustrious families came with its privileges yet she was a woman after all. Merely a clockwork marionette in a world run by men. And her confinement and restrictions had grown as she herself had grown from girl to young woman. Her condition had not served to help at all and had only made matters worse.

Yet Alexander, her beloved husband, had other interests and those were sending her down a new and surprising train of thought.

His pleasure was hers to control, hers to command, hers to decide. This was the case at all times, but during their private time together in her chambers or his, she wanted him to have an additional reminder. She envisaged a leather pouch that would cover his glorious cock and prevent him from obtaining sweet release if and until she decreed it.

She pulled the reins on her phaeton as her horses turned the bend that would take her past the arboretum.

Down there was the spot where she had already enjoyed several enticing scenes with Alexander. Where she had taken control of his pleasure and where he had pleased her most outstandingly with his talented tongue and fingers.

When the leather device arrived, she had plans afoot for making good use of it in the arboretum.

Alexander being the gentleman scientist that he was would surely appreciate the joys of being out in nature, after all.

Belinda turned her phaeton upwards to join the path back to the Abbey.

She knew what she wanted so now it was a matter of asking Alexander.

She thought he would likely be interested. He did so enjoy her way of gentle yet strict control.

A familiar heat built between her legs as she thought of how dashing he would look with his cock encased in a leather covering. A device which only she would have the power to remove.

She smiled to herself. She really hoped Alexander would be onboard with this plan too.

She pulled her phaeton up to the main doors of the Abbey.

In short order, a footman and a stablehand appeared.

The footman assisted Belinda down from the phaeton while the stablehand took care of the horses.

Belinda made her way inside the Abbey.

She turned and said to the footman, "Please arrange for a bath to be run in my chambers."

"At once, your Grace," he replied before giving a bow.

Belinda headed up the stairs and walked down the rabbit warren of corridors that led to her chambers.

Belinda luxuriated as she sat back in the cavernous bath. The warm water lapped around her shoulders. She enjoyed going about in the phaeton, but it was good to clear the grime of the outside world off afterwards. Already, she could feel herself relaxing as the dirt of the day washed away.

Now, it was time to think more about her plan.

She wondered what the best design for the device would be. She knew she wanted it to be made of leather. It was such a sensual yet sturdy material, after all. But what shape should it take?

She had never seen any image of such a device, let alone one in person, so she would have to invent her own design.

What would be most pleasing to her, yet also enjoyable for Alexander and practical to boot?

First off, how would she constrict his glorious cock? A cage was one option. But the more she thought about it, the more it put her in mind of a prison. Not such a happy association for what she wanted to do. Perhaps an all-over covering would be more to her taste? It could be some sort of bag or pouch to snugly cover his cock entirely. Liberating enough that it wouldn't remind her of a Newgate cell. But constricting enough that Alexander would be unable to reach full hardness if and until she decreed it. His pleasure would be under her control. Hers to decide. Hers to command.

But how would she ensure the pouch stayed on and remained in one place?

Probably affixing it to some sort of belt around his hips would work. Yes, it could have straps and buckles and fasteners, a bit like the reins on a horse. Sturdy yet malleable.

Oh, she could hardly wait! Alexander was going to look so dashing in this new device. His pleasure would be under her guiding hand, as it always was, but now there would be an additional level of restriction ensuring she had complete control. When he wore the device, at least.

She looked forward to telling Alexander of her plan. She hoped he would be onboard. The device could be a new and most delectable addition to their roles as Domina and pet. She just knew it would heighten the sensations of their sessions, for both of them.

She wanted to tell him of her plan as soon as possible. At the earliest opportunity.

***

The next day, after luncheon was finished, Belinda and Alexander sat together in the library.

Alexander glanced at some estate paperwork.

Belinda, for her part, palmed through a pamphlet that one of the coachmen had left in the Great Hall after he'd finished reading it.

After a few minutes, Belinda put the pamphlet down. She turned to her husband. "Alexander," she said. "I had a thought yesterday that I'd like to share with you."

Alexander put down his paperwork and gave her his full attention. His expression was hard to read. "Pray, do tell more, Belinda."

"Well, yesterday when I was in my phaeton, riding around the estate, the thought came to me of how wonderful it would be for your cock to be encased in a leather device. So that you are restricted and can only gain pleasure if and when I command it," Belinda said. Before she met Alexander, she might have been very embarrassed to say such a sentence to a man. But over the past several months, she had learnt that being direct with what she wanted was the best option. She should have no fear or shame when discussing such matters with her husband, after all.

Alexander's eyes widened. "That does sound intriguing," he said huskily.

"Have you tried it before?" Belinda asked.

"No, never," he said.

"Would you like to try it though?"

"Yes, I like your idea."

She smiled. "Very well, then let us consider how to make it a reality."

He smiled and his eyes crinkled. "Let us consider that indeed."

Belinda enjoyed seeing that expression on his face. She enjoyed knowing that simply by being herself she had made him happy.

She asked, "Where would one find a leather maker around here? One who understands the need to be the very soul of discretion?"

"That's a good question," he said. "And one that I must admit I don't immediately know the answer to. I'm not familiar with even the leather makers the estate uses to make the horses' reins."

"Well that gives me an idea for something else we could get made," Belinda said with a laugh.

"Belinda!" he said in mock outrage. Then his voice softened. "We can get reins made too, if you wish."

"I would like that very much indeed," she said.

Alexander's cheeks turned a slight shade of crimson at the thought of what Belinda had planned and at how she was developing her own tantalising ideas. He let forth a small cough in a vain attempt to clear his throat that was fast becoming dry. "Your wish shall be my command, Belinda."

"So who should we go to about these leather goods?" she asked, returning the conversation to the main question at hand.

"I'll have to make some enquiries," he said. "There must be someone who can do it, someone we can trust to be discreet. The reins aren't such an issue, any horse could use those. But, as for the pouch." He trailed off.

"That would be hard to explain to most leather makers," Belinda filled in for him.

"It would indeed," he said. "So I will endeavour to find someone who truly understands the value of discretion. And pay them most handsomely. It will be worth it though. Your idea is most inspired."

"Isn't it just," she said.

Chapter Twenty Five

Snowflakes fell outside the window in icy circles about the size of tuppence.

The sun was setting, casting an orange haze above a sky that was rapidly becoming a dusty purple grey.

Alexander stared out of the window and watched the sky change before his very eyes.

Behind him, the beagles slept softly in their baskets.

In some ways, this evening was an evening rather similar to the one Belinda arrived. But he himself was a different man.

He had not thought of himself as a man for whom love mattered much. He never wanted to marry, such was the risk he posed to any woman's heart. Some men in his position might still view marriage as an inevitability, as a means to sire an heir. But ancient families like his always had a long-forgotten twig or two who could one day assume the title. And so he had long accepted that the title would go down another branch of the Faversham tree.

But that was last year. Now Belinda had come into his life, colliding with him in the Landsdowne maze and upending all his beliefs.

Where once he had believed he would forever be a man alone, he could not help but want a certain someone in his life and by his side always. Where once he was content to be the cold-hearted duke that so many on the ton thought he was, now he wanted to shed that reputation in the eyes of a certain young lady.

He had never felt this way before. About anyone.

He had had encounters with women, in those specialised houses in Soho, but those events had only ever been a physical thing. A tit for tat exchange. And most of the time he hadn't even had relations with those governesses. Because an encounter didn't need congress to take place. That wasn't the main attraction for him.

He had certainly never loved any of those women in Soho. As wonderful as they had been.

For a long time, he had thought himself incapable of love. He was damaged goods, inside and out. And surely someone so broken would be unable to love anyone else.

Yet Belinda had shown him he was wrong.

He couldn't pinpoint when this feeling began. That day, when he saw her at her presentation at court, he had glimpsed her briefly and thought she was a beautiful young woman. But that was all. He was only attending out of perfunctory duty and the crowds and the hubbub were at fever pitch, From his spot on the balcony, he could see some of the action but not much. Then, a while later, when he had seen her dancing at the Landsdowne Ball, that was when she had captivated him. When he had stood and watched her, lairing at the side of the room as some might say, and thought she was the most pretty, most vivacious woman he had seen in, well, ever. Later, when he bumped into her in the maze, his immediate thought had still been how beautiful she was. But any thoughts of pleasure quickly turned to horror when Lady Petunia Reynolds came on the scene and set the wheels in motion to deny Belinda a genuine choice of husband. From that point on, Alexander's focus had been on protecting Belinda and ensuring she was safe. That was a husband's duty after all, wasn't it? So that was what he had to do. No matter the cost to his own heart.

He thought the matter was over and done with when he went north to the Abbey. Surely that callous act would push Belinda away from him, would make her never want to see him again and instead live her own separate life. And, for a month or so that was exactly what he thought was happening. He had gone to Yorkshire and had heard nary a word from her. The accounts from the London house ran like clockwork, he could see there were trips to the modiste and to various entertainments. He had been a little pleased to see she was taking an active part in society.

So it had come as a complete shock to him when she had turned up at Faversham Abbey that rainy evening.

And that was when his real problem began. Ever since she had turned up at the Abbey, he could hardly get her out of his head for even the slightest moment.

From morning to night, she was always on his mind. What would she want? What would she be doing? Was there anything he could get for her? Anything he could provide?

Of course, he had tried to fight his feelings. Tried to tell himself that his thoughts were just the natural thoughts of a protective husband. Of a man merely doing his duty.

That had been in early autumn.

Now, winter was well and truly on the way.

Try as he might, battle as he had, he could no longer deny his feelings. But she could never know. She deserved better than the likes of him.

He could never have her. Not if he was to keep her safe. Not if he was to protect her.

Chapter Twenty Six

Belinda trotted along in her phaeton. All around, the moors spread out before her in glorious regal purple. The snow of several days ago was long gone. Though winter had set in, the weather was still tolerable today and good enough for a ride around the Faversham estates.

She turned her phaeton and considered when she would need to head back. Bad weather would be on the way. But for now, at least, the path ahead was clear.

Almost in an instant, the air around her grew foggy. From being able to see all around the moors to barely being able to see even a yard in front of her face.

She tried to keep the phaeton on the firm path. It was a winding section of the route and she could remember it fairly well.

Yet not well enough, it turned out.

She tried to steer the phaeton around where she could have sworn there was a bend in the track. However, she somehow managed to steer off the path and down a steep mound. The phaeton's left wheel got caught on a pile of rocks on the way down. The contraption wobbled awkwardly for several seconds.

The horse neighed in fright and lifted its front legs high into the air.

Belinda screamed. Her very life flashed before her eyes.

Then the phaeton stopped teetering.

For the minutest of moments, Belinda thought the horror was over.

But it was the calm before the storm.

The phaeton tilted and toppled over on its side.

The force of the fall snapped the reins and now the horse was free.

The animal gave another whinny of terror and cantered off into the fog.

Belinda fell against the cold, iron side of the phaeton. Her head slammed against the metal with an almighty thud.

Rain began to burst from the heavens and Belinda's world went black.

***

Alexander heard the roar of thunder and looked up from where he sat at the Great Hall table in alarm.

Where the blazes was Belinda?

She'd gone for a phaeton ride about an hour ago and had said she would be back before the weather turned.

But now the weather had turned and there was no sign of her.

Ordinarily, she would have parked her phaeton in the stable yard and let the staff handle it. She always came back from her rides through the Great Hall, where she'd greet Alexander and head back to her chambers to change.

So why was Alexander sitting in the Great Hall with no sign of his wife?

It didn't make any sense whatsoever.

Uneasiness twisted in his gut. This wasn't like Belinda at all. Something was off.

He got up and began to pace back and forth.

He prayed she had not come to any harm. He prayed that she had only been a little delayed and would be pulling into the stable yard any minute now.

Yes, that made sense, he told himself. She would be pulling into the stable yard any minute now.

He stopped pacing and made his way out to the stables.

Sharp droplets of icy rain hit his face. But he didn't care. What mattered was Belinda.

He cast his gaze around the stable yard. There was no sign of his beloved wife. Nor was there any sign of her phaeton or her horse.

He rushed over toward the stable buildings. "Belinda!" he yelled. Panic brewed in his stomach.

A young lad, not more than fourteen or fifteen, poked his head around an open stable door. "Your Grace," he said.

"Have you seen the Duchess?" Alexander asked.

"No, your Grace. Not since she went out in her phaeton earlier."

Alexander's heart raced at a thundering clip. His throat tightened and despite the cold weather, he was uncomfortably warm.

His worst fears were coming true. Belinda was missing.

Another roar of thunder engulfed Alexander's ears.

Before Alexander had a chance to say or do anything else, thundering hoofbeats reverberated on the cobbles that led from the stables down to the moorland.

The horse's fearful neighing filled the stable yard before the animal came into view.

Belinda's horse was back but she was nowhere to be seen.

Trailing behind the horse were ragged, sodden reins that dragged on the cobbles.

Immediately, Alexander knew what he had to do. He had to find Belinda and he would stop at nothing until he knew she was safe.

He walked towards the frightened horse and pulled at what remained of the reins.

The stablehand rushed out of the brick building to assist his employer.

Alexander said, "Take this horse and see it's calmed and in the stables." Then he strode into the stables and addressed the other servants who were sheltering from the torrid weather. "Men, the Duchess is missing on the moors. Set up a search party."

Then Alexander strode towards one of the sturdiest horses and began to saddle the stallion up.

The other men did the same, working quickly with a sense of real urgency.

In a matter of minutes, every horse and rider was ready.

Finding Belinda wasn't going to be easy but there was no other choice. It was this or let her perish on the diabolically stormy moors.

The men rode out with Alexander at the helm, his face set in the grimmest of grim determination.

As they clattered along the cobblestones, Alexander turned around and shouted, "Men, we ride as one! Follow me!"

The group made its way along the cobbles and out onto the moorland.

Alexander kept them to the main path. He knew that this was the route Belinda habitually took so it was the most logical place to start.

"Belinda!" he called.

His men picked up the call and soon enough, shouts of 'Your Grace' and 'Duchess' rang out alongside Alexander's own desperate cries.

The fog was still thick and the rain still fell in harsh sheets. Alexander and his men would no doubt be drenched by the time they were through, but it was a small price to pay to ensure Belinda's safety.

"Belinda!" Alexander called out across the moorland.

No reply was forthcoming. Only the shouts of his men and the howling of the wind and the driving of the rain filled his ears.

The pack followed the winding path across the moorland in a desperate search.

Flashes of lightning illuminated the sky in almost blinding streaks of purple and white.

After the group had been riding for about ten minutes, the fog mercifully began to fade away. Visibility became a little easier, though it was still tough going what with the torrential rain.

"Belinda!" Alexander called, his voice ringing around the moors.

"Your Grace! Your Grace!" an ostler cried.

"Duchess! Duchess!" other men shouted.

The group proceeded thus until a man at the back grew to a sudden halt and bellowed, "I think I see something!"

Alexander pulled hard on the reins of his horse.

The entire group drew to a halt.

Alexander turned around to face the man who had reported seeing something. "What is it? You saw something?" he asked breathlessly.

"Yes, your Grace," the man said. He pointed down the hill.

Alexander peered down. Unless he was very much mistaken, that was Belinda's phaeton! The green metal of the contraption was most familiar indeed.

Without thinking any further, he bolted down the hill towards it, his men following behind.

Alexander drew closer and his heart sunk. The phaeton was on its side and from where he was, he could see no sign of Belinda. Was she even there?

Alexander raced down the hill, fear striking the very centre of his heart. The rain drove deep daggers into his skin.

After what felt like an hour, but in reality could have been no more than a minute, he reached the phaeton. He lept off his horse and took the final few steps to the phaeton.

Inside, he saw the crumpled body of Belinda. She was bundled up against the floor of the contraption, impossible to see for anyone who wasn't peering directly at her.

Somewhere in the background, one of Alexander's men had taken the reins of his horse.

Belinda's forehead was covered in blood. Her eyes were closed and she made no sound. Was she even still with the living?

Alexander knelt down and reached out towards her. "Belinda," he yelled in desperation.

No response from the woman who lay wounded before him.

He yelled her name again.

Still no response.

Could his worst fears be true? Had she left this mortal coil? Was he to be without the woman he loved?

He reached out to feel for a pulse. He was terrified to find out once and for all if she had left him for good. But he forced himself to do it.

Yes! There was a pulse. A weak one, but she was still alive nonetheless.

He called her name a third time but still there was nary an answer nor even any sign she had heard him.

He turned to his men and bellowed at the top of his lungs, "Men! The Duchess is alive. But she is badly injured. Get help!"

The pack peeled off into two. One set headed for the house, the other towards the York road.

One young stablehand stayed beyond and dismounted from his horse. In his other hand he held the reins of Alexander's horse. He walked both animals down to the phaeton.

Alexander bent down into the phaeton and took Belinda in his arms.

She was breathing softly but had no idea he was even there.

He scooped his wife up and carried her towards his horse.

Then he lay her over the front and mounted the steed.

He turned to the stablehand, who was mounting his own horse. "Thank you, you had better head back to the stables. Let them know they'll need to collect the phaeton once the weather improves.

"Yes, your Grace." The stablehand nodded and rode off as instructed.

Alexander picked Belinda up and wrapped his arms around her. "Whatever am I going to do with you?" he murmured.

Then he rode off in the direction of the Abbey, as fast as he could carefully go.

The ride back was a little easier than on the way down, not least because he now knew for sure where Belinda was and that she was alive. But still he was deeply worried. She had dried blood on her forehead, for heaven's sake! And she didn't seem to register anything that was happening around her.

After a panicked fifteen minute ride, he arrived back at the Abbey. He didn't bother going round to the stables, they were further away and every second counted when it came to ensuring Belinda's safety.

They were outside the kitchen doors.

He called out to whoever was around. "The Duchess is here! I need assistance at once!"

In a matter of moments, a gaggle of footmen and maids appeared. Their faces were grey in shock at the sight before them.

Alexander turned to the maids. "Prepare her Grace's bedchambers, hot water, medical supplies, everything."

The maids quickly darted off to perform their duties.

Alexander addressed the footmen. "Help me get her Grace down and then, one of you take this horse back to the stables."

Alexander dismounted the horse and two footmen worked together to get Belinda into his arms.

Then Alexander hurried inside with her. He strode through the kitchens.

A few servants gawked at the unusual sight.

But Alexander didn't care one iota. He was a man on a mission and his mission was to protect Belinda.

He rushed through the winding servants corridors and cut into the Great Hall. He took the stairs two at a time and then he was up on the balcony. He weaved his way through the maze of corridors until he reached Belinda's chambers. The door was open and he strode through.

The bedchamber was a flurry of activity.

Maids moved around setting out steaming hot towels and piles of linen.

The bedsheets had already been stripped and changed.

Miss Dauntsey stood in the centre directing proceedings. "Your Grace," she said, her eyes wide with shock. "The Duchess is unconscious?"

Alexander nodded. "Yes. But by the grace of God, she is alive." He placed Belinda gently atop the bed. "I have sent men for the doctor, though how that will be in this weather is anybody's guess. We must do what we can for her here and now."

"Yes, your Grace." Miss Dauntsey replied. She turned around and said to the maids, "Sally, fetch the hot towels. And Margery, bring the medical kit." Then she walked towards where Belinda lay on the bed and felt her forehead. "Her temperature feels normal for now. But we'll have to monitor it."

Alexander took the medical kit from Margery. He sat on the bed next to Belinda. Then Sally handed him a hot towel. He dabbed it on Belinda's forehead, wiping away the mess of dried blood.

Doing something like this, doing anything, at least made him feel as though he were helping Belinda in some small way. Made him feel that he had some level of control over the situation and that he could make a difference for her.

Otherwise, the only thing he could do was wait for the doctor. And given the remoteness of the Abbey, he likely had a long wait ahead of him.

Well after nightfall, the doctor arrived.

Alexander had barely left Belinda's side. Not a morsel had crossed his lips since breakfast.

When the doctor entered Belinda's bedchamber, Alexander didn't even notice he had entered the room.

"Your Grace," the greying man began. "My name is Dr Turnbull. Can you tell me what happened to the Duchess?"

Alexander recounted the whole sorry tale while Dr Turnbull nodded and bustled about in his medical case. Then he bent over Belinda's chest and listened to her pulse. "Her Grace's heartbeat is steady, though a little elevated," he said.

Alexander nodded but said nothing.

The doctor placed the back of his hand against Belinda's forehead. "Her Grace's temperature is high. Did she report feeling unwell before she went out on her ride?"

Alexander shook his head. "No, not to me. We had breakfast together and she was fine then."

Miss Dauntsey added, "Her Grace was well from everything I could tell, today before her ride."

The doctor felt around Belinda's forehead with his bare hand again. "Her Grace is not severely harmed from the phaeton accident. However, it appears she is developing a fever." The Doctor turned to Alexander. "Your Grace, the next four or so days will be touch and go."

Once the doctor had gone on his way, Alexander settled down into his vigil.

He sat down on a sturdy leather chair next to her bed.

Maids and footmen brought him an array of food, but he could barely touch a bite.

Instead, his stomach reverberated with an awful, aching sensation. He couldn't think about eating anything while Belinda was at risk in such a perilous situation.

His valet returned to collect the plates about half an hour after they were brought into the room. His eyebrows raised in alarm when he saw that they were all almost full. "Your Grace," the valet said. "Was the meal not to your liking? Could I get you anything else instead?"

Alexander shook himself out of his daze. "No, no. It's all quite alright. Clear this table."

"Very well, your Grace," the valet said and then he set about his task.

Alexander put his focus entirely and intensely on Belinda.

She was all he could think about.

Today's events had been horrifying. It was an accident, intellectually he knew that. But on a deeper level he blamed himself. He berated himself for not being there to prevent the accident, for not being there to protect her. Though quite how he could have prevented the accident once she had made the decision to drive her phaeton around the estate was anybody's guess. Still, maybe he should have gone with her. Maybe he could have spent more money on a phaeton for her, even though there was nothing wrong with the phaeton he had given her.

Through all his thoughts, his stomach kept on turning.

Would Belinda ever wake up? Would she ever be well again?

Or was this the end for her?

His stomach grew tighter and tighter and it was all he could do but to sit there and pray for her recovery.

He wasn't a particularly pious man. Certainly, he had happily wed in the Church of England and he would meet with the estate vicar from time-to-time. But matters of faith didn't go much beyond that for him.

Nevertheless, he began to implore the Almighty to save Belinda. To make her well again. He begged that she would have a swift recovery. He bargained that she would return to him and he made all sorts of promises to the Almighty that he would do whatever it took in return.

He sat like that for hours, until the candle wax burned out completely. He had no idea what time it was.

He closed his eyes for what he thought would only be a second.

The next day, after his valet had managed to drag him away to bathe and to change and to get some food inside him, Alexander returned to his vigil at Belinda's bedside.

On his way in, he turned to the maid on duty and asked, "Has there been any change?"

"No, your Grace. I'm afraid not," the maid shook her head sadly before curtsying and leaving the room.

He sat and watched Belinda for long hours, hoping, praying that something would change. That anything would change for the better. That she would show some signs of awareness of what was going on around her.

His servants tried to feed him meals twice during the day, but he barely picked at any of them. He could think of nothing but Belinda and her wellbeing.

He sat in his chair and clenched his jaw. He wanted to do something, anything to improve her condition but it was all out of his hands. He, a mere man, didn't have the power to control life and death. He had no way of healing her, other than doing whatever he could to provide her the best doctors possible. Even then, nothing was a certainty. They were only mere mortals themselves, after all.

Night eventually fell and still Belinda's condition had shown no signs of change.

Alexander was desperate. "Please, wake up, Belinda." His voice choked. "I love you. I can't be without you. I love you."

Maybe it was just a trick of the candlelight, but for the briefest of seconds Alexander could have sworn he saw Belinda's eyelids twitch open before they drew closed again. No, that couldn't have happened, could it? He must have been imagining things. So desperate was he that his sleep-deprived brain had started to hallucinate that she might have heard it. Yes, that's all it could have been. A mere figment of his imagination.

***

Belinda opened her eyes and the light of the grey clouds beyond streamed into her vision.

She struggled to remember how she came to be here. The last thing she could remember was riding in her phaeton out on the moors. Things had been going fine until the weather took a turn and a sea of fog engulfed her. Then...then...what had happened? She had taken what she thought was the path back to the Abbey. Only she had somehow managed to steer down a steep mound and then the phaeton had fallen down down down. She remembered the frightened whinnies of her horse and being thrown against the side of her phaeton. And then nothing else after that.

"Belinda, Belinda!" an excited male voice cried. It was Alexander.

She turned her head towards him. "Wha-what happened? How am I here?"

Alexander got up from the chair at her bedside and leaned over her cautiously. "You had an accident in your phaeton. Something went wrong, we're not sure what exactly, and the phaeton crashed and you ended up passed out. The doctor says you won't be badly injured but you did develop a fever."

"How long have I been out of it?" she asked.

"Four days," Alexander said.

She looked closely at Alexander and noticed how exhausted he appeared. He had big puffy bags under his eyes and his normally sleek countenance was blotchy. She wondered how many of those days he had spent awake, fretting over her.

With almost perfect timing, Alexander tried to stifle a yawn.

"Alexander, you had best get some rest," she said.

His sleepy eyes widened like an animal being pursued. "What? No, no. I'm fine."

"Alexander," she sighed. "I can tell you haven't slept barely an hour since my accident. It's written all over your face. Please, get some rest and try to look after yourself."

He made a reluctantly acquiescent groan. "Well, I suppose you have the right of the matter."

"I do indeed in this instance, I believe," she said. She gave a weak laugh. "Now please, go and try to get some sleep. I shall be fine here."

"You are most wise," he nodded. "Is there anything I can get for you before I go? Anyone I should call? What do you need?"

"Oh just have Dauntsey come and she can sort out all the rest."

"Consider it done."

Alexander raised himself from the chair.

Belinda beckoned him over and reached out her hands.

He placed his masculine firm palms in her dainty ones.

She squeezed them with a force that surprised him in its strength. "Alexander, thank you. You have been exceptional, I can tell."

"You need not thank me, I could have done nothing else," he said. His hawklike brown eyes bore down onto her, proprietary and desperate and something else she couldn't quite yet place.

He released his hands from hers and took his leave.

While she was awaiting Miss Dauntsey, she cast her mind back to what seemed to be an odd memory. Did she dream it? She could have sworn that at some point in the last few days, Alexander had told her he loved her.

He had never done that in all the time she had known him. And she didn't believe he did love her.

So why was her mind telling her that he had said those words?

Was it wishful thinking on her part?

No, it couldn't be. She didn't love him and she knew that he would never love her.

It must have been a delusion of her fever-addled mind.

A few days later, when Belinda was feeling well enough to sit up in one of the chairs in her chambers, she decided that she wanted to take tea with Alexander.

At first, Alexander had let his overprotective side rule him and he had questioned whether she was yet recovered well enough for such an activity.

But Belinda knew better. She insisted that beginning to participate in normal activities again, even if only in her chambers, and not letting other people treat her as though she were a glass ornament was essential for her recovery process.

And so it was that she had her way and was taking tea with Alexander. She wore one of her favourite velvet gowns and had had Miss Dauntsey apply her hair into one of the fashionable buns she so adored.

"What do you remember? Of recent events, I mean?" Alexander asked.

Belinda sipped her tea before responding. "Well, I remember going out on the moors in my phaeton. And then I think I was trying to turn, only I must've steered incorrectly because then the phaeton went sliding down the hill before it fell on its side, the horse broke loose and I was thrown against the side of the phaeton. Then after that I don't remember much of anything else."

"And nothing else?" Alexander asked.

She nodded. "And nothing else. Until I woke up and you were here."

Alexander sucked his lips in briefly. "That's, er, very good. That you don't remember anything else."

"Why is it good that I don't remember anything else?"

"Er, only because you really weren't well and I'd hate for you to remember any of that suffering," Alexander lied.

Belinda scrunched up her nose. Alexander was being oddly evasive.

Alexander continued, "I'm so glad you are back and over the worst, Belinda."

Alexander stood and stared out the library window. He couldn't keep up this pretence any longer. Already, Belinda had caught him out in a lie before and he didn't want there to be any more lies between them.

When he had lied before and covered up his interest in submission, he had genuinely and whole-heartedly believed that he was doing the right thing by her. That he was protecting her. Yet he had hurt her greatly by not telling her the truth and by not allowing her to decide for herself.

He pinched the bridge of his nose between thumb and forefinger.

There was nothing for it. He had to tell Belinda the truth about that night when he had confessed his love for her in his desperation for her to survive.

He turned around to face Belinda where she sat in one of the plush armchairs engrossed in a book.

She was well enough now to come and sit in the library and peruse some reading material, as well as take the dogs on short walks through the gardens. With every day, she was getting stronger.

Alexander walked towards her.

She looked up at him when she heard his footsteps.

She took in his face with her penetrating gaze.

Alexander stood before her. "Belinda," he said. "There's something you ought to know. About when you were passed out, after the accident. And I don't want to place you under any sense of obligation in the slightest. Only, I think you should be apprised of all the facts."

"That's very cryptic. What is it that I ought to know?" she asked.

"When you were sleeping, I told you that I loved you."

"I thought I heard you tell me so, but I decided it must've been a dream."

Alexander bit his lip before replying, "In any case, I don't want you to feel obliged to do anything. Only I wanted you to know the truth of what happened."

Belinda blinked. She put her book down on the arm of her chair. She didn't know what to say. What she thought had only been a dream was in fact reality. But she could not sincerely tell him she loved him back. What did she know of love? She who had never been in love before. Who was she to say what it felt like to be in love? And could she even expect her husband to love her and for her to love him? It wasn't an essential component in marriages of the ton, after all.

Silence engulfed the room.

Belinda bit her lip and said nothing.

Alexander rubbed the back of his neck in a gesture of self-comfort.

In the end, he took the initiative to break the deadlock. "You can forget I ever said anything, if you like."

Belinda tilted her head to one side. "I don't think I'll be able to forget. However, right now I can't give you any answer worthy of what you just told me. I'm sorry."

"No, no, please don't apologise."

"Very well. I cannot give you any worthwhile answer now, though. Let us speak of other things."

Alexander nodded. "What do you wish to speak of?"

"My violin playing."

"Your violin playing? How is it coming along?" Alexander smiled and walked over to the armchair next to Belinda's. He sat down.

"I'm happy with my progress. It's good to get back into the swing of things. In fact, I might play at Christmas, do some background music during the festivities."

"Yes, that's an excellent idea," Alexander said. "What are you thinking of playing? Any particular pieces?"

"Probably some of the old favourites. *In Dulci Jubilo, God Rest Ye Merry Gentlemen, I Saw Three Ships*. That sort of thing. And then whatever else takes people's fancy."

"I look forward to it very much indeed," Alexander said with a genuine smile.

CHAPTER TWENTY SEVEN

Dearest Belinda,

By the time you get this, it will most likely be Christmastide! Or at least very soon! How exciting to be able to plan and host your first Christmas as the lady of the house. You must write to me afterwards and tell me all about it. I simply insist that I be the first in London to know

Do you know yet when you are coming back to London? Or perhaps even Bath? I will be here in the capital until March, then in Bath for a few months to get away from all the hustle and bustle of the London season.

Your own season doesn't seem so far away, my dear. Though you have grown so much in that time. All of us in the Bournemouth family are so very proud of yo

With every best wish for the Christmas season,

Margaret

The Great Hall was a hive of activity.

Footmen were climbing ladders to hang garlands of ribbons and leaves from the walls.

Maidservants were polishing sets of cutlery and glassware.

Yapping beagles danced around Belinda's feet.

She reached down and gave them a ruffle on the head.

There was a jostling at the little door coming in from the servants' area. Then an almighty thud.

"No, no, go this way," a male voice shouted.

Belinda looked up and turned towards the noise.

The tip of a massive oversized Yule log was poking through the doorway. Four manservants were trying and failing to bring the Yule log through the door. It was a hefty decoration.

One of the footmen inside the Great Hall noticed the commotion and hurried over to assist. With his direction, the manservants were able to bring the monumental Yule log into the Great Hall and set it down in front of the fireplace.

Belinda returned her attentions to the beloved beagles. "Come on you too," she cooed. "Let's go and find Cook. I need to discuss the Christmas menu with her."

Belinda headed through the door to the servants' area, the beagles hot on her heels. She strolled down the narrow corridors until she reached the kitchens.

The door was slightly ajar.

Sounds of hustle and bustle emerged from outside. The clanging of pots and pans, the slamming of cupboard doors and the hiss of flames on the hearth.

Belinda rapped on the door. Technically, as mistress of the house, it was her right to simply walk straight in. But she knew that kitchens were in practice a cook's domain so she didn't want to tread on Mrs Atworth's toes unnecessarily.

In short order, a young scullery maid appeared at the door. She gave a deep curtsey. "Your Grace."

Belinda smiled. "Good day. Can you get Cook for me please."

"Yes, your Grace," the scullery maid replied.

A few seconds passed and Mrs Atworth materialised at the door. She was a stout jolly woman, about fifty years old with grey curly hair that was covered by a mob cap.

"Your Grace," Mrs Atworth opened the door fully. "Please, do come in."

"Thank you. I'm here to discuss plans for Christmas," Belinda said.

"Of course, your Grace. Of course."

Mrs Atworth led Belinda through the bustling kitchen and a series of adjoining chambers.

In one such chamber, the assistant cook was standing by the window icing some little cakes and giving a very questionable rendition of *The Holly and the Ivy*.

"Oh the holly and the ivy,

When they are both full grown,

Of all the trees that are in the wood,

Sweet holly bears the crown," she sang.

Mrs Atworth, Belinda and the pair of beagles entered the Cook's office.

The two women sat down in the upholstered seats by the fireplace while the beagles took their spots on the floor.

"I've confirmed how many family members there'll be for Christmas. Six in total. Myself, the Duke, the Dowager Duchess and the three girls," Belinda began.

Mrs Atworth pulled out a notepad and pencil from her pockets. "Very good, your Grace." She scribbled in the notepad.

There was a knock at the door and a kitchen maid came in bearing a tea tray.

Mrs Atworth gestured to the coffee table between Belinda and herself. "Thank you, Hannah."

Hannah put the tray down on the table and headed back into the kitchens.

Mrs Atworth began to pour the tea. "Can I offer you a cup, your Grace?"

"Oh thank you," Belinda said.

The tea poured, the two women sipped on their drinks.

Then Belinda said, "There's also the villagers and the estate staff. You'll know their numbers better than I would."

And so they spent the next half an hour finalising the Christmas menu plans.

A few days before Christmas, a coachman pulled up with a delivery of supplies from one of the villages over the moors.

The footmen made swift work of unloading the parcels and packages, most of which were destined for the kitchens.

There was one wooden box left in the coach.

A footman leaned in and picked it up. "To His Grace," he read the label.

Alexander walked out to the coach. He had been awaiting a certain special delivery for several weeks now. He hoped it would be in this run, the last such run to the Abbey before Christmas.

"Your Grace," the footman said. "This one's addressed to you. Directly."

"Thank you." Alexander took the wooden box from the footman and headed back indoors. He weaved his way through the Christmas preparations of the Great Hall and made a beeline upstairs for his snug.

Once inside, he firmly shut and locked the door behind him. If this box contained what he thought it did, he most certainly did not want any prying eyes finding out about it. And that included any servants. They might be well-intentioned but a loose pair of lips could lead to a scandal.

He placed the box on the desk and unfastened the latches.

The top layer was full of straw.

He moved his hands through the straw and, just as he had suspected, he found a sturdily-crafted leather object. He pulled it out of the box with one hand.

It was the chastity belt.

And then, beneath the belt, was something else he was looking forward to wearing. A set of human-sized reins and matching harness. He held them in his other hand and stroked the exquisite leather.

He put the belt, reins and harness back in the box and fastened the latches.

Then he unlocked the door and headed out to find Belinda.

At this time of day, she would usually be in her chambers. So he decided to look there first.

A short walk later and he was outside her chamber door. He rapped on it firmly with his knuckle.

Her voice flowed through the oaken door. "Who is it?"

"Alexander," he said.

She bid him to come in.

In short order, he stood before her holding the box.

She raised an eyebrow. "What's this?"

"A special Christmas present. For both of us."

"Oh! Can we open it now?"

"We most certainly can," he said with a smile.

She placed the box on the desk and unfastened the latches.

Delight filled her eyes when she rootled around inside and her hands met what felt suspiciously like a leather pouch. "Oh is it, can it be, Alexander?" she gushed.

"I'll let you see for yourself," he said with a smile.

She pulled out the object from the box completely and turned it over in her hands. "Yes! It is! It is!" she said in glee.

She ran her fingers over the exquisite black leather of the chastity belt. It had straps to hold it securely around the wearer's hips. Attached to the main strap at the front of the belt was a leather pouch. The perfect size for locking away Alexander's penis and having it be under her control and command.

Then she looked in the box again and noticed the reins and harness. She reached in with one hand and touched them in wonderment.

"Do you like them?" Alexander asked.

"Like them? Oh I love them! They are exactly how I pictured them," she said. "Thank you, Alexander. For arranging this, it's perfect."

"You're most welcome," Alexander beamed with pride. It felt good to be able to do something that pleased Belinda. He so badly wanted to impress her, despite his cold-hearted outer shell. "And thank you for coming up with the idea in the first place. You were the genesis of it all."

"I do have some very good ideas, if I do say so myself," she said.

"You do indeed," he replied with a smile.

She kept admiring the new leather restraints. Oh, what wicked plans she had for Alexander while he was wearing these!

Then the annoying wheels of practicalities turned in her head. "Will there be a moment, do you think, when we'll be able to make use of these over Christmas? Will we be able to get away from the crowds?"

"We can do whatever we want," he said. "I know you take the hosting duties seriously, but we can surely snatch a couple of hours to make proper use of your wonderful idea. We are duke and duchess, after all. It's our house and we can do as we please, within reason."

She put the chastity belt back in its box. Then she walked over to him. "You are most reassuring." She took his hand and squeezed it. "I can't wait to use these with you."

"Neither can I." He gave her a rakish grin.

A couple of hours later, the Great Hall was alive with noise.

"No, Diana, no!" Mary shouted.

Diana cackled. "You can't stop me! You'll never defeat me, Lord Tarnisher!"

The Dowager Duchess strode towards the pair, her hands on her hips in a pose of fury. "Girls!" she hissed. "If you don't stop that right now-"

Diana carried on oblivious. "Lord Tarnisher, Lord Tarnisher-"

"Diana!" Mary hissed and gestured to her mother.

Diana turned towards her mother, her mouth gaping open.

Judith stood to the side, watching the proceedings with a slightly wrinkled nose.

Before any of the four could say or do anything else, Alexander's deep voice called down to them from the balcony above. "Mother, sisters!"

The Dowager, Diana, Mary and Judith turned their heads towards him.

"Alexander!" the young girls shouted excitedly.

Alexander made his way down the staircase.

A small smile erupted on the Dowager's lips. She held out her arms towards her son.

Alexander reached the bottom stair and walked forward to embrace his mother.

"It's good to see you, Alexander," the Dowager said.

"I'm glad to see you too," he replied.

Then Alexander went to embrace each of his sisters.

Diana jumped up and down in excitement. "And Belinda, where is Belinda?"

Alexander began "Oh I think she's-"

At that moment, Belinda stepped out onto the balcony.

"Right there," Alexander finished.

Belinda made her way down the staircase.

She exchanged a smile with Alexander.

Then she called out, "Your Grace, Judith, Mary, Diana, so lovely to see you!"

The group exchanged greetings and, soon enough, they headed into the drawing room.

The two youngest girls were seated on a little settee while Judith and the adults were on the upholstered chairs.

A maid brought in tea and a selection of sandwiches and biscuits.

Diana reached forward and helped herself to a jam treat.

Her sisters took her cue from her and dove into the plate.

The Dowager rolled her eyes slightly at them but did nothing. It was Christmas after all, and most of what was happening was for the benefit of the children.

Belinda turned to the Dowager. "How are things in Norfolk?"

"Oh yes they are going well, thank you," the Dowager said proudly. "The girls are enjoying the fresh country air, and it is good for us all to have a change of scenery and be away from the city."

Alexander leaned in with an urgent look on his face. "How is the house? Is everything to your liking? Does it need any work done?"

The Dowager smiled. "It is most charming and we could not be better situated. So well appointed with such excellent staff. I don't see an immediate need for works, though

I daresay there will be a need for something as-yet undetermined in the next couple of years."

"Such is the way of these things," Belinda added.

"Indeed," the Dowager said.

Alexander's face became less urgent. "Well, if you need anything, please do let me know and the estate shall endeavour to provide."

"That is most kind, thank you," the Dowager said.

Before anyone had a chance to say anything else on the subject, Mary drew her attention away from the food. She looked at the assembled adults. "What will we be doing for Christmas Day? Is there to be a party?" she asked in excitement.

The Dowager looked at Belinda with curiosity.

"Yes, we've got a special party planned for Christmas Day," Belinda said. "Lots of people from the estate will be attending and we'll have a real feast."

"Will there be music and dancing? Oh, say they'll be music and dancing!" Diana exclaimed. She jostled herself up and down on the settee in her fever of excitement and anticipation.

Belinda smiled indulgently. "There most certainly will. We've organised all sorts of music and there will be so many jigs, you won't remember what it's like not to be dancing. It's been a lot of work from everyone. A real team effort."

"Ah now," Alexander said. "My wife is being too modest on this subject. She's done the vast bulk of the organisation solo. And always with true skill and aplomb."

The Dowager nodded happily. "Oh it will be so good to have proper parties again. You know," she said to Belinda in a confidential tone which all present could hear anyway, "the estate has not held parties on such a scale, or indeed any sort of ball, since the time of the previous Duke. It's been a long time coming that we have another one."

Alexander's facial expression was unreadable. "Indeed," he said.

The Dowager leaned forward and an excited glimmer shone in her eyes. "All this talk of parties leads me to my next question. Will we be seeing another Faversham Ball soon?"

"Perhaps, mother. But please remember that the Duchess needs time to settle into her role first," Alexander said.

The Dowager waved her hand airily. "Oh I know that, Alexander. But it doesn't hurt to ask!" She put a hand on her chest and adopted a swooning pose. "How lovely it would be to see another ball at Faversham House again. I can well remember what spectacular balls we used to hold when you were a boy, Alexander. How anyone who was anyone attended, all the great and good of our beloved ton, and how refined the whole night was. The ladies swirling on the dancefloor in their beautiful ball gowns, the gentlemen looking oh so dashing and smart. Those truly were the days."

Alexander nodded indulgently. "They were indeed, mother."

⌘

On Christmas Eve, the Great Hall was a hive of activity.

The Yule log burned brightly on the fireplace.

All about the Great Hall, people from across the estate mingled and chattered around the mammoth trestle tables. There were the servants from the Abbey, the tenants from the other side of the moor and the Favershams themselves.

Anastasia sidled up to Belinda. "Well, this is quite a celebration. You have outdone yourself, Duchess," she said breezily.

"Oh, thank you," Belinda said.

Anastasia took a generous sip of her cup of mulled wine.

Alexander strode towards the two women, the three Faversham daughters following in his wake.

"Mother, mother," Diana cried.

The Dowager turned to her daughter. "What is it?"

"Is it time for the presents? Oh, is it time for the presents?" Diana said.

"Well," the Dowager began slowly. "Since it's Christmas Eve, you may have one present. As a prequel to the main celebrations."

Diana clapped her hands together with glee and squealed. "Yes! Yes! Yes!"

"But, it is one present and one present only. Each," the Dowager said.

The other Faversham daughters cheered.

Alexander said to his mother, "I left the girls' presents under the tree in the drawing room."

"Like always," his mother returned with a smile.

Then Alexander turned to Belinda. "Would you like to lead the way?"

Belinda laughed. "Alright." She addressed the Faversham girls. "Follow me, your Christmas Eve presents await!"

The little group made its way through the Great Hall and down a side corridor. It was much quieter in here, away from the hustle and bustle of the estate crowds. The strains of the festive music grew quieter and quieter the further away the Faversham family got from the main festivities.

Belinda led the group into a drawing room where a pile of Christmas presents lay wrapped on the table.

The girls clapped their hands in delight.

"Oh how wonderful," the girls cried.

Belinda took the Dowager aside and said, "Are there specific ones they are meant to have for today?"

The Dowager nodded. "Yes, the ones in blue wrapping."

Almost simultaneously, Diana called out to the room at large, "Which ones? Which ones are for today?"

Belinda and the Dowager replied in unison. "The blue ones!"

Alexander and the girls laughed.

The Dowager continued. "They each have tags with your names on."

The girls descended on the table, picking out the blue wrapped presents.

"Oh this one's yours, Diana," said Judith.

"And here's mine," said Mary.

Once all three girls had their respective gifts, they turned to their mother. "May we open them please?"

"You may," the Dowager said indulgently.

The girls tore at the wrapping and, in short order, they were holding their presents.

Diana received a new hat. She plopped it on her head with a flourish and started posing in it. "How do I look?" she asked.

"Fabulous!" Judith said.

"I love it!" Mary added.

As for Judith, she received a selection of new books. "Oh these are just what I wanted, thank you."

And Mary received a whole set of clothes for her favourite doll. "Oh, oh, how lovely!" she exclaimed.

After all the girls had admired their presents and expressed their thanks, it was time to catch up on the family news. A conversation that lasted for several hours.

On Christmas night, the Great Hall was a hive of activity.

In the corner of the room, a ragtag band was playing festive music. Someone from the kitchens was on the tin whistle, a couple of villagers were on some drums and Belinda herself was there, playing the violin.

"Oh, it's Belinda!" Mary cheered.

"She *is* playing well," the Dowager remarked.

Alexander smiled. The violin had proven itself to be an excellent gift. He hadn't even realised the violin was something she enjoyed so much. How little he had known about her! But it was clearly something that brought her a lot of joy. And he so dearly wanted to make her happy.

He turned to his mother. "She is indeed. An accomplished violinist if ever I heard one."

Belinda and the rest of the ragtag band moved on to another piece. *In Dulci Jubilo*.

The festive tune swelled and filled the room.

Some of the maids and women from the village joined hands and jived to the traditional tune.

The room was alive with merriment.

Today was unlike the refined balls of the London social season, but was nonetheless a highlight of the year for the Faversham estate.

Here and there, guests chanted and sung along to the pieces the band played.

Belinda rarely delivered a performance to so many people, and certainly not in such a raucous environment. During her girlhood, she had played to small groups but always in a more formal setting. Being up here, playing as part of a ragtag band for the villagers, made for a refreshing change.

CHAPTER TWENTY EIGHT

Belinda awoke on St Stephen's Day as the clock on her mantlepiece struck ten.

After yesterday's busy Christmas activities, she had slept like a log. When she had clambered into bed soon after midnight, she had shut her eyes and was comatose to the world. It came as no surprise, therefore, that she felt very refreshed and rejuvenated this morning.

She didn't bother reaching for the servant's bell. As was tradition in the Faversham household, the servants would be taking the day off.

Instead, she got out of bed and made her way to her washstand.

It was time to perform her morning ablutions and prepare herself for the day ahead.

The task done, she set her mind to what she could do today. She knew the Dowager and the girls were planning to rest in the guest chambers before a family walk in the late afternoon. That left several hours before either her or Alexander had anywhere they needed to be. Trust his smart devising.

She opened her chamber door and padded down the corridor. It was time to find her husband.

Along the way, she didn't see a single soul. All the servants were taking the day off and those who had family or friends nearby had gone to visit them. And the Dowager and her daughters would be in their guest chambers.

Before she knew it, Belinda was knocking on Alexander's chamber door.

It swung open to reveal the handsome face of her husband.

"Belinda! To what do I owe this pleasure?" he asked.

"Well, since we have a few hours before the walk with your mother and the girls, I was thinking why not take advantage of the peace and quiet and try out the belt," she said.

"I like your thinking." He swung open the door. "Please, come inside."

She duly did so. Her satin skirts hung loosely around her while the neat line of her bodice and what it concealed caught Alexander's eye.

He shut the door behind her.

Belinda drank in Alexander's gorgeous figure. He was freshly shaved and in a fine cotton shirt and beige pantaloons. On his feet he wore brown slouch boots.

He took her hand and placed a reverent kiss atop it. "I have what you are seeking."

He led her towards the sideboard underneath the window. Then he opened one of the doors and pulled out the box with the belt, reins and harness inside.

He offered her the box. "Would you like to do the honours?"

"Thank you, Alexander," she said. She took the box from him.

She put the box down on top of the sideboard and turned her attention to the latches.

She removed the belt from its casing and held it in her dainty hands. Its supple leather was delightsome. And would be even more delightsome wrapped around Alexander's gorgeous cock. Beneath the belt were the harness and reins which sent wicked frissons of lust through her when she laid eyes on them.

She looked across to the fireplace. It was roaring away. Yes, the perfect heat to have Alexander before her in all his glory on this winter's day.

She turned her gaze towards him. "Strip," she said.

"Yes, Domina," he replied. His hands moved to his cravat and untied the plum damask knot. He folded the cravat and placed it on the sideboard. Then he unbuttoned his waistcoat and removed it.

Belinda's pulse began to race a little. The sight of him was most pleasing to her eyes.

As if he knew precisely what she wanted, he removed his white cotton shirt. It joined the cravat and waistcoat on the sideboard.

Now, half of him was bare before her.

Belinda smiled a little to herself. The sight of this most dashing man and he was hers, all hers!

Next, he bent down and removed his slouch boots one by one.

And finally, his pantaloons.

A grin erupted on Belinda's face at the sight before her.

Every inch of him was perfection. From his athletic arms to his well toned chest and down to his strong legs. His face was so noble with its hawk-like eyes and aquiline nose. Not forgetting, of course, his most wondrous cock.

How Belinda adored the shape of his cock and how pert and erect it could become.

Right now, his cock was beginning to stir against his leg and it was growing comfortably hard. But he was not fully erect yet.

And, Belinda smirked, he wouldn't be fully erect until she decreed it.

For today, she held the power and control.

Belinda relished the sight in front of her.

He was absolutely stunning.

She shifted the box in her hands. "Come, it's time to put these on. Follow me."

She walked over to the settee and sat down.

He trailed behind her and came to stand in front of her, uncertain.

She placed the box in her lap. "Stand in front of me, arms behind your back, pet."

He duly did so.

Then she removed the chastity belt from the box and brought it forward to his cock. "Here, I'll slip this here." She did up the fastenings on each side of his hips.

Leather quickly encased him. His cock twitched at the sensation, but because of the snugness of the chastity device, he had nowhere to grow. He bit his lip. The sensation was already maddening and he had barely been wearing this belt for even a minute.

Belinda grinned at him. This was her vision, brought to life. He looked just as gorgeous in the device as she had imagined that day in her phaeton.

Then she reached inside the box again and pulled out the harness and reins. She raised herself to her feet and took a few steps towards him. "And now it's time for a little something extra," she said wickedly.

His eyes widened and he let forth a moan of need.

She fastened the harness around his waist and attached the reins to it. The leather straps accentuated his finely toned muscles. Belinda adored how the tough leather contrasted with Alexander's smooth skin.

Taking the reins in her hands, she made her way to sit back down on the settee.

She reached out her left foot towards him and stroked it up and down his calves.

He jolted at her touch and let forth a whimper of delight.

"Now, pet, come and join me." She patted the cushion next to hers.

He duly did so with a shy smile on his face.

She pulled him by the reins towards her and wrapped her arms around him. "Kiss me," she said.

He bit his lip in anticipation. Then he leaned forward and took her face between his strong, masculine hands. He placed a searing kiss between her lips.

Belinda's heart began to beat faster and faster.

He tasted like mint and molasses. Like pure masculinity. He was absolutely delicious.

She kept the reins in her hands as she slackened them and ran them over his skin. Beneath her dainty hands, his toned muscles felt firm and oh so well formed.

Alexander let forth a moan of contentment.

Belinda giggled a little inside at the thought of what the ton might say to see the cold-hearted duke like this.

Here he was, naked except for a chastity device and restraints, completely at her mercy and under her command. His pleasure was hers to decide, hers to control. He would serve her with his body and obey every order her devious mind could devise.

She had tamed the beast. She had tamed the wolf.

And she loved that fact.

When she had had her fill of his kiss, she drew her mouth back.

Alexander whimpered at the loss.

"Oh, pet," she said. "We are only just getting started."

She moved the reins so that they were both in her left hand. Then she pulled on the reins and drew her closer to him.

He groaned with desperate need.

She glaced the fingers of her right hand up and down his well-toned chest. Her fingers caught the leather straps of the harness here and there. Leather against his skin was simply a wondrous combination!

Being this close with him made an intoxicatingly fizzing sensation erupt within her.

She brought her mouth to his and claimed him in another searing kiss.

He writhed on the settee at her touch.

She saw his needy reaction and giggled into his mouth with glee. Oh, this was most excellent!

She murmured into his ear. "Now, pet, I want you to touch me."

He ran his hands up and down her sides. Slowly. In just the way he knew that she liked.

A delicious tension began to build within her. Though soft fabric covered her, she could still feel the tips of his fingers as fiercely as if there were no barrier between her skin and his touch. "Yes, pet, exactly like that," she said.

He kept his gaze focused on her. His desire to please and to serve was unmistakably evident in every move he made.

She dropped the reins. Then she wrapped her arms around his waist and drew him closer. "Oh pet, your hands feel so wonderful." She drew him forward for another kiss.

He tasted like molasses and mint.

When she had had her good and full fill of every crevice of his mouth, she pulled back and said, "Now, pet, it's time for you to worship me with that sweet tongue of yours."

He bit his lip in anticipation. "As you so command, Domina."

She leaned back against the arm of the settee, her neck propped up by plush damask pillows.

Alexander bent down and dove into her skirts.

He ran his hands along the inside of her thighs.

She let forth a giggle of delight.

Then he placed gentle kisses along each of her thighs, first the left and then the right.

"Oh yes pet," she moaned.

He moved his attentions to the spot where her legs met.

She was soaking wet already.

He ran his tongue up and down her sopping slit. His cock twitched helplessly against its strict restraints.

Then he moved inwards to her plump labia.

She spread her legs wide, wide, wide for his tongue. Ready to claim every ounce of pleasure. As was her right as his Domina and his wife.

His tongue found her pleasure pearl and moved around in skillful circles.

Belinda was already so close to the edge that it would only take a few moments of his attentions to send her into that precipice of pleasure. And, sure enough, that blissful sensation built and built within her until she was falling down down down into the pool of ecstasy. How she loved her sweet pet's skillful tongue!

He kept up his focus on her clitoris.

She bucked her hips upwards to meet him. That delicious pressure grew again within her and another orgasm rippled through every inch of her body.

She felt like the queen she was.

She looked down at him through hooded, commanding eyes. "Pet, that was most delicious."

He preened at her praise. "Thank you, Domina."

She raised herself so that she was fully upright. "And now, it is time for your reward, my sweet pet."

She leaned across to his belt and unfastened the straps. The leather pouch fell away. She took the device and put it on the floor. Then she leaned into Alexander's ear. "Show me how you pleasure yourself, pet."

"Domina -" he groaned.

"I know you can do it. Do it for me, pet," she said.

He duly did so. He moved his hands to his cock and took himself in rough strokes.

Belinda looked down at his glorious cock. "That's it, good boy," she praised.

Her words spurred Alexander on. He moved his hands faster and faster up and down his shaft. His fingers were like a tight vice around his cock. The pressure of the need for release built inside him.

He turned to her with pleading eyes. "Please, Domina, may I come?"

"Not quite yet. I want to see you touch yourself more first," she said firmly.

"But Domina -" he whined.

"But nothing!" she snapped, her voice taking on a harshness she had not used before so far today. "I know you can do it, I know you can be my good pet. So show me."

His cheeks reddened at the chastisement. He wanted more than anything to please her so he continued his attentions to his cock.

Belinda licked her lips in delight at his obedience.

The muscles in his neck strained to keep himself under control. He was so close, almost too close to the edge.

Belinda let him work himself into a frenzied sweat, all the while she kept her watchful eyes upon him. She loved to see him like this. The cold-hearted duke broken with desire and under her command.

His whole face was flaming scarlet by now. Such was his focus on obeying her orders and restraining himself from release through his own sheer willpower.

A pleasant warmth spread throughout Belinda's core. She could sit and watch him all day. But alas, she knew that even the strongest willpower has its limits against the might of biological imperative. She decided to show mercy upon him. "Come. For. Me."

He looked at her quizzically, unsure if he had heard her command correctly or if his need-addled mind had hallucinated in a desperate attempt at obtaining sweet release.

She nodded firmly. "That's it. Come. For. Me." She leaned in and claimed his neck in gentle, teasing kisses.

He needed no further instruction. In mere moments, release spread throughout him and he spilled his seed on his chest.

She looked down and a wicked idea formed in her head. "Now, how shall we clean you up?" she said. "I know, you can taste yourself."

He let forth a groan of need.

She dipped her index finger in his seed and brought it to his lips. "That's it pet, have a taste."

He parted his lips and let her enter him.

He suckled obediently on her finger until all the juices had melted away into his mouth.

"Good boy, that's it," she cooed.

She removed her finger from his mouth and picked up some more of his seed.

Together, they repeated the process until his stomach was fully clean.

"Well done, pet," she said. She placed a proprietary kiss on his cheek. "Did you like that?"

"Oh I loved it, Domina, thank you," he replied, his eyes shining bright.

"I am most glad," she giggled. "Now, we don't have long before we have that family walk."

"Ah, so many commitments. I wish we could stay here instead, just you and I," he said.

"We will have time enough for that, once Christmas is over. But for now, let's right ourselves and get ready for the afternoon ahead. We'll get some luncheon too."

He nodded and, ever the obedient pet, went to follow her commands.

CHAPTER TWENTY NINE

A week after Twelfth Night, when the rest of the Favershams had headed back down to Norfolk and the estate workers were back in their homes, Belinda and Alexander had an afternoon to themselves.

The hosting duties over for their first festive season together, there would be no interruptions whatsoever.

Belinda relished the sight in front of her. Her gorgeous husband stood at attention as though he were on a parade ground. Well, this afternoon in this office he was on her territory, on her parade ground, and he had better do all he could to pass muster. She sat on the plush chair and ran her hands along its smooth varnished oaken arms.

"My, my, my, what a delectable sight you make, pet," she cooed.

He kept his gaze on her and his cheeks reddened a little. "Thank you, Domina."

She gave a nod of acknowledgement. "You are so dashing, pet, that I would like to inspect you more closely. Come here and stand in front of me."

Alexander strode forwards.

Belinda adored how graceful he was when he was in motion. His firm, muscular legs hinted at his strength and athletic prowess.

He came to a halt in front of her.

Belinda drank in the sight of him. He was toned and his skin was supple and sleek. Every inch of him was hers.

"Turn around in a circle for me," she said authoritatively.

He did as she commanded.

She relished how gorgeous he was. Every inch of him was beautiful. His pert buttocks were truly wondrous! And his back was so strong and smooth.

He turned back around to face her, his hands at his sides in the position of ease.

"Fabulous, pet," she complimented.

Alexander preened at the praise.

Belinda reached over to the side table next to her chair and grabbed a now-familiar wooden box. She unfastened the latches and opened it to reveal Alexander's chastity device, harness and reins.

She quirked her lips in a salacious smile. A frisson of excitement built within her belly. Though she enjoyed playing with the harness and reins, today she wanted to put a razor sharp focus on his chastity obedience.

She reached into the box and pulled out the leather chastity device. "Here, pet, let's put this on you."

Alexander shuffled forward slightly so that he was within arms' reach of her.

She looked up at him and saw that he too had a smile on his face.

She reached for his glorious cock and encased it in the snug leather pouch of the chastity device. Then she wrapped the accompanying belt around his hips and fastened it securely. Now his pleasure was at her mercy and at her command.

"How does that feel, pet? Is it comfortable?" she asked.

"Yes, Domina, thank you, Domina," he said eagerly.

"I am most glad to hear it." She gave a satisfied nod. "Now, get on your knees." She pointed to the floor.

Alexander scrambled to comply and, soon enough, he was kneeling in front of Belinda. His hands were in his lap and his head was tilted upwards to meet her gaze, exactly as his Domina required during scenes like this.

Belinda placed the wooden box back on the side table and turned her attentions solely onto the man who knelt before her.

"Oh, you are just the most beautiful picture, pet," she said.

He blushed a little at the compliment.

She continued speaking, "So beautiful in fact that I find I cannot resist the very thought of you. But since you are all locked away in that device of yours, I cannot help but take matters into my own hands."

Alexander let forth a heady, whimpering mix of frustration and anticipation.

Belinda reached upwards through her skirts and petticoats. Their velvet and satin teased against her skin.

She inched her hands over her thighs and towards that special place between her legs. Her fingers moved through her thatched mound to find her sopping slit and then journeyed onwards through her folds to her pleasure pearl. She rubbed her finger around and around her clit, the delicate circles teasing her in just the way she liked. She didn't want to orgasm just yet. She wanted a build up and to eke out every ounce of pleasure that she could.

Alexander watched the proceedings with wide eyes. His cock strained against its leather enclosure but the snugness of the pouch meant he was unable to reach full hardness.

She moaned a little at the ripples of pleasure that began to emanate from within her core.

Alexander could not help but want to be the one giving her such pleasures. "Please, Domina, let me worship you."

But such an outburst was of course against the rules of their scenes together!

She shook her head and tutted. "Careful, pet. If you carry on like this, the next time we head south, you'll be riding in the carriage all the way to London laying on your stomach. At every staging post, at every inn, I will have you cut a new switch and present it to me so I can refresh the reminder into that delectable rump of yours. Just think what a pretty shade of crimson your rump will be."

He bit his lip and lowered his gaze.

She took his chin between her thumb and forefinger and tilted his face upwards so his eyeline met hers. "No, you do not look away. What is the rule, pet?"

He willed himself to look into her eyes and replied, "I am to maintain a reverential gaze when my Domina is speaking to me, Ma'am."

"As you should," she nodded.

She moved her finger round and round over her clit and let the delicious sensations wash through her body.

She was on that precipice of sweet climax. She was dangling around, teasing herself and bucking her hips as each jolt of pleasure ricocheted around her very being.

She adored this sensation. It was wonderful to be fully at one with her body. And, despite all the difficulties she had endured over the years, she was still able to get some kind of pleasure from her physical being at a time like this.

Round and round she moved her finger. The waves of pleasure rippled around her core. Until finally, finally, she decided to let herself feel the ultimate delight.

Down, down, down she fell into that pool of pleasure. Ecstasy swelled throughout her body again and again and she bucked her hips thoughtlessly. It was no longer an intellectual exercise but a burning need she could not help but fulfill.

She was a lady and she was staking a claim on her own body. On her own being, in every way.

She stopped moving her hand and let herself relax as the pleasant sensations began to ebb away a little.

She came down from the heights of her climaxes and cast her gaze down at Alexander.

He looked flustered and teetering on the edge of desire himself. But the belt he wore meant he would not experience sweet release if and until Belinda decreed it.

She liked what she saw. And now, having helped herself to lots of delicious orgasms, she wanted to have her way with Alexander in a way she knew he would enjoy.

She leaned forward in the chair and tilted his chin upwards.

"Pet, I think it's time you get a reward," she said.

"Thank you, Domina," he uttered.

"Now, stand up."

He quickly obeyed her order, his hands at his sides.

She reached forward and unfastened the buckles of the belt. Then she took the pouch away, leaving his glorious cock free in the open air.

It stood proud and, very quickly, fully erect.

Belinda licked her lips a little. He was always such a tempting sight!

"Go and lay on the bed, on your back," she said.

He swiftly did as she bid.

She put the belt down on the side table and followed him over to the plush, four poster bed. She reached into a heavy wooden bureau nearby and pulled out a set of sturdy, leather cuffs and straps.

She returned to him and tied each of his limbs to a bedpost.

Then she glaced her fingers along his legs.

He let out a whimper of need.

She chuckled gently. "Patience, patience, dear pet."

Then she transferred her attentions up to his arms.

Goosebumps appeared on his bare flesh.

He gazed up at her through hooded eyes. "Please, Domina," he rasped.

"All in good time, pet, all in good time," she said.

She removed her fingers with all rapidity.

He jolted upwards at the denial of her touch. "Please, Domina," he groaned.

She giggled and returned her hands to his arms.

He let forth a moan of relief that almost crossed the boundary into pleasure.

"You are so beautiful, so smooth, and you are all mine, mine, mine," she crowed.

She relished the sensation of his sleek, toned arms beneath her fingers.

And when she had had her fill, she turned her attentions to his chest. Though this was by no means the first time she had seen his bare chest by now, she still marvelled at how perfectly formed he was and how wonderful he was to the touch.

He let forth another whimper of desire. He needed her and only her. He would only ever need her, more than he needed air to breathe.

Belinda could see from how every inch of his body quivered, from how his heart rate audibly pulsated, from how his breath raced, exactly how much he needed her. And she relished that fact. It made her feel powerful. It made her feel in control. When she had first learned of his secret desires for submission, she had struggled to understand how someone else who wasn't a twisted monster would want to dominate him. Surely that was only the wish of someone who was cruel and selfish. But she had quickly come to realise that it could be freeing for a woman like her. For a woman who had been beholden to the desires of others her whole entire life. It was good to be the one in command for a change.

She withdrew her hands from his chest.

He let forth a needy moan at the removal of her touch.

"Ah, now, now," she cooed. "I have something even better in store for you. Something that I do believe you are going to enjoy very much indeed."

She turned around and made her way over towards a sideboard by the window. She reached inside and pulled out two of her newest, most favourite possessions.

Her black leather gloves. They were of medium thickness, not so thin as to be ever-so delicate kid leather and not so thick as to deny her the flexibility she craved during these sessions, and they went up to the point where her wrists became her forearms.

She brought the leather gloves over her dainty hands and fingers with a satisfying snap.

She wiggled her fingers and admired how stylish and svelte they were in the snug gloves.

Before she met Alexander, she had seldom ever thought about leather.

But now she loved the concept. It was most enticing indeed.

Alexander, for his part, loved the leather gloves because Belinda loved wearing them. What made her happy, what delighted her, made him happy and delighted him too.

She grabbed a bottle of oil and poured it over her leather-clad hands.

The black leather of the gloves shimmered like a diamond in the candlelight.

She made her way over to where Alexander lay on the bed.

He looked so wanton. He was tied spread-eagle, with his knees bent upwards, to each of the four bedposts.

His gaze was trained on her, his pupils wide and his deep brown eyes hooded with desire.

"Now, pet, it's time for your favourite part," she said.

He bit his lip. "Thank you, Domina."

Slowly, oh so slowly, she pushed her little finger into his small puckering hole.

Though they had done this a couple of times together before, and he had had some experiences with the governesses of Soho, she wanted to warm him up properly.

He moaned at the welcome intrusion. "Domina-"

His muscles tensed a little around her finger, gripping for purchase and enhanced sensation.

She could feel the warmth of him enwrapping her through the leather of the glove.

She wiggled her finger around inside of him.

"Domina, please," he moaned again.

"Oh, you like that?" she cooed. "Well, I'm only just getting started."

She removed her little finger from him entirely.

He whimpered at the loss of her touch.

But before he had time to think of anything else, she moved her index finger so that it was at the edge of his puckering hole. She ran her finger around the rim in teasing circles.

It was all he could do but buck his hips upwards in response to her tantalising touch.

She thrust her index finger inside him.

"Oh, yes, Domina," he groaned in delight.

A smile erupted on her face. She loved seeing him in such ecstasies.

She stroked her finger around inside him. Inch by inch, she made her way towards his prostate.She brushed against the delicate organ.

"Do you like that pet?" she murmured.

"Oh, yes I do, thank you, Domina," he said.

"Then tell me how it feels. I want to hear exactly and precisely what you are feeling. Don't be shy, now."

"It feels...wonderful, Domina. As though you are claiming every part of me. As though there is no part of me that is beyond your touch, beyond your command," he breathed.

She stroked her finger a little more firmly against his prostate.

His hips jerked upwards involuntarily. "D-Domina!" he exclaimed.

She chuckled. "That feels good, yes?"

"So, so good," he said. "You...your hand...you make me feel so alive. I exist only for you, Domina."

As the delicious pressure built inside of him, he could not help but shutter his eyes a little. But he remembered her command to maintain a reverential gaze at all times and opened his eyes a little so his hawk-like eyes focused on her through hooded lids.

"Good pet, that's my good pet. You are doing so well," she said.

He looked so wonderful, so strong yet so under her command and so wanton for her. Only ever for her.

She leaned forward and wrapped her other hand around his glorious cock.

He gasped in surprise and delight at this new development.

She stroked her thumb over the top of his cock, all the
while keeping up her attentions on his prostate with her
other hand.

"D-Domina," he groaned. He was growing more and
more overwhelmed with pleasure.

But just when his body was about to give out and sur-
render to the ecstasy of sweet release, Belinda withdrew her
hand from his cock.

He yelped and again his hips bucked up involuntarily.

She giggled.

"Please, Domina," he begged, his voice wracked with
need and desire.

She brought her hand back to his cock and began to claim
it in a tight vice of strict strokes.

But just when Alexander was about to reach climax, she
again withdrew her hand.

"Not just yet, pet," she giggled.

It was all he could do but whimper and buck his hips at
the denial.

She returned her hand to his cock and this time, she
decided to show mercy upon him.

She stroked the top of his cock several times and then
applied rough pumps to his stone-hard shaft. All the while,
she kept up her attentions on his prostate with her other
hand.

His toes tightened in anticipation. His heart was beating
at fever pitch. He was so very close now.

Belinda sped up her strict pumps to his cock.

"D-d-domina." His voice was shattered.

Then, he bucked his hips again and again and again. His climax washed through him and everything around him in his world was her. Her. Her.

He came down from his climax and his heart rate began to slow down.

Belinda stepped back, removed the gloves and placed them atop the sideboard. Dauntsey could handle them later. Belinda knew she could rely on her absolute discretion.

But now, it was time for Belinda to focus on caring for Alexander after what was an exhilarating yet, for him, exhausting experience.

She bustled around and undid the fastenings on his hands and feet.

She fetched a pitcher of water from the sideboard and poured him a glass.

Then she patted the pillows above his head. "Scooch up," she said.

He did as she bid.

She gave him the glass of water.

He took greedy, needy sips.

"That's it, Alexander, you did so well," she praised.

He looked up at her with a tired smile. "Thank you, Belinda. For everything. You are incredible."

***

"Did you really mean it, darling?" he asked later when they were in his chambers after supper.

"Mean what?" she replied.

"The part about my riding in the carriage all the way to London laying on my stomach and having to cut a switch at every inn."

Ice water flooded through her veins. Had she gone too far? Scared him off for good? He could have used his safe word, it was true, but she still had a responsibility to lead the situation and pay attention to his needs. Oh heavens, she had messed this one up.

"I am truly sorry, I did not intend to frighten you. Please, I implore you to forget I ever said such a thing," she said.

"Darling, I loved it! I do not ever want to forget." He crouched down next to where she sat on the settee and took her hands in his own. "In fact, I was wondering if you might be willing to try it for real?"

She let out a gasp that turned into a wicked smile. "You really would? You are serious?"

"I am."

"Then, dear husband, you had best ensure your switch cutting skills are up to scratch."

Alexander's eyes brimmed with gleeful delight. "I shall do my utmost."

"Make sure that you do." She leaned down to face him and claimed his mouth in a searing kiss.

CHAPTER THIRTY

U p in the snug, Alexander sat at his desk and scratched at the parchment with his quill.

This was the last piece of correspondence he needed to sign today. It was a letter regarding the printing house and the need for expansion. With all the political turmoil in Britain and the rest of Europe, cartoonists, writers and pamphleteers of all kinds wanted to publish more and more. So it only made sense for the Faversham printing house to grow to meet the demand.

Alexander signed his name at the bottom of the letter, put down his quill and leaned back in his chair. He stretched his arms above his head. The business of the day over, it was time to turn his mind to other, more pleasing matters.

Belinda appeared in his mind's eye. She was doing a brilliant job in her role as Duchess of Faversham. Christmas had gone without a hitch and he knew his mother and sisters had enjoyed it. Belinda's suitability to be Duchess didn't only extend to festive planning and playing the hostess, however. She had exhibited tact and diplomacy with all the staff since her arrival at the Abbey. She had a real head for numbers and was excellent at the books. But even more than all of those virtues, he reflected on how she had stood up to him several times and how she was willing to question him. Even if sometimes her way of questioning wouldn't have been what he had desired.

Oh, that night! That infamous night that would live etched in his memory forevermore!

He had been on his way back to the snug, ready for an evening's quiet reading. When he went to climb the stairs, his eyes had been met by a most unexpected sight. A blazing light beneath the closed door of the snug. He had raced up the stairs in double-quick time.

Was there an intruder? Was it one of the servants? Was the room on fire?

His heart pounding, he had opened the door to reveal a sight he had never dreamed of in a million years.

Belinda. She had been sitting on the floor with his secret literature box. Around her were what looked like several books, including *Fanny Hill*, and his collection of governesses directories. In her hand, she had examined one of his many discipline titles. One he had in fact been hoping to peruse that night in private. But Belinda had had it in her very hand! And to make matters worse, she had seemed to be *reading* it!

Cold horror had flooded through every inch of his body.

He had wanted to protect Belinda from him and his interests so badly that he had completely overlooked the possibility that she might go looking for herself. That she would disregard his privacy in her quest for the truth.

He had seen flashes of red that night. How dare she root around in his private space? How dare she go through his possessions without his permission.

And yet, could he really hold it against her on a significant level? He had left her in the dark from the get-go in their marriage, after all. Moreover, he held far more power than she did. It was within the very basic legal structure of marriage in this country. So, could he really expect her to sit back and do nothing and let him leave her in the dark, in a tightly assigned place, for however many years they would remain married? Potentially, for the rest of Belinda's entire life?

Since that infamous night when she had discovered his secret, things had gone better than he had even dared to dream. Belinda knew him and understood him and accepted him for who he was. She had shied away from neither him nor her own desires.

The one thing he did not have that he longed for more than anything was Belinda's heart. Her love.

But he had everything else a man could ever want. He would not allow himself to be greedy and wish for anything more. It wouldn't do to tempt the fates of fortune.

When he was a much younger man, before his father had died, he had never really considered love or marriage. It hadn't been something he had dreamed of. His mother had been devoted to his father, that much was true. But his father, well he had so often been absent from the family on what Alexander had assumed was ducal business but was really, in significant part, thanks to his gambling addiction, that Alexander had never truly gotten the measure of his father's feelings for his mother. So Alexander could hardly say that his parent's marriage was some great shining example that he had long hoped to emulate.

And when, as a young man, he had realised where his personal interests lay, he was so shocked at himself that he couldn't fathom how any lady of the ton could ever love him. What right did he have to love? What right did he have to be understood and accepted for who he was, flaws and all?

He had disgusted himself sometimes. Surely the role of a gentleman of a ton, not to mention a duke, was to lead and not to be led? Was to be the powerful one and not give up his power?

It was appalling. It was a scandal just waiting to be released. Certainly, there might be other men who visited those specialised houses in Soho but they weren't dukes. They weren't peers of the realm. They weren't society's designated leaders, for heaven's sake!

Try as he might, he could not change his desires. He could not force himself to be another person. And so, when he was only in his early twenties, he had made the decision never to marry. The title could go some other way, perhaps one of his sisters would bear a son or there would always be the inevitable distant branch of the family tree to pick up the slack.

So he had resolved to protect all the ladies of the ton and never marry. He would instead let the gossips paint a largely baseless picture of him as the cold-hearted duke. All it took was a poker-faced veneer, a few hard stares here and there, and always lurking around the sides of the dance floor rather than taking part himself. The motormouths of the ton had done the rest. And so it had been for years. Until that night in the Landsdowne maze.

To confound it all, he, the fool, had only gone and fallen in love with the poor young chit of a girl! She had caught his eye when she was presented at court several months before. That, however, had been admiration of her sparkle. He hadn't known anything about her personality at the time or what she stood for. Now he did know both of those things and fight it as much as he could, deny it as much as he had, and he could not stop himself from loving her.

If he could do nothing else, if he could be nobody else to her, he had to be her protector. Now he was her husband, he had a duty to protect her above all others, above even himself. So he would protect her at any cost, even the cost of his own heart and his own chance at happiness. She didn't need his foolish declarations. What good would they be to her? The only good he could do for her was to protect her. From all things and especially, above all, from himself.

CHAPTER THIRTY ONE

Dear Belinda,

I was so delighted to receive your last with all your news about Christmas. It certainly sounds like you had a wonderful time at the Abbey.

You asked me how things are at Pembroke Hall. It's going well. We are still planning out the renovations with a view to getting them started in the spring. They should take most of the spring and summer. So I would love for you and Faversham to be able to visit next autumn.

Have you been keeping up with any of the pamphlets lately? I couldn't believe what Lord Queensworth published the other week, about his economic views. It was most shocking and diabolical! I really hope his views don't gain purchase with other gentlemen of the ton. The Baron wasn't impressed either.

Yours,

Mary

Belinda leant out of the window and felt the cool winter's air hit her face. She cast her eyes to the horizon.

A familiar dark green carriage was making its way down the sweeping, steep drive.

She watched until the carriage was a few minutes away from the house. She turned and ran down the stairs and into the entrance hall. She burst through the doors and out onto the gravel.

The Faversham carriage pulled up in front of her and Alexander leapt from it. "Belinda!" he exclaimed happily.

"You're back," she said with a smile. "Did your trip go well?"

"Yes, very well, thank you." He turned back into the carriage and pulled out a sturdy leather box.

At first, Belinda took it for some sort of travel chest. Perhaps storage for paperwork.

Then she heard a mewing sound. And, on closer inspection, she realised that the object her husband had in his hands was not merely a conventional portmanteau. It was, in fact, a travel case for some sort of animal. It had leather sides with mesh windows and a sloping roof.

Alexander walked towards her. "I've got someone I'd like you to meet." He gestured to the carry case in his hand.

"Ooh, who might that be?" she cooed.

"It's a young cat, a few months old and orphaned recently in the village across the way. I remember you wanted one when we saw Mr Crimplepaws at the tea rooms. So, here he is," Alexander said.

"Oh how wonderful, thank you," she said.

"Let me show you him inside."

Together, they made their way into the house and headed for the Great Hall.

Along the way, the household's newest addition mewed and scratched at the mesh.

"He's a livewire now," Alexander said. "I think he doesn't like being carried around in this case much. I had him out loose with me in the carriage and he was a lot calmer then."

Belinda bent her head towards the travel case. "Poor thing. We'll have you out and about soon, don't you worry."

They arrived in the Great Hall.

Alexander placed the leather case gently on one of the dining tables. He unfastened the latches and lifted out a young black cat.

Belinda's eyes widened with delight. "Oh, hello, darling! Aren't you a pretty one," she cooed at the cat.

"He is very handsome," Alexander agreed. He placed the cat on the table.

Belinda turned to her husband. "Does our new friend have a name yet?"

"No, not yet. The honour of naming him goes to you."

Belinda tilted her head and considered the cat. "Hmm...what shall we call you?"

The cat let forth several enthusiastic meows.

Alexander stroked the cat.

The feline's meows turned into relaxed purrs.

Belinda said brightly, "I know, you look like a 'Gus'. I'll call you 'Gus'!"

Alexander smiled. "Gus it is then." He bent down and murmured at the animal. "Hello, Gus."

Gus gave a satisfied purr.

"Where shall we put him?" Belinda asked.

"I was thinking he could roam around the house, perhaps sleep in your chambers if you like."

"He might make a good mouser too."

Alexander nodded. "That he may. He's the best hope we've had in a long time. I certainly hope he'll be a damn sight better at it than those beagles. No fight in them at all. Gus, on the other hand, seems like he's already a spirited soul. He might enjoy the outlet of being a mouser."

Gus meowed and strutted around the table. He surveyed his new kingdom.

A few days later, the beagles' dog basket was in front of the fireplace in the library.

Belinda sat in an armchair nearby, with one eye on her book and the other on the three occupants of the dog basket.

Alexander wandered into the room.

Belinda looked up at the sound of his footsteps on the creaky floorboards.

Alexander asked, "What are you reading?"

"*The Castle of Otranto* by Walpole," she said.

"Any good?" He asked.

"So far I'm enjoying it. I like a good gothic setting, all those spooky castles and ghostly activities."

"Ah! A similar setting to the Abbey then."

"Yes, it's got that gothic sensation." She furrowed her brow and then clapped her hands together and said brightly, "Are there ghosts here? You never told me this place was haunted!"

He quirked his lip in wry amusement. "I've never heard that it was. Though I suppose there's always a first time for everything."

"Aw, that is disappointing to hear! But I shall keep my ears peeled for ghostly clanking suits of armour heading down the hallways on a stormy night."

He nodded. "A wise decision."

The room fell into companionable silence for a minute or so.

The flames on the fireplace crackled away.

Then Alexander broke the lingering silence. He gestured to the dog basket and its occupants. "And what of these three?"

The two beagles sat sleeping in their usual positions. But in the middle there was a most unexpected new occupant. Gus the cat. He was wedged between the dogs, fast asleep and purring soundly.

Belinda gestured to the pets. "This trio, they're thick as thieves already."

"I am most glad to hear it." He waited for a few beats before continuing. "When I first brought Gus home, I had no idea how he would interact with the beagles. Back when I was a boy, we had several cats and they never mixed well with any of the dogs."

She smiled knowingly. "These three, they're so different to that. They barely spend a moment apart."

Alexander's lips formed a small smile. A cat and two dogs getting along famously in the Faversham household? This was a most unheard of occurrence, most unheard of indeed. And as for the fact that Alexander Faversham was smiling? Well, that was almost as rare an occurrence. But most heartily welcome nonetheless!

❧ · ✦ · ❧

CHAPTER THIRTY TWO

Belinda felt groggy and cramps were stabbing her belly.

She sighed. Why did this have to happen every month?

She lay on her bed and groaned.

Ordinarily she would take laudanum in these situations, but frustratingly she was out of her supply. She'd have to send one of the servants to York for more and even the fastest horse would take the better part of a day to make the round trip. That wasn't time she had to waste. She needed relief now!

As she was groaning on the bed, feeling very sorry for herself, there was a knocking at her bedchamber door.

"Who is it?" Belinda called out weakly.

Miss Dauntsey's voice rang through the door. "It is I, your Grace. May I come in please?"

"Yes," Belinda called.

The door swung open and Miss Dauntsey entered. When she saw Belinda's state, concern overtook her features. "What's wrong, your Grace? You do not look well."

"Ugh, it is my period," Belinda said. "And I do not have any blasted laudanum." Belinda waited a few seconds, then said, "I'm sorry, Dauntsey, you don't need to hear such language from me."

Miss Dauntsey waved her hand. "It is quite alright, your Grace. I've heard far worse in my time. Should I fetch His Grace? Is there anything I can get for you?"

"Yes, please get him," Belinda said. "And have someone bring up some willow bark tea."

"Very good, your Grace." Miss Dauntsey bobbed a curtsey and scurried out of the room.

Belinda rolled over, clutched her stomach and groaned. She lay waiting for about ten minutes until there was another knock at the door.

A couple of seconds passed and Alexander entered the room.

He rushed to Belinda's side. "Belinda! What's happened?" He leaned over the bed and reached out to her.

Miss Dauntsey entered the room and deposited a tea tray on the wheeled table.

Alexander called over to her. "Thank you, wait outside please."

Miss Dauntsey curtsied and left the room.

Alexander stroked Belinda's hair.

She whimpered. "I've no laudanum. And these cramps hurt. Oh Alexander, what am I to do?"

He sat next to her and continued stroking her hair. "I'll have a man ride to York immediately. I know that doesn't help for the here and now though. Is there anything else you've tried other than laudanum?"

"The willow bark tea maybe helps a tiny bit, mentally. Other than that, there's been little of use."

"Have you tried climax? I don't mean to be facetious, but I've heard it might help with taking one's mind off some of the pain in situations like this."

"I suppose it's worth a try." Belinda paused to consider the matter further. "But won't it create rather a mess? Staining and such?"

"If you like, you could use a bath. I can have my servants run one for you."

Belinda nodded and said in a small voice, "Alright."

Alexander leant forward and placed a kiss on her forehead. "I won't be long." He stood up and wheeled the tea table over to the side of the bed. "Here, try some of this while I'm gone." He poured her a cup and set it on the table. Then he strode out of the room.

Muffled, unintelligible conversation that Belinda assumed was Alexander and Miss Dauntsey wafted in from the hallway.

Belinda propped herself up and took the teacup in her hand. The earthy taste filled her mouth. She didn't expect it to do much for her cramps, but at least it would help her to relax somewhat.

She sat and sipped on the beverage and tried to focus on something other than the pain.

After about a quarter of an hour, Alexander reentered the room.

"One of our men is riding to York right now. I'm so sorry, Belinda." He ran a hand through the back of his hair. "I should've been better prepared. This won't happen again, I assure you."

Belinda gave a tiny smile. "Well, I am the first wife you've ever had. I can't expect you to be too well-practiced in these matters. You will have time to learn, I am sure." She cocked her head a little. "Now, about this bath you spoke of?"

"That should be ready very soon," Alexander said. "Are you finished with your tea?"

"Yes."

"Very good. I shall take you to your bath then."

He walked over to the bed, bent down and scooped up Belinda in his arms.

Her eyes widened in surprise. "Alexander!" she yelped. "What are you doing?"

"Taking you to your bath, your Grace," he said matter-of-factly. "But my bathroom is through that door." She pointed to the other side of her bedchamber.

"So it is, your Grace. But you'll be bathing in *my* bathroom today."

"What? Whyever did you set up that?"

"It'll be less disruptive to you than having servants clanging about with pails of water right by your bedroom given you're already hurting."

Belinda snuffled. "Oh, right." Alexander's words made sense, though the idea that the servants rushing around would potentially make her suffering worse hadn't really crossed her mind. Such was her unfortunate state.

Alexander carried her down the web of corridors to his own chambers.

Belinda shut her eyes and tried to focus on feeling calm.

They came to a halt outside Alexander's chamber door.

The room was full of the hustle and bustle of servants.

Alexander turned to one of the footmen. "Is the bathroom ready?"

The footman nodded. "Yes, as you requested, your Grace."

"Very good," Alexander said. Then he addressed the room at large. "Everyone, please depart."

A chorus of 'your Grace' filled the room and then, in a matter of seconds, Alexander and Belinda were alone.

Belinda opened her eyes and blinked at the light of the room.

Alexander gave a reassuring smile and carried her into his bathroom. "I'm going to put you down now," he said.

He knelt down and helped Belinda to her feet. Then he went to close the door.

Belinda cast her gaze around the room.

Alexander's vast bathtub stood brimming with sweet-smelling water.

What took her by surprise, though, was the array of candles dotted on every surface throughout the room.

"Would you like some help?" Alexander asked.

"Please," she replied regally.

Alexander made his way over to her. Then he undid the ties at the back of her dress. "Step out," he said.

She duly did so and her dress glided to the floor.

Alexander picked it up, folded it and put it away neatly in the cupboard.

Then he unlaced her petticoats and stays and repeated the process.

Belinda stood before him in all her glory but he knew that this was not the time to revel in how enchanting she was. Instead, he had a responsibility to look after her.

He offered her his hand.

She took it gladly and allowed him to assist her into the tub.

"I'll leave you to it," Alexander said.

He headed towards the door. He was about to turn the handle when the sound of Belinda's voice stopped him in his tracks.

"Will you attend to me?" she asked.

Alexander turned around to face her. "Are you sure?"

"Yes. In fact, I do believe it will help me most greatly." She bit her lip in anticipation.

"As you so command," he said.

He walked towards her.

She stood, so ethereal in the candlelight, and held her hands out to him. "Please, assist me into this bath," she said.

"It would be my pleasure." He took her hand and helped her get into the bath.

She relaxed as the warm water sloshed around her. The aroma of something she couldn't quite place filled the air.

Alexander stood at her side still fully clothed.

Belinda bit her lip before saying, "You know, I think you should remove your shirt. In fact, it would please me greatly, pet."

His eyes widened briefly before he broke into a smile. He was delighted that Belinda was asserting what she wanted. "As you so command, Domina."

He unbuttoned his billowing white cotton shirt, folded it and placed it next to her dress.

"Come here, pet," she said.

He knelt by the bathtub.

She drank in his dashing figure. Desire built within her for this man, her handsome husband. "Touch me, pet", she said.

He dipped his hand into the balmy bathwater and reached down.

She spread her legs wide and placed one foot on each side of the tub,

Alexander brought his hand to the space between her legs and found her clit. He began to apply firm pressure in circles to the sensitive spot. He knew that Belinda needed the immediate relief of climax today. He switched it up and rubbed up and down with rough strokes.

Soon enough, her hips began to buck up and down. "Oh pet, just like that," she moaned in pure delight.

He kept up his attentions, her hips writhing all the while to maintain the best position.

She felt a delicious pressure building within her.

With every stroke from Alexander, the wonderful sensation spread to every inch of her body until it was all she could do but release the pressure and allow herself to fall down down down into that palace of pleasure. "Pet...don't stop...don't stop," she commanded through hooded eyelids.

Alexander kept up his motions, moving faster and faster to ensure Belinda received the maximum amount of pleasure possible.

She felt the exquisite pleasure growing inside her again. And again, she moaned in ecstasy as her orgasm radiated throughout her.

Alexander brought her to orgasm so many times that she lost count.

Eventually, she said, "Thank you, pet. You have provided me with the most wonderful relief. But alas, this water is getting cold and I should like to rest."

Alexander helped her out of the tub and dried her off with a heated fluffy towel.

She looked down at him from where he was drying her feet and asked, "Say, what was that lovely perfume that was in the bath?"

"That's a mix of jasmine and frankincense." He rubbed between each of her toes with fastidious attention.

"Oh, it does smell very nice," she said dreamily. "I should like to bathe with that again more generally."

"That can be arranged, Domina," he said with a smile.

He pulled a bathrobe from the cupboard and wrapped it around her. Then he reached into the closet, retrieved his shirt and put it on.

"How do you feel?" he asked.

"Better now, thank you."

It was true, Alexander's attentions had taken her mind off the pain and now she found that it didn't hurt as much as it had before. "Though I am rather sleepy," she added with a smile.

"I expected as much," he nodded.

"I should take you back to your chambers."

"Yes please, pet," she said.

He opened the door before lifting her so she was cradled in his arms. Then he headed out of the bathroom, through his chambers and into the corridor. A few minutes later and they were in Belinda's bedchamber. He deposited her gently on the bed and tucked her in.

"Thank you, pet," she murmured sleepily.

She must have been ever so tired as the next thing she could remember was opening her eyes and the room being in total darkness.

She turned her head to the main windows. Moonlight streamed through the latticed panes.

She lay and considered the events of the day. She had been in so much pain earlier from her cramps and the frustration at being out of laudanum had been intense. Alexander's idea, however, had proven to be most worthwhile indeed. The sweet relief he had brought her to again and again had soothed her and quelled a not insignificant proportion of her pain.

She was feeling less groggy now, though not her full self.

Her stomach rumbled. She hadn't eaten since luncheon.

She propped herself up on the pillows and rang the bell for a maid.

A few minutes went by and then Alexander entered the room.

Belinda laughed. "You're not a maid!"

"No, I'm not," he said. "But I told the staff to let me know when you had awakened."

There was a meowing sound from the hallway. Then Gus bounded into the room and leapt onto the bed.

Alexander lit a candle on the bureau near the door.

"How are you feeling?" He asked.

"A fair amount better, thank you," she said. She stroked Gus affectionately on the back.

"I'm glad to hear it."

"Though I am getting hungry now."

"Never fear, I'll have the servants bring something. What would you like?"

"Ooh, has cook any roast chicken? Or sausages?" she said. "Or some sort of good meat, whatever she has to hand."

Alexander nodded. "I shall be sure to ask. Surely she will have something of that nature. Can I get you anything else? Some reading material perhaps?"

She tilted her head in consideration. "Yes please, I've got *the Mysteries of Udolpho* on the go. I left it in the library last I remember."

"I'll get that for you."

"Thank you. That is all for now," she said with a small smile.

"As you so command." He gave a playful bow and exited the room.

CHAPTER THIRTY THREE

Belinda looked at Alexander through hooded lids. Her whole entire being was brimming with desire.

From where he knelt on the floor in front of her, Alexander could see her swooping velvet skirts and satin bodice. She was a beautiful vision, his Domina.

She crooned down at him, "Now, pet, rub my feet."

Alexander smiled to himself. This was one of his most favourite activities in all the world. He took her left foot between his hands and placed firm circles on the sole.

Belinda let forth a moan of contentment.

Alexander continued his ministrations, sometimes focusing on the ball of the foot, and other times the heel and arch.

"That's good, pet. You are most talented," Belinda cooed.

Alexander's cock lifted at the praise. He switched his attentions to Belinda's other foot, repeating the process of firm circles applied to every inch of the sole.

Belinda moaned in delight. Eventually, she said, "You are most skilled at giving foot rubs, pet. But now I would like for you to worship my cunny with that sweet, devious tongue of yours."

"At once, Domina," Alexander said.

She pulled her skirts up part way and he dove in.

The velvet of her skirts was like a sensuous tickle against the bare skin of his back.

Alexander groaned against the soft skin of her calf. He placed reverential kisses to each leg, alternating sides until he reached that glorious, secret place betwixt her legs.

Then he placed firm circles, with his hands, on her calves and to the backs of her knees.

Belinda let forth a moan of delight. "You do that so well," she praised.

Again, Alexander's cock couldn't help but stir at her honeyed words.

And now it was time for the best part of the evening.

He nuzzled against her thatched mound. Oh how he adored this reminder that she was all woman, woman, woman!

Then he moved southwards to her glorious cunny.

She spread her legs wide, wide, wide for his tongue. She was going to stake her claim on her pleasure.

He moved his tongue between her soft, fleshy labia.

She was sopping wet already.

With gentle deftness, he found her pleasure pearl and placed soft kisses upon it.

Belinda shivered in anticipation.

Alexander smiled into her cunny. He was glad that she was enjoying herself, that she was able to feel such pleasures within her own body. And he rejoiced in the fact that it was his privilege to give those pleasures to her tonight.

He suckled on her clit with a featherlight intensity.

Alexander relished how sweet Belinda's cunny tasted. It was like molasses and strawberries and something he couldn't quite place. She was truly a delicious woman.

Belinda gasped in pleasure at his ministrations. "That's it, just like that, pet," she said.

Ever the obedient submissive, Alexander did as he was bid and kept up his attentions on her clit.

She moaned again and again and again as climax after climax rippled throughout her body.

Eventually, Belinda opened her eyes and looked down towards Alexander.

His well-toned buttocks and legs poked out from beneath her skirts.

"You've been most excellent at your worship this evening, pet. I think it's time you have a reward. What do you say, pet?"

Alexander removed his head from Belinda's velvet skirts. He looked up at Belinda with reverence. "Yes please, Domina," he said huskily.

"Very well," Belinda said. "You may join me on this settee. And lay down on your back."

Alexander climbed up and obeyed Belinda's instructions so that was on the settee with his back propped against the armrest.

Belinda gazed down at him with an affectionate smile on her face. "Spread your legs, pet."

He complied with swift eagerness.

She turned around on her side of the settee so that she was facing directly opposite him. Then, without any warning, she brought her feet towards his throbbing, hard cock. She glaced the sole of one foot over his cock, so that she could just barely feel his smooth silken skin and the delicious hardness underneath.

Alexander let forth a surprised whimper.

Belinda giggled. She brought Alexander's cock between her feet and teased him with exquisitely gentle movements.

At Belinda's touch, Alexander helplessly felt a delectable warmth build within him. He adored being here with this wonderful woman and being with her in ways he never thought possible.

Chapter Thirty Four

Dearest sister,

I am coming up to Edinburgh next month. If you are at Faversham Hall then I would be delighted to see how you are going. Do let me know if you'll be present and I shall make the necessary arrangements with all manner of expediency.

I remain your most affectionate brother.

Xavier

Belinda scrawled an affirmative reply and sealed the parchment with the now familiar Faversham emblem of a ducal coronet and two bulls as supporters. Then she placed it in her outgoing correspondence box, ready for a footman to collect and send it on its long journey southwards.

She lifted herself from the chair and padded to the door. It was time indeed to find her beloved husband for their phaeton ride.

It was a brisk morning. The air was fresh over the moorland and the upper branches of the silver birch trees rustled in the crisp gusts.

Inside the phaeton, however, Belinda was toasty warm underneath the heavy tartan blanket around her legs.

Alexander sat next to her with his hands on the reins.

Belinda enjoyed being here with him like this;. Despite herself, she had come to find that he wasn't the cold-hearted duke so many on the ton said he was. Or at least, his reputation wasn't the whole story. He had a fierce loyalty and an overwhelming sense of duty. His need to protect her was second to none, even though it had disastrously misfired at the start of their marriage. So much had changed in the past six months since she first came up to Yorkshire. In fact, she could hardly imagine her life without Alexander now.

"I have a landowners meeting to attend in Newcastle. It's three days carriage ride away, so I'd understand if you'd rather stay here. But would you like to come with me?" Alexander asked. He deftly steered the horses round a bend.

"Ah yes please," she said. "Perhaps we can try my idea with the birching?"

"I do like the sound of that."

"And I shall enjoy seeing Newcastle. I've never been further north than Yorkshire before. In fact, I'd never been further north than Norfolk before I came up to Faversham Abbey."

Alexander turned and looked at her with slightly widened eyes, for a beat, before returning his attention to the path ahead. "Really?" He asked. "I must say, you have far more courage than I ever estimated."

Belinda quirked an eyebrow and guffawed in surprise. "You do flatter me with faint praise, sir."

"Alright, I'll admit that I put that clumsily. What I should've said is that I wouldn't have expected you to journey somewhere to which you'd never been before to try to find someone you barely knew, especially when -" Alexander broke off and sighed ruefully before continuing - "The person in question had made a real rum show of how he treated you. A very poor show indeed."

"That is true," Belinda said with seriousness. "Which makes it a sign of my tenacity. Whatever happened, I had to know for myself. I wasn't going to spend my whole life waiting and not knowing. Even if you had turned me away, at least I would've tried." Her voice turned lighter. "And if you had turned me away, I would've simply gone back down south and made my way through the entire stock at Cookson's. Plus other bonbons of London."

Alexander wasn't sure whether or not he should laugh, so he decided to keep a straight face. "Other bonbons of London?" he questioned.

"Yes," she replied with a smile. "Other bonbons of London. The Everaline Club. The theatres. Vauxhall Gardens. Those last two we simply must go to when we're back down south."

"We shall go there, don't you worry about that," he said.

"I look forward to it."

The pair went along in companionable silence for a few moments.

Then, Belinda said, "There's so much I wish for us to do together, so many places I wish for us to go." She rubbed one of her dainty hands affectionately on his muscular, well-formed thigh.

Alexander let forth a moan of pure excitement and anticipation.

All things would come in good time. Yes, all in good time.

Chapter Thirty Five

"Dauntsey won't be coming with us," Belinda said from the library settee. "She's hurt her ankle and cannot walk easily for the moment." She reached down to where Gus sat next to her and gave him an affectionate pat.

"That's a shame. Are you sure you still want to come? It might be more difficult if you don't have your lady's maid with you," Alexander said as he stood by the fireplace.

Belinda rose from the settee and made her way over to her husband.

"Ah, it won't be much of a bother. Most women in this country don't have a ladies maid at all, and there'll still be the footmen." She smirked and gave Alexander's pert buttocks a firm squeeze. "And you too of course, my gorgeous husband."

"That's very true, my sweet wife." He brought her dainty hand to his lips and placed a reverential kiss atop it.

A couple of days later, when the carriage was fully loaded and Miss Dauntsey was tucked up in her Faversham Abbey bed, it was time to begin the journey to Newcastle.

The first part of the ride, through the moorland near the estate, was unremarkable enough.

Half a day's travel saw them reach the village of Little Potterington where they spent the night at an unassuming coaching inn.

Given the time of year, not many other people were around when they walked through the dingy taproom.

"This way, your Graces," said the portly innkeeper. He led the couple up a sturdy set of oaken stairs and along a whitewashed narrow corridor.

When they reached a large brown door, the innkeeper drew to a halt. He unlocked the door and swung it open. "The master suite, your Graces," he said with pride. Then he handed the key to Alexander. "The maids will be up with some victuals within the half hour. And please, if there's anything we can help with, do let us know. I trust you will be most comfortable here." He gave a deep bow and headed back down the corridor, leaving Alexander and Belinda alone.

Belinda turned to her husband and said, "Come with me. I have a most delightful idea."

"Do you, now?" Alexander murmured with a wicked smile upon his face.

"Yes I do," she said. She took him by the hand and led him towards the settee close to the fireplace.

They sat together side by side.

Belinda reached out to his toned, muscular knee and placed firm, proprietary strokes atop it.

He tilted his head towards her and murmured in her ear. "So, what was this most delightful idea of yours?"

"Well, do you recall when I spoke of giving you a birching?" she asked with a grin.

He bit his lip. "I do recall that conversation, yes."

"What do you say if we try it now?"

"I would like that very much indeed," he replied, his eyes shining bright.

She took his hand between her own and placed a fierce kiss atop it. "Then we have no time to waste, my sweet."

He broke into a broad smile and gave a nod.

Belinda gestured to the writing desk on the other side of the room. "Go to the desk, unfasten your breeches and then bend over and brace yourself, pet."

Alexander raised himself to standing and made his way over to the desk. Then he did precisely as his beloved Domina bid and assumed her desired position.

Belinda remained on the settee and cast her gaze over the delicious sight in front of her. She loved it when Alexander was like this, following her every command and doing his utmost to be a good pet for her. And he was oh so easy on the eye as well, with his toned body, dark hair and hawk like features. She could sit and stare at this gorgeous man all day. But the night could only ever be this young once and she wanted to make sure she had time for the main event. The long-anticipated birching at an inn.

She ached to get her hands on him.

She raised herself from the settee and padded over to her pet. She reached towards his pantaloons and pulled them down so they were around his knees. Then she rubbed her hands along his well-toned thighs.

He whimpered at the touch. "Domina -"

"Don't worry. I've got you, pet," she cooed. "You're safe in my hands, these hands of mine."

She relished the way he felt beneath her dainty hands and fingers. Every delicious inch of him was hers hers hers. From the tips of his toes to the hairs of his head and all points in between.

She continued her firm attentions on his thighs before moving upwards to his buttocks. Like his thighs, his buttocks were well-toned, fine specimens of masculine power. How wonderful they were!

But even more than to feel the deliciousness of his thighs and buttocks, she wanted to make sure they were good and properly disciplined. That they and their owner would well remember who was in charge. It was time to apply the birch.

She removed her hands from Alexander.

He moaned at the loss of her touch.

She sauntered over to the travelling chest Alexander had neatly packed. She rummaged through it and found the velvet bag she was looking for.

A small smile quirked on her face.

She undid the rope ties of the velvet bag to reveal a sturdy wooden switch, about eight inches long. She took it in her hand. It was supple to the touch.

She swished it a few times in the air. There was a surprisingly deceptive amount of give within its birches.

Alexander tilted his head towards the sound. His cheeks reddened when he realised it was the switch.

Belinda nodded and strode over towards him. "Oh yes, that is exactly what you think it is. It's for you, pet."

She rolled up his shirt so it sat just above his buttocks. "Are you ready, pet?" she asked.

"Yes, Domina," he replied.

"Very well." Without further ado, Belinda brought the birch down on his shapely buttocks.

It resounded with a thwack.

Alexander let forth a deep moan that was half surprise and half delight.

Belinda giggled. "You like that, do you pet?"

"Very much indeed, Domina."

"Then you leave me no option but to oblige you." She brought the birch down again on his buttocks, slightly harder this time.

He let forth another moan.

Then, before Alexander had a chance to regain his breath, Belinda brought the birch down thrice in quick succession. Each time, the birch left a rosy pink mark behind on his skin.

Belinda marvelled at her handiwork.

She brought the birch down again on Alexander's buttocks, one two three four five.

Alexander let forth a stammering groan.

Belinda kept up the strokes of the birch until his arse was cherry blossom pink all over. She drew back and put the switch down on the desk.

She rubbed a reassuring hand on Alexander's back. "There, all done," she cooed in Alexander's ear. "You did so so well, I'm very proud of you, my sweet pet."

He turned his head towards hers a little. His cheeks were red with exertion and his eyes were slightly hooded. But he hadn't been crying.

Belinda hadn't wanted to exert more force than she needed to have her desired effect. After all, this session had been about firm discipline and a reminder that his Domina was in charge. And she had certainly made sure Alexander knew that fact.

Alexander opened his eyes fully and focused his hawklike gaze upon her. "That was incredible, thank you."

She gave a satisfied smile. "I'm very glad you liked it."

Alexander straightened himself up and turned around to face her. He took her in his arms and placed a fierce kiss on her lips.

Belinda wished she could kiss Alexander like this morning, noon and night. He was the most wonderful man in her mind. But her duchess' duties and the journey to the landowner's meeting awaited her tomorrow. So she would take all the pleasure and delight she could with Alexander tonight.

CHAPTER THIRTY SIX

T he carriage pulled up on the cobblestones with a slight jolt.

It had been a rough ride through the moors ever since Little Potterington and the weather was unrelentingly harsh.

Belinda twitched back the damask curtain and peeped out. Not that she could see much of anything at all, what with the raindrops pattering down the window and the black of the night beyond.

Alexander stroked her thigh through her heavy velvet cloak and glanced out through the window. "You stay here, darling, and I'll talk to our men about what we are to do tonight."

"Of course," she said with a smile.

Alexander opened the carriage door and darted down onto the cobblestones. Then, he quickly shut the door behind him.

Belinda was alone for the first time in hours. Yet she did not feel afraid. She was inside, safe though not very warm, and Alexander would not do anything to let her come to harm. That she knew for sure.

She heard men's voices conferring outside. That must be Alexander and the coachmen.

"Diabolical weather tonight, your Grace," bellowed one of the Faversham men.

"Yes, yes -" Alexander began.

But Belinda did not hear much else of what he said as his voice grew fainter and fainter. Probably he was heading towards a coaching inn, in search of some rooms for the night.

Somewhere in the background, a horse neighed.

Perhaps it was in a stable nearby, she told herself.

Then there was a shout. It sounded like a man's voice. She couldn't make out the words that were said, but whoever it was sounded angry.

Belinda's stomach grew uneasy. Something here didn't feel quite right.

Another shout, this time from a different man's voice. Again, the words themselves were unintelligible but the tone was furious.

A church bell clanged overhead in the ferocious wind.

Then there was the sound of some jostling, followed by an almighty thud.

And more male shouting.

And then something she hadn't wanted to hear at all. The sound of Alexander yelling. This time, she could make out the words.

"No, stop that!" Alexander bellowed.

Belinda's stomach twisted even tighter now. Who was Alexander yelling at? And why? What did he want them to stop?

Another man said something in reply. It was muffled and Belinda couldn't make him out over the howling of the wind.

Then Alexander shouted again. "Unhand me, you bastard!"

The next sounds Belinda heard were some punches being applied to somebody's flesh, followed by the crunching thud of a body hitting cobblestones.

And then a voice that wasn't Alexander's jeered, clear as day, "There you are, your Grace. See if you can get yourself out of that one, whether it's from a bastard or not!"

Belinda's heart lurched in horror. She had to do something. Anything.

She recalled that Alexander kept a pistol in the drawer underneath the seat. He had expressly told her it was only for absolute emergencies. In fact, she couldn't recall ever having seen him fire any sort of gun. Unlike Edgar and Xavier, her husband was not one for shooting pheasants or grouse.

She reached down and opened the wooden drawer, finding a sturdy pistol within. She took the pistol in her hand and peeped out of the curtain to her left. Two cloaked figures stood in menacing poses. She did not recognise them. Whoever they were, they looked like bad news. At their feet lay a figure sprawled on the cobblestones. A very familiar figure indeed.

Without hesitation, she flung the carriage door open and clambered down onto the street. It was difficult to see much of anything through the driving rain, though the footmen seemed to be nowhere in sight. Just the four of them, then.

Her, Alexander and the two shadowy cloaked figures looming above him.

One of the figures had stepped on Alexander's leg, pinning him to the slippery ground.

The other, about eight inches taller than the first, stood to the side and leered down over her husband.

"Give us all your money," the taller one bellowed in a crisp accent, not too far removed from what one would hear on the playing fields of Eton.

"I will, I will," Alexander gasped in agony.

Belinda grimaced to hear the pain in his voice.

Alexander continued speaking, "I wasn't carrying any, other than what you've already taken from me."

The taller figure let forth a derisive splutter. "Eight guineas? Do you seriously expect me to believe a lord such as your fine self carries only eight guineas with him? Don't make me laugh."

"In fact," the shorter figure said, "I bet twenty guineas that you have hundreds of pounds in that there fancy carriage of yours." Despite his affected working class grammar, his cut glass tones gave the game away. It was all a ruse, he was just as high class as his partner in crime and almost as much of a toff as Alexander himself. They were a bunch of frauds, the pair of them. And terrifically stupid to boot. As if anyone would not be able to see right through them.

"No, no, there's nothing in the carriage, it's not worth your while," Alexander said.

"Oh no, I don't believe that for a second," the shorter man said. "I bet it's full of riches -"

"Or even some pretty lady." the taller man interjected.

"No, no, it's just me. Me and my men here tonight," Alexander ground out. "You already saw them go inside the inn, to make arrangements with the landlord. Just me alone now. You've got me where you want me, boys."

"You're lying," the taller man said.

None of the three seemed to have heard her as they carried on with their argument. Good, that gave her the upper hand in one important area. The element of surprise.

With light, prowling steps, she made her way towards Alexander and the cloaked figures.

When she was about two feet away, she pulled the pistol from her cloak and pointed it towards the assailants.

Then with all her might, she shouted, "Stop, or I shall shoot! Believe me, gentlemen, I am not afraid to end your lives tonight."

The cloaked figures turned towards her, the one who had been standing on Alexander's leg releasing him from the trap as he did so.

Shock overtook their features. In the dim light of the moon, their faces had a deathly pallor.

She held the gun steady, all the while battling with herself internally to conceal her terror. "I mean it! Now, go!"

The two assailants didn't need to hear any more. They turned tail and scarpered. Their footsteps echoed on the cobblestones, loudly at first and then fainter and fainter until, at last, all was silent and Belinda and Alexander were alone together.

Alexander turned his head towards Belinda and squinted up at her through the dimness of the night.

Belinda gasped at the sight that met her eyes. It was much worse than she had at first assumed. Alexander's face was a mess of blood and mud. His lip was puffy and he was sporting a mighty fine black right eye.

"Belinda -" he began.

She lowered herself so that she was kneeling beside him on the cobblestones. Her dress was going to get soggy, but she didn't care. Alexander was safe and that was what counted.

She reached out to him and touched his bleeding face.

Alexander seethed a little in pain. "Don't, please, it hurts."

She withdrew her hand as though she had touched a roaring open flame. "Sorry," she said. "I just can't bear to see you like this." Her lip quivered but for now, she held herself together. She needed to stay strong for him, to not let him see her concern and how terrified she was. He was the one who had been so viciously attacked, after all. Now, her focus had to be on helping him and not on her own emotions.

"Could you help me up?" he said.

"Oh of course, of course," she said. She bustled to assist him, wrapping her arm around his shoulders and offering him her hand.

He grasped onto her and slowly raised himself to his feet.

Once he was steady on the ground, he let go of her.

She examined him closely from this new angle. He looked rather the worse for wear. But he also at least seemed able to take control of himself. He was not as badly hurt as she had feared. Still, her cheeks were clenched and her stomach was twisting itself into knots. Her heart beat twenty to the dozen underneath her gown.

Alexander took her in his arms. "Belinda!" he growled. "That was bloody, bloody stupid. Don't you ever do a thing like that again." Then his voice softened. "But also rather brilliant. Thank you."

He leaned down and placed a kiss upon her forehead. "I mean it though, don't ever do anything like that again. You could have been killed."

At that moment, two of the Faversham footmen emerged from the door of the inn.

"Your Graces, please follow -" the first footman said. He broke off when he saw the agitated stance of his employers.

The other footman's mouth widened in shock when he saw Alexander's bloodied and bruised face. "What's happened?" he asked.

"Some footpads," Alexander said.

Two sets of eyebrows shot up.

"Your Grace, which way did they go?" one footman asked.

"Yes, tell us and we'll apprehend them. I'd like to give those jokers a taste of their own medicine, give them what for," the other footman said.

Alexander held up placating hands. "No, no, it's quite alright. Thank you for your concern, but there's been enough fighting for one night and I won't have you risking yourselves on my account. I'd rather we all get inside and put this behind us. Please set the horses and carriage in the stables and then have the rest of the night to yourselves."

The footmen looked sceptical.

"Very well, your Grace. If you are quite sure," the first footman said.

"But if you change your mind, I would really like to set my hands on them," the other footman added.

"We both would," the first footman said.

Then the pair bowed and went to get things in motion with the ostlers.

Belinda took Alexander by the hand and together they headed towards the inn.

Once they were inside, Belinda found a maid and mentioned the Faversham booking.

Alexander, meanwhile, hung back in the shadows. It wouldn't do to let all and sundry see how he'd come off the worst in the run-in with those footpads. Too many awkward questions.

The maid smiled and said, "Please follow me, your Graces."

Less than a minute passed and Alexander and Belinda were entering a wood panelled chamber with a dining table laid near the hearth. Close to the bay window, a four poster bed draped with yellow and cream damask sat imposingly. A flaming candle stood in each corner of the room.

Belinda turned to the maid. "Can you send up a bowl of warm water and some soap, please. Also whiskey or another spirit, whatever you have to hand."

The maid nodded and gave a curtsey. "Yes, madame." Then she left the room and Alexander and Belinda were alone together again.

Belinda shut the door and made her way over to where Alexander stood.

She wrapped her arms around him.

He took her within his arms and nuzzled his face into her hair.

Together, they stood like that for several minutes. Neither saying a single word the entire time.

Belinda felt her eyes begin to wetten. Outside in the street and when dealing with the maid, she had been able to hold herself together and keep her emotions at bay. But now she and Alexander were the only two people in the room, she could no longer wear the impassive visage of a duchess on display.

Her lower lip trembled and quivered. Without thinking, she let out a sob.

Alexander reached up, with one hand, behind her neck and began to stroke her scalp.

She kept sobbing and his shoulder began to grow wet from her tears.

"Please don't worry, I will be fine," he said gruffly.

"How can I not worry? I love you, don't you know it!" she sniffled.

Alexander's mouth gaped open in shock.

If Belinda hadn't been in tears and if her husband's face wasn't covered in blood, mud and wounds, she might have laughed. As it was, it was all she could do but fight to stay present in the situation, to stay present for Alexander.

For his part, Alexander could not help but let a note of rapturous joy seep into his voice. "Is this true? That you love me?"

"Yes," she said firmly through her tears.

"Then do you see what this means? We can live together happily as one," he said in tones of wonderment.

"I hate how this has happened, that you found out like this." She gulped. "I do not think I even realised myself tonight. Which is terrible. But I could hear you were under threat and I knew, I just knew that I would do anything, anything in all the world to save you from harm."

Alexander gave a soft smile. "It doesn't matter how you came to realise. What matters now is that we don't have any impediment to being together properly, forever."

"But I will probably never be able to bear you an heir. Is that not an impediment?"

"No, it doesn't matter to me. The title can always go another way, through another line of the family. And who is to say I'd even be able to sire a child with anyone else. I've never fathered a child before. What matters to me, Belinda, is you, us together. That's what I care about."

"Are you quite sure? That this is what you want?" she asked.

"More sure than anything I've ever been in all my life," he said.

Her tears had begun to dry. She lifted her hands upwards and took his chin between her hands. "Oh Alexander, we will truly be together as one. I love you so so much."

"And I love you, my darling." He kissed her on the forehead.

A knock at the door broke them apart.

Belinda rubbed at her eyes to prepare herself for the servants.

Alexander looked at her with concern. "I'll get it." He made for the door.

"No, it has to be me Alexander. When your face is as badly beaten up as yours is right now, the inn staff and servants are only going to ask questions."

"But Belinda -" Alexander interjected.

Another knock at the door.

"Please, let me do this," Belinda said.

Alexander sighed internally and then gave a nod of assent. "Very well." He turned away and cast his eyes towards the sleeping area.

Belinda cried out, "Enter!"

The maid from before, accompanied by another maid, came in carrying several platters of food. A third maid followed them with a bowl of hot water, soap and some sort of bottle of spirits.

The maids placed their food cargo on the sideboard and the rest on the long table and then left as quickly as they had arrived.

Belinda walked over to Alexander and placed a gentle hand on his shoulder.

He turned his neck a little so he could get a better look at her.

"Please, let me take care of you," she said.

He nodded and turned around to face her. Then he took her free hand in his. He brought it to his lips and placed a fierce kiss upon it.

Together, they made their way over to the long table and sat down on the bench next to it.

Belinda took a towel, dipped it in the bowl of hot water, and dabbed it against Alexander's muddy, blood-sodden face.

In the flickering candlelight, some of his wounds appeared less severe than they would have in the cold light of day. Even so, Belinda couldn't help but wince at how they covered so much of his face.

With gentle strokes, she cleaned away the streaks of mud and blood.

He began to bear a stronger resemblance to himself.

"There, that's better," she said. "How do you feel now?"

"A little less dazed, perhaps. But please don't worry about me, I can handle it."

"Alexander," she said sternly. "I know you can handle it. However, I don't want you to suffer unnecessarily." Her voice became gentler. "Would you like some laudanum? I have some in my travel bag."

"No, no, it's quite alright," he said.

"As long as you're sure."

"Yes, I'm sure," he replied.

She kept clearing away the mess of blood and mud.

Eventually, his face was clear of the grime.

Belinda gave a small nod of satisfaction at her handiwork. She put the cleaning supplies down on the table and pushed them away. "Would you like some food?" she asked.

"Yes, please. I'm starving. I can't remember when I last ate," Alexander said.

Belinda nodded. She went to get a plate for Alexander.

But before she had a chance to finish standing up, Alexander said, "I'll get it, don't worry."

Alexander raised himself to his feet, fetched two plates from the sideboard and placed them in front of his and Belinda's chairs. Then he brought over the platters.

They served themselves small pork pies, pickled onions and slices of cheese.

Morning broke and outside the birds began to chirrup.

Inside their room at the inn, Alexander lay asleep enwrapped in Belinda's arms.

Belinda had woken up first. She cast her mind back to the night before. It had been full of drama.

She had never before witnessed such a violent attack. Her life had been sheltered and cocooned. When she had heard those men threatening Alexander, she had feared for his very life. And seeing all that blood on him had been truly harrowing. Yet, she had risen to the occasion and had made sure he was cared for. Most unexpectedly of all, which she would never have predicted in a million years, the events of last night had led her to admit to both Alexander and herself what her soul had known for a long time. She loved Alexander Faversham. Wholly and completely. And with her declaration, she and Alexander would truly be husband and wife. A new chapter in their lives was beginning. Even in the darkest of events, a sliver of light had fought through.

She got up from the bed and padded to the windows. She pulled one of the shutters back ever so slightly and peeped out at the word beyond.

Unlike last night, the street was serene and peaceful. A few agricultural labourers trundled their carts, ready to head off to the day's work on the fields and farms beyond.

There was no sign of last night's footpads. Even so, the sight of the street below made her stomach twist. She felt uneasy. What if the footpads came back? What if they were still lurking elsewhere in the village?

From the bed, she could hear a shuffling sound. Alexander was rousing from his slumber.

He sat up and called out to her groggily. "Belinda, what are you doing?"

She turned around and gave him a small smile. "Good morning to you too, dear husband."

He let out a laugh. "Good morning, darling wife! Why are you out of bed, prowling around by the windows?" He gestured to her loosely with his right hand.

Belinda's face took on a more serious expression. "This doesn't feel right. Us hanging around here, after what those cursed footpads did to you. I don't think we should hang around."

"I can see your point," Alexander said. "We should have breakfast here and then get back on the road. Back to the Abbey. I'd really rather just get home after last night's run-in with those bastards."

Belinda nodded. She made her way over to the bed and placed her arms around Alexander. "Yes, I think that's very wise indeed, dear husband."

"And I would much rather spend time with my beautiful wife than in some stodgy landowners' meeting." He placed a kiss on her cheek.

She giggled. "Alexander!"

"Well, it's true. If the events of last night have shown me anything, it's that time is limited, all our time is limited, and things can change at any moment, often on the back of factors we can barely even control. And so I don't want to waste time on things that don't matter all that much. I'd far rather spend my time with the people that matter, doing the things that matter."

"So no landowners' meeting tomorrow?" she asked with a grin.

"No, no landowners' meeting" He kissed her on the cheek. "That can wait. I'll send an apology and perhaps send a representative instead to the next one."

"You are most wise indeed," Belinda said. She took Alexander's hand in her own and placed a searing kiss atop it. "Can I get you anything this morning?" she asked.

"Let's just get ready, have breakfast and go," he said. "I'll go and talk to our men and then we'll be on our way soon.

Belinda nodded. Despite the dramatic and confronting attack of the night before, she felt that she and Alexander had found a new forward. Together. United as one. And she could hardly wait.

⁂

Back at Faversham Abbey, after a rushed ride through the moors, the Great Hall was a flurry of activity.

Belinda and Alexander made a beeline for the stairs.

The butler scurried after them. "Your Graces, can I make any arrangements?"

Belinda turned to him. "Yes, please have the maids prepare my chambers for his Grace and I."

The butler gave a bow. "Very good, your Grace." He bustled off to perform his task.

Belinda and Alexander headed to his chambers. Best give the maids a chance to get things up and running.

Once the door was shut behind them and they were away from the eyes of the servants, Belinda took Alexander within her arms. "Here, let me look after you," she said.

Alexander let himself go limp in her arms.

The last couple of days had been intense and stressful beyond belief. Everything between the pair had turned out alright in the end. But the journey to get there had been a painful one.

He placed a kiss atop her head. "I should look after you, too," he said.

"We can both look after each other," she said.

He held her tighter. He mumbled something into her hair that she couldn't quite discern.

They stood like that for several minutes, saying nothing and simply being in one another's presence.

Eventually, Alexander broke the silence. "It's so good to be home with you, my darling," he said.

She rubbed her hands soothingly across his back. "I love being here with you, my sweet Alexander. Is there anything I can get for you?"

"Maybe we should ring for some refreshments."

She nodded and broke apart from him briefly to pull the servants' bell cord. Then she returned and he took her in his arms.

They stayed like that until a servant knocked at the door.

CHAPTER THIRTY SEVEN

A week later, when Alexander's wounds had mostly healed, Belinda and Alexander were in the herb garden.

She pushed him against the stone wall of the garden.

Not a soul was around, per Alexander's command given to all staff earlier in the day.

The air was brisk today but the imminent coming of spring made being outside bearable.

Besides, Alexander had always wanted to do something like this, so he wasn't about to let a little cold spoil things.

Belinda's velvet skirts rustled as she leaned against him.

Alexander felt their movement against his legs. It was funny, on so many occasions had a lady's skirts brushed against his legs, when he was seated next to them at banquets or in a carriage. Yet it wasn't until Belinda that such a simple sensation built a burning need within him. Drove him wild with desire.

Belinda reached down to the spot where Alexander's legs met and ran her hands around the white cotton fabric of his pantaloons.

He groaned in delight at the unexpected sensation.

She giggled and leaned forward to murmur in his ear. "Oh, you like that do you, my sweet pet?"

"I do. Very much indeed, Domina," he said.

She ran her fingers around his pantaloons in a pitter patter, raindrop rhythm.

He let forth another groan. His hips bucked wildly towards hers.

She smiled in self-satisfaction. She loved to have Alexander like this beneath her hands, all needy and desperate with desire.

"Well, let's see how you like this," she said mischievously.

One by one, she undid the buttons on his pantaloons and the front fell down to reveal his sturdy cock.

It was already growing hard and rising to stand proud and erect.

Belinda looked down and licked her lips. He was oh so tantalising when he was like this.

She took Alexander's glorious cock between her hands.

He felt smooth to the touch, yet with a rough masculine power lurking beneath the surface.

She revelled in how he was so wonderfully formed.

She ran her fingers up and down his shaft.

He bucked his hips forwards at her touch.

Then she gripped his cock firmly between her palm and fingers. She pumped several times up and down, up and down, up and down.

He let forth a moan of desire.

She kept up her pumping motions on his shaft. She loved to have him under her control. It made her feel powerful and strong. "Oh you are mine, all mine," she cooed.

He gave a needy whine in response.

She giggled. She decided to switch things up and tease him. She took her hand away from his shaft.

He whimpered at the loss.

Then she glazed her fingers over the end of this cock. His precum was sticky beneath her fingers. She ran her fingertips around his slit so softly that she barely touched his skin.

But Alexander still moaned in delight at her teasing touches.

"That's it, I've got you," she crooned.

"Please, Domina." His voice was strained and tight with lust.

"Oh, but you are so pretty like this. All nice and hard and desperate for me. I could do this all day."

Alexander shivered at the intoxicating blend of her words and her feather-light touch.

Belinda kept up her attentions, enjoying his squirming and whimpering all the while.

With each touch of her fingers against his cock, Alexander bucked his hips in an attempt to be ever closer to his Domina.

Eventually, she took pity on him. She took his cock firmly in her grip and pumped. Slowly at first, then she built faster and faster into a frenzied crescendo.

His cheeks were scarlet red by now. He roared in wild abandon and spilled his seed on his chest and her hand.

Belinda giggled and reached inside her cape. She pulled out a cotton handkerchief and deftly cleaned her hand and Alexander's body.

She leaned into his ear and murmured, "Did you like that, my sweet pet?"

"Very much indeed, Domina," he said.

She nodded. "I am glad." She put the handkerchief away inside her cloak. "You may dress yourself."

Alexander duly did so and before too long, he was fully clothed. Nobody who had not witnessed their earlier escapade would have had any idea of what wicked delights had just transpired.

Belinda rubbed his back in soothing circles. "Come inside," she said. "We had best get you warm. And I should like to rest by the fire with you."

Alexander leant down and placed an affectionate kiss atop her forehead. "I should like that very much indeed, Domina."

Belinda took Alexander's leather gloved hands within her own and led him around the herb garden and up towards the house.

Soon enough, they were at the doors and crossing the threshold.

Belinda turned to a waiting footman. "Have a fire lit in the library please. And some hot chocolate brought up."

The footman bowed and hurried off to attend to his tasks.

Belinda pulled Alexander in for a searing kiss and took him within her arms.

She relished how he tasted of mint and molasses.

Once they had had their fill, the pair broke apart.

Alexander grinned shyly. He was feared on the ton, the cold-hearted duke, but here with his wife he was a lion tamed. Exactly the way he liked it.

Belinda pulled the servant's cord.

Mere moments later, a maid appeared from a side door. "Your Graces?" she asked.

"Here, please take our coats and cloaks," Belinda said.

The maid bustled around and did her job, before swiftly removing from the room and leaving the Favershams alone together again.

"Come, let's go to the library pet," Belinda said.

Alexander beamed internally at those words. They touched a deep chord somewhere inside him.

The fire blazed in front of them. It made for a real contrast to the brisk world outside.

Gus lay in front of it on one of his favourite blankets. Every occupant of the Abbey was doing all they could to get away from the chill this afternoon.

Alexander sat in just his shirt, pantaloons and socks.

Belinda, for her part, kept her velvet dress and stockings on.

Alexander's arms were wrapped around Belinda. She leant into his chest and placed her ear over his heart.

She could hear the steady, even beats of his heart. A re-assuring rhythm that all was well and all manner of things would be well.

She reached a hand up to his face and placed gentle strokes on his cheek. "I love you so so much, Alexander."

"And I love you too," he said with a smile. He drew her closer to him.

"Before I met you," Belinda said, "I had hoped to find love. But it seemed like such a distant proposition. So to find it and to find it with you has been truly wondrous."

"You had more faith than me. I hadn't even allowed myself to dare to think I could find such a love. You are truly a blessing, Belinda." He leant down and placed an affectionate kiss upon her forehead. "And now I cannot imagine my life without you."

"You won't ever have to again. We are going to be together forever. And ever."

"I cannot imagine anything better, darling." He placed another kiss on her forehead.

"Oh we are going to have the most wonderful life together, I just know it," she said. "We can be here at the Abbey, or sometimes down in London or Bath. We shall have phaetons and nature explorations and balls."

"And visits to friends and our animals and music and art."

"Of all kinds."

"Of all kinds," he agreed.

"And not forgetting Domina and pet. There will be lots and lots of that on the horizon," she said.

"No, we cannot forget Domina and pet."

She stroked his cheek with delicate yet proprietary movements.

Alexander chuckled. "You have it all planned out. And I like it. I really really like it. I like a woman who knows what she wants."

"Then it is most fortunate that I am your wife."

They lay close together on the settee and were at peace with the world. Though it was most unexpected and a long time in the making, their love was unbreakable and was bound to last the test of time.

CHAPTER THIRTY EIGHT

Horse hooves beat on the gravel.

Belinda and Alexander made their way through the main doors and out onto the driveway.

In the distance, a carriage in the familiar Weatherby purple made its way down the hill.

Alexander placed a protective arm around Belinda, his bruises from the footpads now faded away almost completely. He placed an affectionate kiss on her cheek.

The Weatherby carriage drew nearer and nearer until it drew to a halt outside the doors of the Abbey.

Xavier didn't bother waiting for the footmen to position the steps beneath the carriage door. Instead, he leapt down from the carriage with pizzazz in his step.

Trust her brother, thought Belinda.

Though she didn't see it from where she stood, Alexander quirked his lip briefly in wry amusement.

"Hello, brother!" Belinda exclaimed.

"Good afternoon, Weatherby," Alexander said.

"Hello Favershams!" Xavier made his way over to the couple. "And may I say how well and fine you both are looking."

Belinda laughed. "Thank you, brother."

"It's a pleasure to see you," Alexander said. He gestured behind himself. "Please do come inside."

Later that evening, when Xavier had received a most comprehensive tour of Faversham Abbey and a hearty dinner, the three sat around the fireplace in the retiring room. This wasn't a place Alexander and Belinda used much, they had little need when it was just the two of them, but it was perfect for hosting close family guests like Xavier.

The trio supped on a deep tawny port as they lounged about on the plush upholstered chairs.

Alexander reached down to the beagle nearest him and gave him an affectionate ruffle on the head.

The dog barked happily.

Xavier laughed. "He's a lively one, isn't he? I didn't even know you kept beagles, Faversham. How did that come about?"

"Now, I've had these two for five years or so. You know, I've never much been one for hunting but they were leftover from a litter the squire across the other side of the moor had. He didn't feel he needed so many pups to form a new pack of hounds. And these two -" He gestured to the dogs on the floor - "being the weakest in the litter, were not what the squire wanted to keep."

Xavier took a swig of port before saying, "I wouldn't have thought you'd have it in you, Faversham. You are a man of surprises."

Belinda grinned and leaned forward. "He is indeed. Many surprises indeed."

"And Belinda, is she full of surprises too?" Xavier asked playfully.

Alexander gave a tiny nod. "Yes, that is a fair way of putting it."

"Well, disclose them man! What surprises are they?" Xavier brought his glass of port to his lips again.

"Xavier!" Belinda exclaimed in mock outrage.

Alexander shook his head in jest. "As for that, I am not at liberty to disclose."

"Yes! A lady's secrets are her own!" she yelped again and then laughed.

"They are indeed. They are indeed," Xavier said sagely.

A small smile formed on Alexander's lips. He liked being here with Belinda. What was more, he could see how much her brother Xavier meant to her so for her to be able to be herself with him, and freely and openly in the presence of her brother, meant a lot to him.

⁕ ⁕ ⁕

The next day, when all three awoke with slightly sore heads from their previous night's port consumption, Belinda and Xavier sat on the settee in her chambers.

Belinda turned to her brother. "I've got a phaeton, would you like to go for a spin? I'll show you around the estate," she said.

"Yes, that sounds fun," Xavier said. "By the way, since when did you have a phaeton?"

"Alexander got me it, back in the autumn. I wish I'd had one earlier, they really are fun. Just don't ride them in the fog, that's my recommendation."

Xavier raised an eyebrow quizzically. "Don't go riding in the fog?"

"Yes, I speak from experience. I took a tumble riding in the fog, back in November."

"A tumble? Were you hurt? Are you alright now?" Xavier was flabbergasted.

"I was hurt, a bit. I banged my head and was out of it for four. I'm better now though," she said.

His face slackened into relief. "Well, I'm very glad to hear it!" he exclaimed.

"Maybe I shouldn't have just told you all that, it might not inspire much confidence." She gave a wry smile.

Xavier guffawed. "I should tell you about my carriage accidents!"

"*Your* carriage accidents? Clearly we don't talk enough."

Xavier laughed. "Clearly! Well, lead the way to your chariot of fire."

A short while later, they were in the stableyard.

Grooms and lads hustled up a bay mare to Belinda's phaeton.

Xavier took a three-hundred-and-sixty degree walk around the contraption. He let out an approving noise. "This is very nice. Yes, very nice indeed. You've done well with this one."

The phaeton's green metallic sides shone enticingly in the sunlight.

Belinda admired her carriage. Xavier was right, it was very nice and she had done well.

The horse now hitched up properly, Belinda and Xavier got into the phaeton.

She took the reins.

Soon enough, they were on their way out to the moorland.

"Are you out here often?" Xavier asked.

"Yes, I try to get out here at least every other day. Weather permitting. Once I'd recovered from the accident, it was one of the first things I wanted to do," she said.

"And did you do it?" he asked.

"Alexander was really hesitant for me to do it. But he knows I'm my own woman. So I did, within six weeks of the accident. Being out here, on the phaeton, it's too freeing for me to give it up so easily."

"I remember, when you were much younger, how much you loved horse riding."

"I did, yes. Riding out around Renfregh, that was one of my favourite things in all the world back then." She smiled at her moment of nostalgia. "It was once my condition started, when I had to stop horse riding, that was hard."

"I remember," Xavier said solemnly.

"But now I have the phaeton, it's a way for me to recapture that old feeling of the freedom that comes from riding about in the open air."

"I know that feeling well," he said.

They rode in silence for a few beats.

Then Belinda said, "I'm hoping to take the phaeton round at Renfregh, when we're next down there. Really go back to where my love of riding all started."

"That's an excellent idea," Xavier said with a smile. "Say, does Edgar know you've got this phaeton?"

"I did mention it in one of my letters to him. He was supportive and keen on me driving round Renfregh. Though I didn't tell him of the crash," she said.

Xavier's eyebrows raised. "So he doesn't know? Do you need me to keep it a secret?"

"No, it's fine. Alexander handled telling him. I knew Edgar would take it very hard and so I figured getting the reassurance from a Duke would carry more weight. I'd rather let my public face handle difficult conversations like that."

"Faversham is your public face?"

"Yes, it's one of the perks of being married to a Duke. I often like to handle things myself, but sometimes leaning on the ducal title makes life a little easier," she said.

Xavier chuckled, "I can only imagine what it would be like to have the name of a duke to lean on."

"Well, you have the name of an earl to lean on for many things."

"That's true. Only it doesn't come in very useful when I need to explain myself to said earl for some transgression or other."

"No, it doesn't. That's when you would need to get yourself a duke or maybe a marquess to come to the rescue."

He laughed. "That would be rather handy."

Belinda steered the phaeton round the bend that led towards the arboretum.

"This truly is beautiful country," Xavier said. "I can see why you love coming out here."

"It is indeed," she said. She was so happy here like this, riding next to her brother. With Xavier's visit, her two worlds, Weatherby and Faversham, had met truly and he had been able to see her as the duchess she now was. Yet she would always remain his sister, Belinda.

⁂

The fire in the library crackled.

Belinda and Xavier sat in front of it in plush armchairs.

"How is Edgar getting along?" Belinda asked. "We've exchanged some letters, but I can't help but feel it's mostly cursory. On both sides."

"About the same as ever," Xavier sighed. "He's running the estates well enough. But all the responsibility, it weighs him down."

"What can any of us do there, I suppose," Belinda said.

"I don't know if there's really anything we can do. I'm realistically the only one who potentially could, in our immediate family. And Edgar wouldn't want me sticking my oar in. There can only be one Earl of Weatherby at the end of the day."

Belinda pondered for a few moments, before saying, "It sounds like Edgar could do with a wife."

"Yes, it rather does." He took a sip of his port. "He's never really shown interest before, at least not to me, though."

"Judging by the season just gone, he isn't without his admirers on the ton. But he seems to spend most of his time glowering at the edges of ballrooms rather than taking part in the marriage mart proper. While I suspect at least some of his glowering was borne out of a desire to scare insalubrious suitors away from me-"

"It was, yes."

Belinda gave a small laugh before continuing. "I thought so. Yet also some of the glowering I believe is due to his discomfort and disinterest in the whole thing. As with so many bachelors on the ton, his appearances at the balls often seemed perfunctory."

Now it was Xavier's turn to laugh. "That's very well observed."

"Perhaps next season will be Edgar's season to make it all less perfunctory. Then again, there's no need for him to rush. No Countess at all is better than a bad one who will serve to drag him down," Belinda said.

"I concur."

Belinda tilted her head. "And what of Philomena? She seems in sour spirits judging by the letters I've received from her."

"Sour spirits!" Xavier exclaimed. "You can say that again. She doesn't seem to be happy about much of anything at the moment. Though it could be down to her age. And all the changes that have come about in light of your marriage."

"Yes, my being the first Weatherby to fly the nest and all that," Belinda said. "It's a difficult age, sixteen. Sometimes it simply has to be lived through. Though I wonder, does Philomena have much to do with Virginia and Margaret?"

"Not as far as I know. They were always closer with you, I thought."

Belinda nodded. "Yes, that's fair. I've always been close with them in a way I don't recall Philomena being. In recent times, they've been particularly helpful to me during the season and in the early days of my marriage. I think it's worth Philomena meeting with them, maybe they can help her get through some of these difficult years. As they are difficult years for any woman, not just Philomena. I'll write to them both."

"You are very sage. In only a few moments you've worked out some sort of plan to help Philomena that the rest of us hadn't figured out in months," Xavier said.

"It comes with experience," Belinda said with a small smile.

⁂

The day before Xavier was due to leave and resume his journey northwards to the Scottish capital, he and Belinda sat in her chambers.

A steaming pot of bohea tea sat on the table in front of them.

Gus was lying on a rug near the fireplace, unconsciously stretching himself out to take full advantage of the warmth from the flames.

Xavier turned to Belinda. "These past several days, I've come to realise something," he said.

"Oh, and what's that?" Belinda asked.

"How well suited you and Faversham are," he said.

Belinda smiled and nodded ever so slightly. "That came as a surprise to me too. Though she didn't mean it at all, Petunia Reynolds' meddling had a good outcome for probably the one and only time."

"Yes, the one and only time," Xavier chortled.

Belinda took a sip of her tea.

Xavier's face grew a little more serious before he continued speaking. "I do mean it though, you and Faversham seem much more well-fitted than any of us thought you would be, if I'm honest."

"Well, the moral of the story here, I believe, is that someone's reputation can precede them. But it doesn't mean that said reputation is the full truth." She took another sip of her tea before continuing speaking. "And on the matter of reputation, the whole concept is so flawed. The ton, in fact our entire society, places such great emphasis on a woman's reputation. That's why Alexander and I had to marry, after all, even though I hadn't actually done anything to jeopardise my reputation. Other than be in the wrong place at the wrong time with Petunia Reynolds on the scene. As for Alexander's reputation, I have come to learn so much of it isn't true at all and the rest has been twisted and exaggerated over the years by busybodies galore."

Xavier looked again at his sister. Yes, there was the intelligent young woman he knew so well. But now she had been changed by her marriage and she had new insights to offer. Insights and perspective on a wide world and way of being that to him, a bachelor, remained a mystery. He didn't think he wanted to marry yet but seeing his sister's marriage was making him think a little about the kind of bride he might wish to wed at some point in the future.

Belinda's voice broke him away from his thoughts. "Would you like another cup of tea?" she asked.

"Yes, yes please," he replied distractedly. His time with the Favershams had certainly given him a lot to think about.

From his spot on the floor, Gus rolled over and dozed on, oblivious to the pensive thoughts of the man a few feet away.

CHAPTER THIRTY NINE

The carriage trundled its way up the driveway. The horses strained against the steep gradient but soon enough they would be onto the easier roads of the moorland.

Inside, Belinda sat enwrapped in her luxurious bronze-colour velvet travel cloak.

Right next to her was Alexander.

They were on their way to Morworth Hall to visit Eunice and Percival. The Devitts, Violet and Michael, would also be there.

Belinda ran her dainty hand across his thigh, relishing his fine muscular formation all the while. Back and forth, back and forth she ran her hand.

Alexander let out a small moan. He tried to conceal it with a cough.

But Belinda was wise to exactly what her darling husband craved. "Oh you like that, do you? No need to be shy about it, dearest!" she purred.

"Yes, Domina," he said through hooded lashes.

"I am most glad to hear it," she said.

Her hand made its way upwards towards his groin. Then she glaced her fingertips over his cock.

He shuddered and let forth a needy whine.

She rejoiced at the sight of the bulge in his pantaloons. It was she who did this. She was the one who had made her husband, the very paragon of propriety, into a quivering pool of desire. Yes, the power and control were *hers*.

Alexander let forth another shuddering groan.

Belinda smiled to herself at his wanton reaction. His gorgeous cock was like satin under her dainty palm. How delectable!

She leaned across and claimed his neck in a searing kiss.

Alexander moaned at the delicious sensation of Belinda's sweet lips on his neck.

The carriage clattered on through the moorland.

Outside, the wind was whipping up a gale. But inside, the Favershams were warm and oblivious. Simply enjoying one another's company and the joy of being together as one.

Belinda pulled away from Alexander's neck for a few seconds. "Oh, you are most glorious like this, pet. Most glorious indeed."

Without further ado, she dove back into Alexander's neck and resumed her fiercely proprietary attentions.

Alexander let forth a moan of pleasure.

Belinda grinned into his neck. He was her husband, her pet and her love. And he was under her command, ready and willing to obey her every order.

When she had had her fill of his oh so delicious neck, she pulled away slightly and ran her hands down his chest in teasing strokes.

She moved her hands over the bulge in his pantaloons. A light touch that he could barely feel. But that drove him wild with desire.

"Please, Domina," his voice juddered.

"Oh I shall give it to you when I am good and ready. Don't you worry about that," Belinda said. She leaned into his neck again and nipped at him, all the while moving her dainty fingers around his cloth-covered cock with delicate strokes.

Alexander let forth a yelp of need.

Belinda giggled. She loved to have Alexander like this. At her mercy. At her command. Bound to obey her and to serve her. She kept up her wicked attentions.

Goosebumps of desire began to form on Alexander's forearms.

Belinda moved her hands to the buttons at the front of his pantaloons and undid them one by one. Her fingers met his bare naked flesh.

She ran her fingers along his silken skin. How she adored every inch of him. He was perfectly formed and he was all hers hers hers.

She reached down and her fingers met his cock. It stood hard and proud and erect. She ran her fingers around the slit, teasing and testing his responses.

He whimpered with desperate need and looked at her through hooded eyes. "Domina -"

"I've got you, I've got you," she cooed.

She ran her fingers up and down his shaft in pitter patter raindrops.

He shivered with desire.

She kept up her teasing motions for another minute or two. Then she leaned into his ear. "I know you like that, my sweet pet."

"Yes, Domina," he breathed.

"And I know you want sweet release."

He nodded desperately.

She continued. "But first I should like for your deviant hands to please me."

Alexander let forth a groan of sheer lust. "That can most certainly be arranged, Domina."

"Very well. Show me what you are made of."

She removed her hands from his cock and leant back against the plush carriage seat. She spread her legs wide and looked at him with expectant eyes.

A rakish grin overtook his features. He leant across and reached down to the place where her legs met. He ran his fingers through her soft bush.

She mewed a little at his touch.

He moved his fingers towards her slit and reached through to the plump folds of her labia. She was getting wet already.

He ran his fingers through her labia and reached her innermost core. With skilled deftness, he found her clit.

She bit her lip. "Yes, that's it pet."

He rubbed around her clit in teasing circles.

This was exactly what Belinda liked. Though she was wet before, Alexander's attentions made her completely sodden.

She bucked her hips upward, hungry for ever more of his touch.

He kept up his attentions on her clit.

A delicious pressure began to build in that special place between her legs. She let herself feel every inch of it fully. She did not want to deny herself even the tiniest little mote of pleasure. And, soon enough, she was falling down into that palace of pleasure. Her orgasm rippled through her and the exquisite ecstasy reached even the very tips of her fingers and toes.

She gazed at him through hooded eyes. "That's very good, very good indeed, pet."

He beamed at her words of praise. He kept up his motions on her clitoris, moving his finger sometimes in circles and other times up and down and in random shapes and patterns.

Belinda loved it all. Another orgasm built within her to a crescendo of pleasure. And then, when she had come down from that intoxicating high, another climax built within her and again she was falling down down down into that wondrous pool of pleasure and delight.

She lost count of how many times she reached those epic heights, such was her abandon to the power of sensation and the claim she staked over her own body.

When she had well and fully claimed her fill, she gazed down at Alexander. "That was most excellent, pet. You really outdid yourself. Now I do believe it's time for your reward."

She leaned down and placed a fierce kiss on his lips. Then she said, "Come, let me take care of you."

He removed his fingers from the space between her legs and licked her juices clean from his fingers. A contented smile overtook his features. "You taste truly delicious, thank you Domina."

She giggled. "I am glad you like." Then, without giving him any further warning, she reached over to him and took his shaft in her hands. Her grip was firm and authoritative.

She pumped, slowly at first. One. Two. Three. Four. Five.

Alexander bucked his hips upwards at the delicious sensation of her domineering hand around his hard and erect cock. He let forth a needy groan.

Belinda sped up her rhythmic motions.

Alexander let forth another moan of desire. "Domina, please -"

"All in good time, my sweet pet, all in good time," she soothed.

She pumped faster and faster.

Alexander's cheeks grew cherry red. His hips bucked wildly and then suddenly stilled. He spent his release against his stomach.

Belinda removed her hand from his glorious cock and drew him towards her in a proprietary embrace.

"Did you like that?" she asked.

"Oh I loved it," he replied.

She laughed and placed a fierce kiss upon his cheek. "I am most glad to hear it, pet."

The carriage rumbled onwards to the east and inside its occupants were at one with each other and at peace with the world.

After a journey of half a day, the Faversham carriage pulled up at the front of Morworth Hall.

The Viscount and Viscountess of Morworth, Percival and Eunice, were out the front ready to greet them.

Alexander exited the carriage first, before turning around to hand Belinda down.

The quartet exchanged warm greetings.

"Come inside, come inside," Eunice said. "The Devitts are already here. They arrived about an hour ago."

The Morworths led the way to a cosy drawing room with lemon-coloured walls.

The Devitts, Violet and Michael, stood up to greet them.

Belinda looked around the room. It had been a while since she had visited a country residence other than Faversham Abbey. In fact, not since before she was engaged when she had spent a few weeks at Virginia's house in Shropshire. She was looking forward to the days ahead and what they might bring.

The next day, the quartet sat around the dining table enjoying a luncheon of egg and cress sandwiches, beef soup and roast chicken.

They finished up their meal.

Then, Percival said, "Eunice and I have some entertainment planned. Gentlemen, if you'd like to follow me."

Eunice picked up where her husband had left off. "And ladies, please come with me."

In short order, the group peeled off into two.

Percival, Alexander and Michael headed off to the estate's wetlands.

Unlike so many of their compatriots on the ton, none of the three men cared much for shooting or hunting. Instead, they enjoyed scientific study of nature and so each man's main estate played host to a special place where they could engage in their beloved pastime. Alexander had the arboretum and Michael had the lake. But today it was the turn of the Morworth wetlands.

The three stepped out into the fresh air.

Michael cast his gaze to the heavens. "Looks a fine day today."

Alexander nodded. "What do you say about walking down, while the weather is mild?"

Michael nodded too.

"Agreed," Percival said.

A short while later and they found themselves at the wetlands.

Percival turned to Alexander. "So, you are a married man at last."

Michael said, "You know, for the longest time I never thought I'd see the day."

Alexander replied, "Well, we all have Lady Petunia Reynolds and her penchant for ludicrous rumours to thank for that."

Michael lifted his binoculars to his eyes and searched across the horizon. Then he put them back down. "But how is married life treating you?"

Alexander gave a small smile. "Much better than I had ever hoped, I must say."

Michael said, "So it seems Lady Reynolds' meddling and cantankerous ways were finally good for something after all."

Alexander said dryly, "Or at least they had a positive, if unintended consequence."

Percival laughed in delight. "I knew it! I knew it! You and Belinda were well-suited from the start. I could see from how you couldn't take your eyes off her at the Landsdowne Ball, when she was dancing with Lord Walthamstowe."

Alexander's cheeks reddened a little. "I had hoped you hadn't noticed."

Percival guffawed again. "I certainly did!"

"And so did I," Michael added. "It was as plain as day to anyone who had eyes."

Alexander pinched the top of his nose briefly. "I can't imagine many in the ton had such eyes though. I let my reputation precede me."

Percival clapped Alexander on the back. "That's the spirit! But seriously," his voice turned less the jester and more the solemn, caring friend, "I am glad you are with someone with whom you are very well suited."

Alexander gave a small smile and nodded. "Yes, it has been a most pleasant surprise indeed."

Michael said, "Finding a spouse with whom one is well suited is no easy feat. Violet and I are most fortunate in that regard. So I do congratulate you on your good fortune with Belinda."

Alexander picked up his binoculars and scanned the horizon. Perhaps he would spot something today. Or maybe not. In any case, he was a different man to the last time he had paid the Morworths a visit. And he was much the better for it, thanks to his most unexpected bride.

A sudden flash of tawny red through the binoculars drew him away from his inward ruminations. He focused on the tawny red. Could it be? Yes, it was! The rare red kite. He had only seen one of these before in his whole life, back when he was a boy. They used to be ubiquitous during the Middle Ages, and Shakespeare had viewed them as vermin, but nowadays they were rare. So Alexander prized this chance to lay his eyes on one, carrion-hunter or no. Yes, this was a most pleasant surprise indeed. Like several things over the past year.

✦ ✦ ✦

Over in the house, Eunice led Belinda and Violet down a corridor lined with massive portraits. Rows upon rows of bygone generations of Morworths bore down on the three women.

"Where are you taking us?" Violet asked.

"Ah, now that would spoil the surprise, ladies," Eunice replied. "But I have it on good authority that you are both going to enjoy what I have planned."

Violet giggled. "Well, we shall hold you to that, shan't we, Belinda?"

"We shall indeed," Belinda replied with a laugh.

A few more steps down the corridor and Eunice brought them all to a halt in front of a carved pink and white door. "Ladies, welcome to my salon," she said. She swung the door open to reveal a cosy room with wooden beams and big French windows. Pale yellow and pink wallpaper lined the walls.

Violet's eyes widened. "Eunice, it wasn't like this the last time I was here! Wow!" she exclaimed.

"I know. I really wanted a salon so I thought 'why not?' And here we are," Eunice said.

Belinda looked more closely at the contents of the room.

Plush couches in a rainbow of pastel colours were scattered around hither and thither. In front of the largest couch, which would comfortably fit five or six people, there were three easels in a row on a low table.

"Oh, what is this all about?" Belinda asked. She had a fairly good idea and she did enjoy painting and drawing, but she wouldn't have predicted this as the afternoon's entertainment.

Eunice clasped her hands together in excitement. "I have organised a painting session. With a little bit of a twist."

Violet quirked an eyebrow. "Oh, have you now?"

"I have indeed," Eunice said proudly.

"And what, pray tell, is the twist?" Belinda asked.

Eunice strode over to the servants' bell by the door and gave it a tug. "We are about to be joined by one of the north's most accomplished female artists. And while you are welcome to paint whatever you wish, our special guest can teach you how to paint a Greek god. Such as Adonis."

Belinda brought her hand to her mouth and let out a giggle.

Violet exclaimed in mock outrage, "Eunice! You can't corrupt young brides such as Belinda and I!"

Belinda was cackling by now. "Oh, I think we are quite capable of corrupting ourselves!"

Violet and Eunice laughed.

"Oh, most certainly we are," Violet said.

At that moment, a group of maids carrying paint sets and a whole smorgasbord of delicate fruits, sandwiches and macarons entered the room. A footman followed behind with a tray of beverages.

The trio helped themselves each to a glass.

Belinda enjoyed the sweet taste of the hot chocolate as it hit her tongue and swirled about her mouth.

Violet took a sip. Then she said, "This hot chocolate really is something. Eunice, your cook has outdone herself."

Once the three women had finished their beverages, there was a knock at the door.

The butler entered. He bowed to the group. "Your Grace, my ladies, Miss Edwina Palmerston."

Belinda recognised that name. Miss Edwina Palmerston was one of Britain's most celebrated artists. Though as a woman she was excluded from certain aspects of the Royal Academy, she had exhibited at the Academy's summer show every year for the past decade and she was sought after for commissions by many leading families of the ton.

A woman in her late thirties entered the room. She wore a pale brown dress made from twill and satin and in her hands she carried a large leather case.

"Miss Palmerston!" Eunice exclaimed. "Welcome, welcome! Oh it is so good to see you again."

Violet raised a quizzical eyebrow. "You are already acquainted?"

"Oh yes. Miss Palmerston was my painting instructor for several years, before I wed. And she still gives me lessons every so often," Eunice said.

Miss Palmerston exchanged greetings with Belinda and Violet.

Then Eunice clapped her hands together. "Let us start, let us start!"

Miss Palmerston walked to a spot facing the easels and placed her case on the table. She gestured to the easels. "Please, take whichever one you like."

Belinda stood at the middle easel with Eunice on her left and Violet on her right.

Miss Palmerston led them through a guided painting session. First, the torso of a most well-toned gentleman. Then his head and arms.

Violet peeped around to see Belinda's canvas. "Ooh, what's yours like? He is most dashing!"

Eunice's ears pricked up. "I say, your Grace, you do have a very good eye for gentlemen!"

Belinda giggled. It was true, her painting of Adonis was most enticing. And, if she did say so herself, she did have a knack for choosing handsome gentlemen.

Miss Palmerston walked behind the three canvases. "Your Grace, my ladies, you have all most splendidly outdone yourselves."

The four women all laughed. It was true, each painting captured something special in its own unique way. But every painter had achieved her own likeness of her Adonis. This was an afternoon very well spent, indeed.

A few days later and Eunice and Percival stood in their great hallway, ready to see off the Devitts and the Favershams.

The six exchanged farewells with promises to see one another soon at the Devitts home near the coast.

The Faversham carriage pulled up at the doors and Belinda and Alexander climbed into it.

They were off, trundling down the road back to the Abbey.

Belinda turned to Alexander. "You really are a man of surprises, you know."

He nodded. "I know."

"Just think what the ton in London would say if they knew about everything you get up to here in the north."

"Ah, now that would be too much for them to handle," he said wryly.

Belinda laughed and leaned back into his arms. "You are quite right, dearest."

CHAPTER FORTY

As the dying gasps of winter turned into the first days of spring, Belinda and Alexander stood together in the Great Hall and discussed preparations for heading south.

"Once we're through with the bulk of the lambing, I think we can head off," he said.

"Yes, as long as we are back in London by Whitsun then it is all the same to me," she replied. She took Alexander by the hand. She revelled in how firm and masculine his fingers were between hers.

He nodded. "Then that settles it. We'll wait until most of the lambing is done and then go down south."

Gus let forth a meow of agreement from the spot where he sat on the floor.

"Are you looking forward to being back in London?" she asked.

"In a sense, yes. It's not been a place where I've been comfortable most of the time. But that's in the past. I'm happy to be there with you. And I'm looking forward to experiencing the many bonbons of the place with you, as you once put it."

"Alexander!" she exclaimed in playful outrage. "I was hoping you had forgotten I used such phrasing."

"I like that you used that phrasing. I find it rather endearing." He squeezed her hand.

"It will be fun, though. Seeing London together, properly. The Vauxhall Gardens. Astley's Amphitheatre. And the opera. Though there is something else I am hoping we can do in London, that's not sightseeing. Something that the Faversham family hasn't done in a long long time."

"And what would that be?" he quirked a teasing eyebrow.

"Hosting our own ball. At Faversham House."

"We can do that. The finances are in the black and healthy."

"Then I look forward to hosting. What about this summer?"

"Whatever you think best," he said with a smile.

And so Belinda set herself about planning what she knew would be one of the most talked about social events of the year. How the ton would be amazed to see the cold-hearted duke and his timid and uncertain bride hosting a fine event that would be a night full of surprise and delight.

❧❧❧❧❧❧ ❦❦❦❦❦❦

Spring broke across the moors.

Belinda stood at the back gates of the gardens and marvelled at the beauty of the land.

She took a deep breath and inhaled the fresh country air.

If someone had told her a couple of years ago, back before her one-and-only season, that she would one day be a Duchess and most happily married, she would have struggled to believe them. Certainly, when she was younger she had dreamt of love. But she had known that for many women, including those of Britain's most privileged classes, love was not guaranteed at all. The most many could hope for was an arrangement where they'd find security and position.

In Alexander, Belinda had found a most unexpectedly suitable husband. More than she had allowed herself to hope for.

They would be heading back down to London in a matter of weeks. As husband and wife really and truly, and not just as a marriage of mere convenience to save her reputation.

Going back down to London would mean returning to the familiar world of the ton. It would be a return to the balls, the gossip and the theatres of Covent Garden. The Everaline Club. Vauxhall Gardens. Astley's Amphitheatre. Lots of things she had missed, in part, while she was at the Abbey. She was looking forward to dividing her time with Alexander between London, Yorkshire and perhaps also the Bath townhouse.

Becoming the Duchess of Faversham had given her the space to explore a darker side of herself she hadn't even really realised she had. However, it was a side of herself she liked and had no need to hide from Alexander.

Footsteps crunched on the gravel behind her.

By now, she could recognise those footsteps anywhere on earth.

She turned around to see Alexander walking toward her. Her heart leapt at the sight of him. He was so suave and dapper in his black pantaloons, waistcoat and great coat, plus black riding boots. He was everything she had never known she wanted.

"Belinda!" he called out to her. "You are looking most beautiful today."

She giggled. "You told me the same at breakfast."

"Well, it's true. So it bears repeating." He closed the final few steps between them and came to a halt at her side.

"My sweet Alexander," she said. She reached behind his neck and pulled him into a searing kiss.

He closed his eyes and let himself feel the bliss. The joy of this moment.

Eventually, they broke for air.

He looked at her with a deliciously wicked glimmer in his eye, full of promise of the delights to come. "We'll be on our way to London tomorrow. Where you will be one of the leading ladies of the ton, no doubt. But before we head off, what do you say to make use of all this rural privacy while we still have it?"

"I say that is a most excellent idea!" she exclaimed with brimming joy.

"Then I shall make it happen," he said with a smile.

He deftly steered the phaeton down the moorland towards the arboretum.

Belinda sat at his side, enjoying the spring day.

The bulk of the lambing now over, Faversham Abbey's fields were home to a sea of young lambs and their mothers.

Belinda said, "I shall miss this. Being here at the Abbey with you."

"Well, we can come back anytime we like," he replied with an affectionate smile.

"Oh I know that," she said wistfully. "Only it will be hard to leave. After everything we have experienced together here. But I am also looking forward to being in London with you."

"And I with you."

They pulled up outside the entrance to the arboretum. The place would be entirely theirs for the rest of the day, Alexander having forewarned the staff not to come near under any circumstances.

The horses trotted along under the boughs of the newly verdant oak trees. A few flower buds sprouted here and there and in a matter of mere weeks, the arboretum floor would be covered in wildflowers.

Belinda rubbed her dainty hand across Alexander's cotton-clad thigh.

Though his skin was shielded from her fingertips by the fabric barrier, every touch zinged through him like a fizzing jolt of electricity. Alexander was on edge already and they had but barely even begun.

He brought the phaeton to a halt in a pleasant clearing. "Please, Domina," he said in a juddering voice.

Belinda giggled, "Oh, there is plenty of time yet, my sweet Alexander!"

He bit his lip in anticipation.

She continued glacing her fingers across his thighs.

He moaned in shivering delight.

Then she withdrew her hands from his legs.

He whimpered at the removal of the delicious sensation.

Belinda brought her dainty hands to his face and pulled him towards her for a searing kiss.

"You are mine, Alexander, and don't you ever forget it," she said with a growl.

"No, Domina, I shall never forget," he moaned.

"Very good, my sweet pet," she said. She claimed his mouth in another searing kiss.

She slid her hands down his neck, her fingertips like electricity on his bare skin. She moved her hands over his chest and back.

He let forth a moan of need. "Domina," he uttered.

Her hands reached his thighs again, and again she laced her fingers over his well-formed muscles.

He moaned again.

"Remove your boots," she ordered.

He swiftly moved to obey her command.

She moved her hands upwards and unbuttoned his pantaloons. "Help me remove these," she commanded.

He duly did so and shuffled out of the pantaloons.

Belinda looked down and admired his strong, well-formed legs. It was all she could do but admire their tantalising, masculine form. He, her beautiful husband, was hers forever, every inch of him. She drew her eyes upwards until she reached that glorious space where his legs met. Instead of an immediate view of the bare skin of his cock, she was treated to the vision of him encased in black leather. Oh how she loved to see him like this! Her idea of the harness brought to life. His pleasure under her power .Under her control. Under her command.

She brought her hands to his thighs and glaced her fingers all around them.

Alexander shuddered. "Domina, please, that feels so good," he said.

"I know, my pet, I know," she replied with a wicked smile.

She stroked higher and higher until she reached the space where his thighs met. She ran her fingers teasingly by the crevice.

Alexander began to buck his hips, desperate for her touch.

Just when Alexander's bucking was about to reach its apex, Belinda removed her dainty hands from his body. Tempting as his cock was, she had another plan in mind before she would consider allowing his sweet release.

He looked at her through hooded lids. "Domina, how may I serve you?"

"Oh pet, you do show such wonderful initiative," she cooed. "No, worship me with those talented fingers and then that tongue of yours."

He opened his eyes more widely and looked at her with true reverence. "Yes, Domina."

With that, he moved his hand up through her skirts and petticoats to find that wondrous place between her legs. He ran his hands over her mound and found her wet with need. With expert deftness, he entered her, moving past her plump labia to find her pulsing clitoris.

She gasped at his touch.

Slowly, oh so slowly, he moved around her pleasure pearl in delicate circles.

Belinda made little moans of delight. Her legs twitched at the blissful sensations radiating from her core. She grew wetter and wetter until she was sopping slick with desire.

She looked down at Alexander with the gaze of a woman who knew precisely what she wanted. "Pet, your fingers are most skilled. I am impressed."

Alexander beamed at the praise.

Belinda continued speaking in her honeyed tones. "Now, what can you do with that pretty pretty mouth of yours? Why don't you show me?"

"Oh, thank you, Domina," Alexander said huskily.

She lay herself down on the phaeton's plush leather padded seat and spread her legs.

Alexander dove into her sea of skirts and placed soft kisses to the insides of her thighs. He worked his way up to the beautiful spot between her legs. She tasted like forest fruits and something he couldn't quite place. He relished her. Round and round he moved his talented tongue, teasing her plump labia and delighting her achingly needy clit.

Again and again, she climaxed on his face and he loved every second of it.

Her voice was a little breathy, but still in command. Still in control. "That's so good, pet. What a skilled tongue you have."

Belinda's breathing grew heavier and her heart rate increased with each delectably exquisite orgasm.

Alexander kept up his worship. His cock strained against the confines of his chastity device, but he was focusing all his efforts on her pleasure. That was what was truly delicious about this day!

Eventually, Belinda looked at him with flushed cheeks and barely a hair out of place. "You are truly outstanding, my sweet Alexander." She rubbed her fingers affectionately through his hair.

He purred at the relaxing sensation and continued with his attentions.

Belinda reached down a little to his ears and played with them.

Alexander wasn't sure which was better. When his Domina played with his hair or his ears. Nonetheless, he loved it all. He craved her touch ever so.

Belinda said, "Now, my pet, I do believe it's time for me to have my way with that delectable cock of yours."

She ran her fingers through his hair. Then she lifted herself up into a seating position. "Come, sit next to me, my pet." She patted the space next to her on the leather padded bench.

Alexander moved to sit alongside her. Even though Belinda had climaxed again and again while he remained snugly restrained in his chastity device, he was far more dishevelled than she was. Her cheeks were flushed to a shade of pink while his were more crimson.

Once they were both upright, Belinda leant across to him and moved her dainty hands all over his knees and thighs.

His cock strained something fierce against the leather constraint of the chastity device.

"My, my, how dashing you look like this," Belinda said.

The praise made Alexander's cock twitch within its leather encasement.

He grinned at the sensation.

She moved her commanding hands upwards towards his cock and its dastardly surroundings. She stroked the skin around his hips.

He jolted upwards in pleased surprise. "Domina," he moaned. "That feels so good."

She laughed affectionately, "My, how responsive you are, pet."

He bucked a few times, an involuntary movement of his finely-cut hips.

Belinda smiled to herself. She looked up at Alexander's face to see his eyes were shut already.

He was in a world of anticipation.

Belinda looked back down at where her hands rested and pondered what she would do next. She bit her lip. Yes, that would be a most delectable idea! She ran the palm of her hand over his leather-bound cock.

He let out a yelp of surprise.

She giggled a little. Round and round she moved her palm over his chastity device.

Alexander bucked his hips again, straining for his Domina's touch.

Belinda carried out her devious plan. She quickly moved her hand away from his cock.

He strained against the empty air, desperate for a release that was nowhere to be found. "Please, Domina," he moaned.

"Oh my sweet pet. You know it would not be appropriate for me to simply give you release immediately. There is sweetness in the waiting," she cooed. She continued rubbing her dainty hand over his leather encasement.

Sometimes her circles were consistent, lasting for what felt to Alexander like an age. And other times, they were over far too soon as she teased him again and again by removing her touch whenever she pleased. With every teasing removal of his Domina's touch, Alexander grew more and more needy. He so craved release. Yet he also craved to please his Belinda, his Domina.

When he thought he was almost going to come apart at the seams with desire, Belinda finally showed mercy upon him.

She moved her hands to the fastenings around Alexander's cock.

One by one, the leather restraints fell away to reveal his cock in all its glory. It was red, pulsating with a level of need so intense that it brought tears to the corners of Alexander's eyes.

Belinda placed the chastity belt on the floor at her feet. She loved it. It had brought them together, in ways she had not even been able to imagine. Truly, it was one of the best ideas she had had in a long time.

Alexander's cock was released from its physical restraints. Nonetheless, his cock still remained under Belinda's loving, strict command. He was not at liberty to obtain sweet release unless and until she decided to decree it.

His cock was bolt upright and oh so hard. Everything pulsating within him was on edge with desire for Belinda and everything she was driving him to feel in this moment.

Belinda rubbed her palm around the top of his cock. "There, is that better, pet?"

"Yes...Domina. Thank...you, Domina," he stammered.

She giggled. "I am glad you like it." She kept up her attentions on his erect staff.

He let forth a moan of need. Her touch was incredible. Every time her flesh met his, it was as though it were the first time he had ever been touched in his entire life.

All of a sudden, Belinda withdrew her hand.

Alexander yelped at the loss of her touch. "Domina, please -"

"Now, now. Patience is a virtue, pet," she said.

He harrumphed in frustration.

Belinda quirked an eyebrow. "I won't tolerate that attitude. Show any more of it and this all stops now."

"Yes, Domina, sorry Domina. I understand," he breathed.

Belinda nodded. "Make sure that you do." She returned her palm to his cock.

He bucked his hips upwards in desperate desire for her touch.

She ran her palm round and round the top of his cock. Then she switched things up and took his shaft between both of her hands. She squeezed it firmly several times.

He moaned again, a heady mix of need, pleasure and desire.

She kept pumping on his cock with firm, slow strokes.

Goosebumps formed on Alexander's flesh.

Belinda maintained her strict rhythm. She loved it when Alexander was like this, under her command and under her hand.

He bucked his hips upwards again. He wanted her. He burnt with desire for her.

With a little giggle, Belinda quickly withdrew her hand.

He could not help but whimper at the loss of her touch. But this time, he knew better than to demonstrate impertinent frustration.

Belinda smiled and nodded. "Very good, what a polite pet you are."

She traced her fingertips around his groin, being careful to avoid his cock and relishing the sleekness of his skin and his perfect formation.

He shivered in response.

She quirked her lip in amusement. Then she ran her fingertips along his cock. Up and down, pitter patter, pitter patter, like raindrops. She moved her fingertips all around every inch of him.

All the while, he let forth desperate moans and whimpers.

She gripped her hand around his cock and pumped hard, with strict, vicelike strokes. Faster and faster she moved until he was a wreck beneath her palms.

He bucked his hips upwards again and again in time with her hand. He was close, oh so close, almost on the edge of release. He was nearly there.

But all of a sudden, Belinda removed her hand.

Alexander whimpered.

"Not just yet, pet, not just yet," she cooed.

She leaned in and claimed his neck in a series of searing kisses.

Then she stepped back and admired her handiwork.

Alexander was wracked with lust and desire. His cheeks were bright scarlet, his eyes were hooded and his hips were bucking aimlessly into the chill spring air.

She smiled. Not that Alexander would see it. But in celebration of her handiwork. At her skill and ability to bring the cold-hearted duke to heel. Many on the ton would not believe it, and no one was ever going to know, but she was the woman who was capable of bending Alexander, Duke of Faversham, to her will.

She decided to take mercy on him and at last grant him sweet release.

She returned her tight grip to his throbbing cock and pumped vigorously. "That's it, come for me my pet, come for me," she crooned.

In mere moments, Alexander was climaxing into her hand. Every inch of him was alive with sheer pleasure.

His climax ended and his hips stopped bucking.

Belinda removed her hand and wiped it on a nearby handkerchief. Then she cleaned Alexander up too.

She took him in her arms and murmured in his ear, "I love you so so much."

"And I love you, my darling." His deep baritone was like honey in her ear. "You were incredible."

"As were you," she said.

He took her hand between his and brought it to his lips. He placed a reverent kiss atop it.

"I want to spend forever with you," she said.

"We shall, darling, we shall." He placed another kiss atop her hand.

Then she pulled his face towards her own and claimed his mouth in a passionate kiss. In this moment and in this place, all was right with the world.

Epilogue

Miss Dauntsey put the finishing touches on Belinda's bun. An intricate array of small gemstones and pearls adorned the hair of the Duchess.

"There, your Grace," said Miss Dauntsey.

"Thank you," said Belinda.

Then, as if on cue, there was a knock on the door.

Miss Dauntsey went to open it and gave a curtsey when she saw who was waiting on the other side.

Alexander's rich tones filled the air. "Your Grace may I come in please?"

Belinda turned her head to her husband and gave her assent.

Miss Dauntsey took that as her cue to give another curtsey before quickly disappearing down the corridor.

Alexander shut the door behind him and made his way over to his wife. He took her dainty hand in his masculine grip and placed a reverent kiss atop it.

"How are you feeling, darling?" he asked.

"Ah good, looking forward to it," she replied with a smile.

When she looked like that, she took Alexander's breath away. She was ethereal, radiant, a queen of the Golden Hour and everything he had ever wanted. Oh, how he counted himself as the luckiest man alive!

Belinda tilted her head towards his own. "And you, dear husband, how do you feel about all this?"

"Well, my reputation for enjoying balls is not widespread amongst the ton. I am, however, looking forward to seeing you in your element." He placed another kiss atop her dainty hand. "You are going to do such a brilliant job tonight, darling. I am sure of it."

"Thank you, Alexander," she said with a warm glimmer in her eyes. "Shall we head down to the ballroom? It won't be long until the first carriages arrive and I should hate to miss greeting our guests. It would be incredibly rude of me."

"Yes, it would be rude. But we could keep them waiting, take our time up here." He quirked his lip in a rakish way.

Belinda let forth a hearty laugh. "That does sound tempting, my sweet. Alas, we have committed ourselves and duty calls." She rose to her feet.

"Ah, but first, think of the scandal we could cause," said Alexander with a grin.

Belinda let out another giggle. "A scandal indeed! I shall give you a scandal, your Grace!"

She placed three firm swats on his backside.

He let out a yelp of surprise. Quickly, it turned into a moan of pleasure.

"Now, come along, my sweet Alexander," Belinda said.

He gave a relaxed grin, his cheeks ever so slightly flushed. "I do love you, you know that darling."

"And I love you too, my gorgeous husband." She placed a kiss on the top of his hand.

Alexander placed a protective arm around her waist and they made their way towards the door.

Couples swirled around the ballroom, dressed in all their finery.

Xavier was there, in the company of the Dowager Viscountess of Milton. They were clearly having a good time and enjoying one another's company, but Belinda had the sense that it was only a temporary thing.

Edgar, for his part, was dancing with one of the Earl of Burbank's daughters. Belinda doubted that it would even go beyond one dance.

Virginia and Margaret were there too, with a different gentleman on their arm for each dance.

The Dowager Duchess of Faversham was dancing with a man Belinda didn't recognise. In any case, the Dowager looked to be enjoying herself.

In the centre of the room, a string ensemble played *Water Music* by Handel.

Belinda walked around the room, delighted in how the night was going. Who would have thought only a year ago that she would be here, on this night, as the Duchess of Faversham hosting one of the ton's most salubrious balls of the year. Everyone would be talking about it tomorrow, and for all the right reasons.

After she'd made a complete circumnavigation of the room, she cast her eyes around to find where her husband had gotten to. She had last seen him when they'd been together in the entry hall greeting the arrivals. Then, Virginia had drawn her in for a conversation about how excellent the decorations were and who were the suppliers and how Belinda simply must put her in touch with them for a soirée she was planning for the autumn. The next thing Belinda knew, she had turned around to talk to Alexander and all she found was thin air.

She cast her eyes around the ballroom for a familiar dark-haired figure.

Ah! There he was, over by the punch table.

She started over to him, dodging the crowds of whirling lords and ladies.

When she was partway to him, he happened to glance up in her direction.

Their eyes met across the ballroom floor.

Belinda felt a heat of desire build within her. Alexander's gaze always had a way of doing that to her.

A few more steps and she was standing straight in front of him.

He reached out and took her hands in his own.

"There you are!" she exclaimed. I was talking with Virginia and turned around and the next minute, you were gone."

He gave a wry smile. "Yes, I got waylaid by the Baroness Chevalier. She was very keen to tell me all about the previous Faversham balls she'd attended. Of which there were many, back in the day. But," he added with confidential relish, "Do you know what she said to me? I think you're going to like this."

"What's that?" she asked.

"She told me this is the best decorated ball she has attended in many years. In fact, she was gushing over it all. And she was asking after the name of the firm you used. I think she'll make a point of asking you personally."

Alexander brought her hand to his mouth and placed a reverential kiss upon it.

Belinda smiled at her husband's attentions and congratulations. "Thank you, pet."

So far, this ball had been very much in the vein of so many others of the ton. Similar music, similar dancing, similar refreshments. Though with better decorations, of course. No doubt her guests were pleased. But Belinda wanted to make this, the first Faversham Ball in many a year, truly a night to remember. She had something better yet up her sleeve.

Alexander let go of her hand and drew himself upright.

The butler, Pentice, sidled up to her. "Is it time, your Grace?" he asked discreetly.

"Yes, please proceed," she said.

"Very good, your Grace." Prentice bowed and scurried off.

Alexander raised a quizzical eyebrow. "Time for what?"

"Oh you will see very soon," Belinda said. "It's a special surprise."

"One I will like?"

"I certainly hope so. I hope everyone here likes it. I wanted to make tonight memorable." She took his hand in hers.

"Well, I look forward to seeing this surprise," he murmured huskily in her ear.

At that moment, the string quartet drew to a halt.

Prentice's voice boomed around the room. "Ladies and gentlemen, their Graces the Duke and Duchess of Faversham are very proud to present a most wondrous spectacle for your entertainment and delight."

After Prentice finished speaking, the lamps in the room immediately went out and the ballroom was plunged into darkness.

A low murmur of anticipation filled the room.

Then, dancing lights appeared on the walls behind the string quartet. But they weren't just the usual orange and yellow flames. There were lights of green, pink, blue and purple.

"Oh this looks fun," one voice said.

"Well, I say!" exclaimed another.

The string quartet picked up their bows and began to play. The sweet sounds of *Cello Suite No. 6* by Bach filled the air.

The lights on the stage began to take new shapes. First a rose. Then a mermaid and on and on through a whole plethora of characters, animals and plants. Sometimes the lights joined together to form a bigger image and, other times, one light alone took the starring role.

Appreciative oohs and aahs could be heard over the music.

Eventually, the light show drew to a close with projections of two bulls which came together to form the Faversham coat of arms.

The room erupted into cheers and applause.

"That was really quite something," a voice boomed.

"I absolutely loved it!" someone else cried.

Alexander leant down and murmured in Belinda's ear. "That was wonderful. Unlike any magic lantern show I've seen before."

She turned around and tilted her lips up to his.

He claimed her mouth in a searing kiss.

When she had had her fill, she pulled away slightly and said, "So much of it's been done before and I didn't want to scare our guests with one of those horror light shows. They're a touring troupe who specialise in these lighter sorts of light shows, with the music synchronised and the newer, chemical colours. They're all the rage in Persia." She gestured to the balcony above, where a group of performers and technicians were packing away their lighting equipment.

"They were an inspired choice. Well done, darling," he said. Then he leaned down and kissed her again.

❦

After the ball, when the last guests had trundled off in their carriages as the dawn was breaking, Alexander and Belinda sat curled up together on the settee in her chambers.

"Darling, that was an absolute triumph," Alexander said.

"Thank you, it was indeed if I do say so myself," she said.

He reached for her hand and placed a kiss atop it.

She took his hand and interlaced her fingers with his. Then she brought their two hands to the spot over her heart, before moving them to the similar place over his own heart.

"It will be the first of many triumphs for you," he said admiringly.

"For both of us. The first of many triumphs for the both of us," she said.

He leant down and claimed her mouth in a searing kiss.

She simply adored how he tasted. Like mint and molasses.

She wrapped her free hand around him and drew him closer.

When they had both had their fill of the kiss, they drew away slightly.

Alexander placed a kiss on her forehead. Then he said, "I love you so so much, darling."

"And I too love you, more than anything else in the whole world," she replied.

He rubbed a protective hand down her spine, stopping at the small of her back.

She moaned a little at the feel of his touch. "I am so looking forward to spending the rest of our lives together," she said. "There is so much I want for us to do together. Here, in London. At Faversham Abbey. All the places we could go. All the things we could do together. As the Duke and Duchess. As Domina and Pet. As Alexander and Belinda."

"I would so like that too. All of those things, darling," he said.

She pondered for a moment. "What should we do first? Other than be ourselves, of course."

"Well, we never had a honeymoon," Alexander said wistfully.

"We still can," smiled Belinda. She moved her free hand away from his back and placed his cheek between her thumb and forefinger. "I have never been to Edinburgh."

"I think you'd like it. It would suit your personality."

"My personality? How so?" she laughed.

"Well it's a little more gothic than much of England. And there's a strong intellectual current. I know London has that, but Edinburgh's got a lot of it too. And a university to boot." He placed a kiss on her cheek.

"Oh, it does sound wonderful. It will be a wonderful adventure. When do you think we can go? In the autumn?"

"Yes, we can finish everything up we need to do down here and then head up there in the autumn. Edinburgh in October will be a little cold but we'll still enjoy ourselves."

"I like the sound of that. In so many ways." She placed a proprietary kiss on his cheek. "Tell me, have you been to Edinburgh before?"

He nodded. "Yes, about half a dozen times over the years. I don't have family up there or anything, and most of my connections are in Yorkshire as you know, but it's a place I've enjoyed visiting over the years."

"And what's it like in your opinion? From your time there, not from a travel guide?"

"Wild and free and very romantic. Like you," Alexander said. He took Belinda's hand from his face and placed it in his own. Then he brought her hand to his mouth in a searing kiss.

Belinda bit her lip. Even after so many kisses, it always felt like he was kissing her for the first time. A kiss from Alexander was guaranteed to make her feel new and fresh and alive.

"I do like the sound of that. Wild and free and very romantic. And what, pray tell, shall we see when we're in Edinburgh?" she looked up at him and gazed into his hawk like brown eyes.

"They've got the Assembly Rooms, of course, more elegant than the ones in Bath. And then there's the Castle and Holyrood Palace. Both unlike anything you've probably seen here in England. Very different architecture to what we have down here. Then there's the New Town, that'll put you in mind of parts of Bath and London," he said. "Plus another bookshop with a specialist section."

"Oh, a specialist section now?" she let forth a wicked giggle.

"And, pray tell, how does it compare to such bookshops in England? From your personal experience?"

"It compares very well indeed," he murmured. "Some similar content but also a lot of titles that are uniquely Scottish. You would really enjoy a visit."

"Or perhaps even more than one visit, if it has so much unique content."

"Yes, only the one visit may not suffice." He placed a kiss on her cheek. "Oh darling, I am so looking forward to our honeymoon. And to the rest of our lives together."

"As am I, my sweet Alexander, as am I," she said.

They joined together in another passionate kiss.

Belinda moaned with delight. She adored the sensation of Alexander's mouth on hers. And she knew he felt exactly the same way about her.

Eventually, they pulled apart for air.

Belinda looked up at him. "Say, before we prepare any more for our honeymoon, what do you say to being Domina and pet this morning?"

"Oh I do like the sound of that, Domina, I like the sound of that indeed," he said with a smile.

"Very well, let us prepare. Innumerable delights await you today, pet."

And with that, they headed hand in hand to her plush four poster bed. Where Belinda claimed Alexander again and again. And Alexander counted himself as the luckiest man alive to have such a wife as her.

And as for Belinda? Well, if anyone were to ask her, she would gladly say that she was the luckiest lady in all the world. Though when her season began, she would never have imagined she would end up married to the cold-hearted duke. But now she could not imagine a better man for a husband. With Alexander, she had found true happiness.

ACKNOWLEDGEMENTS

First off, thank you to you the reader of this book. I hope that you enjoyed it and that you got something out of Belinda and Alexander's story.

To the team at Miblart, thank you for your brilliant work on the cover art.

And thank you to MD for everything.

DISCUSSION QUESTIONS

1. Alexander is highly focused on his desire to protect Belinda. In doing so, however, he ends up harming her. What does his behaviour tell us about expectations of masculinity in England in the late eighteenth and early nineteenth centuries?

2. The power of reputation is a recurring theme throughout the novel. Belinda marries Alexander to save her reputation after the unfortunate run-in in the maze. Alexander has a reputation on the ton as the cold-hearted duke. In what other ways do the characters exemplify that a reputation isn't necessarily the whole truth?

3. Alexander has a reputation as the cold-hearted duke that he himself cultivates. Who do you think started the rumour in the first place? Was it Alexander or somebody else?

4. What was the most surprising or shocking scene in the story and why?

5. Phaeton riding brings Belinda a real sense of freedom. What does freedom mean to you and what makes you feel free?

6. Marriage is a defining moment in the lives of young women of the ton such as Belinda. But it is less of an all-encompassing moment in the lives of young men. What importance do you think marriage has as a milestone in people's lives today?

7. Music is a hobby that brings Belinda a great deal of happiness. What hobbies do you have and how do they impact your life?

8. Belinda assumes that society in the north is behind the times compared to what she knows in London. Her trip to the York Assembly Rooms proves her wrong. How else are characters proven wrong in the novel?

9. Which *Protected by the Duke* character did you find the most intriguing and why?

10. How did the different settings of London, York and Faversham Abbey impact the tone of the novel? What can they tell us about the characters' priorities and mental states?

About the Author

Chloe Willowfield adores all things historical romance. Ever since she was very young, she has been fascinated by how people lived in the past.

When she's not writing, you'll find her enjoying musicals, visiting local cafes or maybe even going on a hike.

You can connect with Chloe on Instagram, TikTok or Pinterest. You can also keep up-to-date by signing up for her newsletter.

Chloe can be reached via email at chloe@chloewillowfield.com. She'd love to hear from you!

SUBSCRIBE TO CHLOE'S NEWSLETTER

Scan the QR code below to subscribe to Chloe's newsletter and stay updated on the latest releases.

VISIT CHLOE'S WEBSITE

Scan the QR code below or head to
www.chloewillowfield.com